UNDER PRESSURE

Also by Sara Driscoll

Leave No Trace

No Man's Land

Storm Rising

Before It's Too Late

Lone Wolf

UNDER PRESSURE

SARA DRISCOLL

KENSINGTON
PUBLISHING CORP.

www.kensingtonbooks.com

KENSINGTON BOOKS are published by

Kensington Publishing Corp.
119 West 40th Street
New York, NY 10018

All Kensington titles, imprints and distributed lines are available at special quantity discounts for bulk purchases for sales promotion, premiums, fund-raising, educational or institutional use.

Special book excerpts or customized printings can also be created to fit specific needs. For details, write or phone the office of the Kensington Special Sales Manager: Kensington Publishing Corp., 119 West 40th Street, New York, NY, 10018. Attn. Special Sales Department. Phone: 1-800-221-2647.

Library of Congress Card Catalogue Number: 2021940066

The K logo is a trademark of Kensington Publishing Corp.

ISBN: 978-1-4967-3504-1
First Kensington Hardcover Edition: December 2021

ISBN: 978-1-4967-3505-8 (ebook)

10 9 8 7 6 5 4 3 2 1

Printed in the United States of America

UNDER PRESSURE

CHAPTER 1

Eye Clean: A jeweler's term for a gemstone that has no flaws visible to the naked eye.

Saturday, July 27, 1:43 PM
Jennings/McCord residence
Washington, DC

"What's this thing made of? Lead?"

Stepping back from the staircase, Meg Jennings studied the two men maneuvering a massive wardrobe up the stairs. The strangled question had come from her partner, Todd Webb, on the lower end of the wardrobe and taking the brunt of the weight, while Clay McCord balanced the top and steered them up the flight of stairs.

"Oak." McCord's voice was slightly breathless. "Been in my family for two generations. They don't build them like this anymore. It'll outlast me."

"It'll outlast me when it slips out of my hands and crushes me on the way down," Webb grated.

Meg took a step forward, already calculating whether she could slip in beside Webb to carry some of the weight, when he glanced sideways and winked at her. She relaxed, realizing that while the piece of furniture was heavy, to a firefighter/paramedic who routinely wore sixty pounds of gear and carried another hundred pounds of hose to run headlong into a roaring fire, this wasn't as much of an effort as he was making out.

"Can't fool me," McCord retorted. "You have to work out for a living. Us journalism nerds have nothing on you big, brawny firefighters. All we have to lift is a keyboard."

"I figured that's why I got the heavy end. And nice try, nerd. I saw the weight set in the truck that's going in the basement."

"That's Cara's. I'm a delicate flower."

"That's you, all right. Now stop dragging your feet. We can go faster than this. But if you tell me to pivot, you get to carry the rest of your stuff in here solo."

McCord's crack of laughter bounced off the unadorned walls. "Deal."

Meg stepped closer to her sister, Cara, who stood at the bottom of the steps, worry digging a crease between her eyebrows. With the same tall, athletic stature, long, straight black hair, and ice-blue eyes, they could almost have been twins, though in reality Cara was eighteen months younger than Meg. Granted, the months-old, pale, inch-and-a-half-long scar over Meg's right eyebrow would now forever differentiate them. "I wasn't sure the two of them were going to be able to manage that piece."

"You and me both." Cara stepped to the staircase and laid one hand on the heavy wood banister as the men crested the stairs and set the wardrobe down in the hallway on the runner. "They're good." Turning, she stared down the hallway to the pile of boxes stacked in the middle of the kitchen. "Want to give me a hand with these?"

"It's the least I can do, considering you did the same for me last month." Meg looked down at the pack of dogs at her feet to find her black Labrador, Hawk, at her knee. "Come on, guys. Let's see if we can find the box with the treats in it." She started down the hallway, trailed by

Hawk, along with Cara's two rescue dogs—Saki, a mini blue-nose pit bull, and Blink, a retired red brindle greyhound. Cody, McCord's hyperactive golden retriever, shot past the group to gallop into the kitchen and then stop, tongue lolling out of his mouth as he waited for them to catch up.

Up until last month, the two sisters had shared a house in Arlington, a situation that worked perfectly for them until they'd both partnered up. Webb had found the perfect compromise for all four of them—a duplex with two identical units located in the Cookes Park area of Washington, DC, only ten minutes from McCord's office at the *Washington Post*, and about fifteen minutes away from Webb's firehouse, Meg's office in the J. Edgar Hoover Building, and Cara's dog training school in Arlington. Meg and Webb had moved in the previous month; now Cara and McCord were moving into their side of the duplex.

"You live and work with a trained scent dog. Let's make this job easy." Cara entered the kitchen and pointed at the stack. "Hawk, find the treats."

His tail waving happily in the air, Hawk trotted toward the pile of boxes, detailing each box as he moved methodically around the pile. Circling to the back side, he sniffed the bottom box, moved up to the middle box, paused, and immediately sat down in his trained alert signal.

"Good boy." Meg circled the pile. She lifted off the top box and set it on the counter, opened the next box down, and pulled out a bag of chicken jerky. "He's such a Lab. He'll do anything for food."

Cara ruffled his ears and bent to place a smacking kiss on the top of his head. "Of course he will. Now reward the good behavior."

Opening the bag, Meg pulled out four large pieces of jerky. "Sit." Three rumps hit the ground simultaneously.

Cara gave Cody a look and he belatedly sat.

Meg gave the dogs their treats and they scattered to different parts of the room to settle down, crunching loudly.

The rhythmic thud of boots muffled by the charcoal stair runner telegraphed the men were on their way down. Webb and McCord came through the kitchen door, both breathing hard. They were both dressed in jeans and T-shirts, but, beyond that, they were the yin and yang of light and dark, as different as the sisters were similar. Out of his turnout gear, Webb had a firefighter's muscular physique, with brown eyes and dark hair trimmed short to fit easily under his helmet, and the no-nonsense outlook of a first responder. McCord, on the other hand, had blue eyes behind his wire-rimmed glasses, slightly floppy blond hair, and a perennially jovial expression. If there was a joke to be made about a situation, McCord would be the first with a zinger.

"Any more pieces like that?" Webb made a beeline for the fridge, opened it, and pulled out two cans of beer, handing one to McCord before opening his own and taking a long series of swallows.

"No, thank God." McCord opened his own beer. "The beds are next, but they're all broken into pieces. Then we just need to put them together."

"Bedroom, master bath, and kitchen." Cara picked up her glass of sparkling water and tapped it against McCord's can. "If we can get those set up today, we can settle in for the night. And then deal with the rest over the next few days."

"We can do better than that." Meg leaned back against the counter. "Todd's on shift tomorrow, but I'll be here. We can get almost everything into place by the end of the weekend."

"Unless you get called to a case." McCord tipped his head back to take a long drink. He set his can down and fixed Meg with a pointed stare. "You're not holding out on me, are you?"

Meg fluttered her eyelashes at him. "Would I do that?" At his derisive chortle, she shrugged. "Okay, I would have in the past. But we have a deal."

Since the first case they'd worked together the year before—when a disgruntled bomber shunned by the world around him had taken out his misery and rage on those he saw as responsible, and had used McCord as a direct conduit to the FBI—they'd worked a number of cases together. As an investigative reporter for the *Post*, McCord had been able to use his research skills, contacts, and dogged determination to make himself invaluable to Meg. They'd solved cases, and while they'd lost a few victims, they'd saved countless lives.

One of those lives had been Cara's.

They'd made a deal during their last case—Meg would share details of her case in exchange for his assistance. He, in turn, would remain silent until the case was closed and would earn an exclusive on the story in reward.

"It's actually been a slow week for the group," Meg said. "Lauren and Rocco"—Meg referred to her colleague Lauren Wycliffe and her border collie, Rocco—"got sent down to Florida to help out after that tropical storm blew through and those kids went missing, and they were afraid there was a kidnapping in progress. Rocco found them. They were lost and scared, but that was the extent of it. Otherwise, it's been quiet lately." She rapped her knuckles on the cabinet door behind her. "Knock on wood, it will stay that way. It's a nice change."

Hawk finished his snack and wandered over to the group.

"Is Brian back yet?" Cara asked.

"This week, hopefully. It's been a long three months, but Brian couldn't bring Lacey in until she was in top shape. There's just too much resting on her performance out in the field. I saw her about two weeks ago, and she's looking great. Of course there's some scarring."

Meg couldn't help but remember the terror of Lacey's injury last April when Brian, out on a search, had been attacked by a cougar and Lacey had defended him, almost at the cost of her own life. Her injuries were severe, but with quick medical care and Brian's steadfast efforts to nurse her back to health, Lacey was making a full recovery. Now it was time to put her to the test.

Meg couldn't have been happier that they were coming back to the team. She'd really missed Brian. They worked together seamlessly; so much so, Craig often paired them together. She'd worked with Lauren and Rocco, and Scott Park and his bloodhound, Theo, over the past few months, but she never felt quite as in-step with them as she did with Brian and Lacey.

"Most of the scarring is hidden in Lacey's fur. More importantly, she moves well. I think what Brian is most concerned about is her stamina. Sometimes these searches go on for hours. He's been jogging with her, working her stamina back up." Meg's gaze dropped to Hawk. "He said she's ready to join Hawk and me on our five-mile misery-loves-company morning runs again."

Cara ran a hand over Hawk's head and down his back. He looked up at her, his tail wagging so hard it repeatedly thumped the side of the boxes. "I bet Hawk will be thrilled with that. He must be missing her."

"He likes working with Rocco or Theo. He's great solo. But he really loves Lacey. And they click together as a team better than any of the other dogs do." The alert of an incoming text sounded and Meg pulled her phone out of her pocket. "Uh-oh."

Webb crossed the room to stand beside her. "What?"

"It's Craig," Meg said, referring to her supervisor,

Special-Agent-in-Charge Craig Beaumont. "I told him I needed this weekend off unless a disaster occurred." She opened the text and read the message. Then read it again as dread and confusion coiled in her gut.

"I don't like that look. What's the disaster?"

"I have no idea." She met Webb's gaze. "He's ordered me to meet him in EAD Peters's office Monday morning at nine." As the executive assistant director of the FBI's Criminal, Cyber, Response, and Services Branch, Adam Peters oversaw the Forensic Canine Unit.

The only time she'd ever been summoned to Peters's office, it had been to be called on the carpet after she'd disobeyed a direct order from Craig.

To this day she stood behind that decision. A madman had been killing women who looked like her in order to kill her again and again. She'd disobeyed Craig's order not to enter a building that was about to be demolished because she knew Hawk could find the victim in the basement and get them all out before the implosion. He had—though only by a matter of seconds. They'd been thrown so hard by the shock wave, Meg came away with a grade-three concussion.

She'd do it all over again, given the same set of circumstances.

You people drive me to drink, and I can't do it on the job.

She remembered Peters's words from the party she'd thrown to celebrate the close of the case and the recovery of her sister after she, Webb, McCord, and Hawk had saved Cara's life. When he was out of his office, Peters was personable and funny. Inside his office, he was pure hard-ass.

"What did you do wrong?" McCord asked.

Cara smacked his arm—hard—and McCord grunted in pain. "She didn't do anything wrong."

"Then why does she have to meet with Peters?" McCord turned to Meg. "Any idea?"

"Your guess is as good as mine."

"Why don't you call Craig to get more information?" Webb suggested. "Rather than worry about it for another day and a half."

"And ruin what's left of our weekend?" She lifted the beer out of his hand and took a long drink, keeping her eyes locked on his, ignoring his raised eyebrows. "Not on your life." She handed him back the can and turned to McCord. "What's next?"

McCord continued to stare at her in silence.

Rolling her eyes, Cara linked her arm through Meg's and tugged her toward the front door. "The beds are next. Come on, they'll catch up to us sooner or later. They always do."

CHAPTER 2

Fingerprint: Any unique identifying characteristic of an individual or a diamond.

Monday, July 29, 8:57 AM
EAD Peters's Office, J. Edgar Hoover Building
Washington, DC

Webb knew her too well. Meg had pasted on a smile for the rest of the weekend, but she'd spent every moment she wasn't occupied with Cara's move fretting about the meeting with Peters. In the end, she was absolutely stumped about why Peters needed to see her.

With only a few minutes to go until the meeting, she strode down the hallway toward Peters's office. Hawk, off leash and wearing his FBI work vest, heeled at her side.

Stop stressing. You'll find out in a few minutes. Nothing to do for it either way.

"Good boy, Hawk. Let's find out if we're on the chopping block and then . . ." She stopped dead and trailed off as two figures turned the corner at the far end of the hallway. Her spirits jolted upward; she'd recognize the tall, dark-haired man and the German shepherd at his side anywhere. "Brian! What are you and Lacey doing here?"

Brian grinned at her as Lacey broke into a half trot at

the sight of Hawk. "Lacey, heel. We're at work." But he compromised and picked up his pace.

Meg met him halfway with a tight hug. "It's so good to see you." She pulled back and studied Lacey as she and Hawk happily greeted each other, bumping noses and circling excitedly. "Lacey looks great." Meg abruptly remembered her meeting and why she was here, instead of on the fourth floor. "What are you doing here? I mean, not in the building"—she pointed to Peters's door—"but *here*."

"Craig sent a text over the weekend saying he wanted to meet me here at nine."

The weight resting on Meg's shoulders melted as all of her stress slid away, leaving only confusion. She might think she'd done nothing wrong, but Brian absolutely hadn't. He'd been on paid leave for several months at this point. "I got the same text." She met his eyes. "So now the question is—why are *we* here?"

"You realize the best way to find out is to go into Peters's office, right?"

"Funny man. You haven't spent the whole weekend sweating over what you screwed up."

"Why would you think that?"

"Because the only time I was called to this office was after the Gettysburg building demolition. Peters was . . . displeased."

"I bet that's putting it lightly."

"In spades. When I got Craig's text, it was all I could think of, but I couldn't come up with a reason."

"I hear you."

"But now you're also here, so that can't be why."

"As I said before, we're standing out here, asking these questions, when we could be in there, why?"

"Amazingly, I've even missed your sass."

"You know it." Brian laid a hand on the doorknob. "Come on, girl. Let's go watch Meg face the music."

"Hey!" But Meg followed Brian into the outer office, feeling lighter than she had since Saturday afternoon.

Peters's assistant showed them through to his office. Bald and dressed in a conservative navy suit paired with a matching tie that shrieked *Fed!* to Meg's eye, Peters sat behind his wide desk in a padded leather chair. Meg's gaze slid to the chairs facing Peters, first falling on the stocky build and familiar craggy face of Craig Beaumont, whom she acknowledged with a nod. Then she turned toward the other chair to find a petite brunette in a tailored burgundy pantsuit rising to her feet, a smile lighting her face.

"Kate!" Meg stepped forward, her hand extended. "This is a surprise. I haven't bumped into you in months. Probably since shortly after we closed the urban exploration case."

Kate shook hands. "It's definitely been too long, but I've been out of state a couple of times on cases." Kate's voice carried the sweet tea–infused lilt of Tennessee. She released Meg and turned to Brian. "Brian, it's good to see you as well."

"Sure is." He shook hands with her and then stepped back as Kate bent to greet the dogs.

"Craig was telling me about Lacey. You'd never know from looking at her that she's been on leave. Is she ready to come back?"

"We both are."

"I'm glad to hear that because I have a proposal for you."

"For us?" Meg exchanged a look with Brian, only to see her own curiosity reflected back.

"Yes. Please have a seat."

Meg and Brian took the two empty chairs, Brian beside Kate and Meg on the opposite side, next to Craig.

"You may be wondering why I called this meeting," Kate began.

Brian couldn't keep his lips from twitching as he flicked a glance in Meg's direction.

"EAD Peters has kindly allowed me to come in with a little cross-division proposal for you," Kate continued.

Peters leaned back in his chair, the leather squeaking quietly as his weight shifted, and studied Meg over his glasses. "I've given Kate permission to borrow you and your dogs for a case she's working on. Beaumont is in agreement."

Craig raised a single index finger. "With the understanding that if something hits the fan and I need you, I can have you back. In the meantime, I'll have Scott and Lauren cover any new cases while you're in Philadelphia."

"Philly?" Brian asked. "What's there?"

"Jewelers' Row." Kate held up a hand, forestalling any more questions. "Let me back up so you can get the whole picture. I'm working on a case with the Organized Crime Program. They focus on transnational organized crime taking place across borders that involves an American component. We've been focusing on Philadelphia, and, more specifically, on the Philadelphia crime family."

"The Italian Mafia?"

"They're sometimes referred to as the Philly Mafia or the Philly Mob. They have their fingers in a lot of pies— firearms trafficking, drug trafficking, money laundering, racketeering, extortion, and murder, to name a few."

"Just a few." The sarcasm in Brian's muttered words was unmistakable.

"We're taking a multipronged approach, with different agents tracking their different areas of business. They're experienced and use their knowledge and skills, and their already-established contacts to ferret out what's really going on."

"What role are you playing in this?"

"They wanted an agent from outside the program for

one particular aspect of the family's operation because it's so specialized. Financial crimes, firearms crimes—unfortunately, there's a lot of that nationally—which take a lot of agents to investigate. However, they're also dealing in conflict diamonds."

Brian whistled. "Yeah, that's specialized. Are we talking blood diamonds?"

"Blood diamonds, conflict diamonds, hot diamonds . . . they're all the same thing. Diamonds mined and sold to finance a war or a warlord. Those diamonds are then sold and move through a number of permissive countries that mix the gems in with legitimate stones, while counterfeit certificates are created for the conflict gems to give them a fictitious provenance. They're then sold to groups that deliver the stones to diamond brokers, who, in turn, sell them to jewelers."

"Do the jewelers know they're getting conflict diamonds?" Craig asked.

"Most of the time, no. However, we suspect there are some who know exactly what they're buying. Especially those who cut their own gems because these are often coming through as rough stones."

"I assume once the jewelers cut them," Meg said, "there's no tracking back to the original stone. They've essentially laundered the stones."

"That's exactly right."

"Why are you investigating these crimes instead of the FBI Diamond Trafficking Program?"

"We're actually working with them. My role is to liaise between the two groups and to lead the Philadelphia investigation into the family's illegal diamond activities. We'll be working with Special Agent Doug Addison from the Diamond Trafficking Program."

"What you've explained so far makes sense," said Brian, "but I don't see where we fit in."

"When I worked with you on the Stevenson case, I got a firsthand lesson on what your dogs can do and was extremely impressed. The way they could take the scent from an old sock or shirt, and search through the worst of environments, to not only find a trace of the scent, but to follow it straight to a victim. Without the dogs, we would have likely lost every senior citizen who'd been taken. With the dogs, even though we were fighting the clock, we saved many of them. That skill interests me."

"You mean specific scent work? Not when they're going after an unidentified scent, but when they're tracking a known scent."

"Yes. I think we can use a little out-of-the-box thinking, as long as the dogs can track inside structures, as well as outside, and through potential crowds." Kate glanced from one handler to the other and then down to the dogs. "Can they?"

"Absolutely."

"You bet."

Kate chuckled as Brian and Meg answered on top of each other. "Perfect. Let me explain what I have in mind and I want you to shoot this down if you think it's not feasible in any way. We have one of our agents deep inside the family. He started off as a low-level flunky, but has worked his way up to being a trusted courier, recruiter, and sometime enforcer. They're about to receive a shipment of conflict diamonds in the next few days, and for once, we're purposely not stopping that shipment from entering the country."

"You could do that?" Peters asked.

"Most likely. We know it's coming from the Democratic Republic of the Congo via India and will pass through New York City on its way to Philadelphia. We could block it right there, but we're going to let it through because if we cut them off in New York City, they'll simply find another way in next time. We want to disrupt the entire chain, and that means discovering who's involved down-stream from the family—the diamond brokers and the jewelers, who may or may not realize what they're buying and passing on to their customers. Philadelphia's Jewelers' Row is second only to New York City's. It's literally a two-block stretch downtown packed with jewelry stores. They move a lot of diamonds, most of which are legitimate stones. But there are too many that aren't. And that's where Special Agent Finn Pierce comes in."

"That's our guy?" Brian asked.

"Yes. He'll be meeting with brokers to make the sale and we want to make the bust as they're in the middle of that transaction. However, Pierce is in deep as 'Angelo Marzano' and has limited contact with us. Needless to say, these transactions are kept under wraps with only those directly involved in the know, and meet locations are usu-ally planned with relatively short notice to limit the time for word of the drop to spread. In this case, while he's the courier, he'll be with someone else, because they won't send one guy off on his own with property that valuable. He'll find out at the last minute where they're going, but won't be able to communicate that level of detail to us. And before you ask, we can't track him electronically. The family has been burned before by infiltrating law enforce-ment or by rival groups trying to steal their business and they now have a zero-tolerance policy. They check even their most trusted guys. If Pierce were to be found wired at any time, he'd be executed then and there, with no ques-tions asked, and no chance for him to even try to explain."

Meg was nodding, already seeing where Kate was go-ing with her argument. "But unless he can strip off his own skin, he'll always be carrying a tracker the dogs can follow."

Kate leveled an index finger at Meg. "And that's my

idea. If we get Pierce to provide sweaty gym socks or something equally smelly for the dogs to use, could they track him?"

"Without question."

"Even indoors?"

"Especially indoors. The top twenty or so layers of human skin are entirely made up of dead cells, and we shed about forty thousand of those cells a day. That's what the dogs track. Outside, you have a variety of surfaces—grass, trees, sidewalks, buildings—and variable air currents to blow the cells everywhere. That's the scent cone the dogs follow—it's narrow at the point of origin until air currents move the cells around in an ever-expanding cone. The dogs know the more concentrated the scent and the narrower the cone, the closer they are to their target. But indoors, the cells just drop. Yes, there are some minor currents—forced airflow or disturbance from foot traffic—but basically, indoor tracking is much less disturbed, so it's a much straighter path for the dogs to follow. But whether it's indoors or outdoors, we can make the search essentially invisible. He only needs to be a few minutes in front of us and the dogs will follow his trail like it was lit by neon lights. No one will see us or know we're following, but we'll arrive before the deal is complete."

"Not quite. You're FBI, but you're handlers, and while I have every confidence in you, when it comes to the arrests, it needs to be done by special agents. You do the tracking. When you get close to the meet, that's when Doug and I will step in. You two are going to be constants in this case, so I don't want you being seen by any of the players. If Doug and I get close enough to be seen, it's already game over for them."

"Do you know when the first meet will be?" Peters asked. "And therefore, how fast will you need the teams?"

"No, but Pierce will keep us in the loop. Arrangements

for the meets will have to be made at least a day or two in advance to make sure all parties are available, so we'll know at least one day before when we need to be in Philadelphia."

Brian's brow was furrowed in a way that told Meg he wasn't totally on board yet. "You anticipate us doing this a number of times?"

"Yes."

"You don't think having the same guy on hand every time they lose a cache of diamonds won't raise suspicion and get him killed anyway?"

"I raised that issue myself, but Pierce suggested a couple of options. For starters, he won't be the only courier. He's going to try to find personal items from anyone who will be a courier, so the dogs can track whoever that might be, not just Pierce. Some busts could take place after Pierce had just left, so the family might not even realize that load of diamonds was confiscated. He also suggested purposely getting busted by us and arrested as another way of alleviating suspicion. We'll have to play each situation by ear, but he's very cognizant he needs to not have a giant bull's-eye on his back. We'll adjust as needed, keeping Pierce's safety as our top concern. Better to let the bust go than to risk him. If the choice is between putting Pierce in jeopardy and losing the evidence at a particular drop, we'll lose the drop. There's always a next time with these people. But you also need to know he's not the only one in danger. If at any time any family member suspects you're following him, or, God forbid, you're law enforcement, they'll take out your dogs right before your eyes. And you'll be next. It's not so much the first search; it's the subsequent searches. Y'all need to recognize the risk before committing to this."

"We do." Brian turned to Meg. "You think this'll work?"

"I do. It's a good thought, using the dogs' skills in a way

that's a little unusual, but could have some significant pay-offs. And we can take precautions. Would we be able to meet the players beforehand?"

"I can take you up to meet Doug today. He can also address any questions you might have about the illegal diamond trade. As far as Pierce goes, I told him I wanted to do a proof-of-concept search. Give his scent to the dogs and make them find him through the most challenging, but realistic, search he can set up. I don't want him out there thinking backup is right behind him, when the dogs lost him a half hour before."

"They won't. But I understand wanting to make sure the concept is solid before we start. We can do whatever you need."

Kate looked relieved. "Thank you. I thought this would work, but couldn't be absolutely certain until I'd talked to you." She turned to Craig and then Peters. "Thank you for lending me the teams."

"You're welcome." Peters sat forward, linking his fingers and resting his folded hands on his desktop. In his position as the EAD of the Criminal, Cyber, Response, and Services Branch, he oversaw both the Critical Incident Response Group, which included the Forensic Canine Unit, and the Criminal Investigative Division, which included both the Organized Crime Program and the Diamond Trafficking Program. It was in his best interest for the two groups to work together to maximize their chances of success. "I know you don't report to me directly, but as this is a cross-division collaboration, I'd like to be kept in the loop as to your progress. The dogs are a vital asset to this branch, but there are only four in the Human Scent Evidence Team. If for some reason this scenario isn't working as well as you hope, I'd like to know ASAP so we can either pull the teams or modify our operational protocol."

"Understood, sir. I won't take up their time except when needed for a search. And I'll loop you into my reports during this case."

"Thank you. Beaumont, anything else you need?"

"No. If Meg and Brian won't be needed daily, I'll keep them on backup rotation. Give me as much notice as you can, and they're yours."

"Thank you." Kate stood and touched Brian's shoulder. "Let's go see if Doug's in his office. I'd like to get you both up to speed immediately. I don't know when the first search will be, but it could be in the next few days, so I want us to be able to hit the ground running."

CHAPTER 3

Rough Diamond: An uncut, unpolished stone often resembling a lump of colored glass.

Monday, July 29, 9:49 AM
Diamond Trafficking Program, J. Edgar Hoover Building
Washington, DC

Kate rapped her knuckles against the side of the cubicle near the edge of the well-lit bull pen.

The man inside held up an index finger, not taking his eyes off his screen. He finished typing his sentence and then swiveled in his chair to look up. Meg pegged him in his middle or late thirties, with pale skin awash with freckles above his close-cropped beard, light gray eyes, and auburn hair, with the slightly shaggy look of a missed haircut. His eyes tracked up to Kate, over to Meg and Brian, and then straight down to the dogs. Recognition dawned.

He stood from his chair, offering his hand first to Meg, then to Brian. "Doug Addison."

"I'm Meg Jennings, and this is Brian Foster." Meg turned to the dogs. "Hawk, Lacey, say hello."

Addison chuckled when both dogs sat and politely offered a paw to shake. He bent to greet each dog and then straightened. "You have a couple of smart dogs there."

"That's nothing," Brian said. "Wait until you see them on the trail. Then you'll be impressed."

Addison locked gazes with Kate. "They've agreed to help us?"

"Yes."

Addison fist pumped the air and then flushed in embarrassment. "Sorry. I'm excited about having you as a new tool in our toolbox."

"We're happy to help." Meg scanned the bull pen, where men and women hurried back and forth and a low buzz of voices floated over the room. "Is there somewhere we can go to really talk this out? Brian and I are in, but we'd like some more background, and Kate said you were the guy for that."

"You bet." Addison craned his neck to peer down toward the end of the room. "Looks like the conference room is empty. Let's grab it."

Meg felt curious eyes follow them as they walked through the bull pen. Even though the Forensic Canine Unit wasn't new, its teams were usually out in the field, and if they were in the Hoover Building, they were usually only in their own area, so it often seemed like other office staff members were surprised to find a dog in their midst.

Addison held open the door of the conference room as the handlers, dogs, and special agent entered; then he pulled the door shut behind them.

Brian scanned the conference room, with its long, oblong table surrounded by black-and-chrome chairs, and leaned into Meg. "Craig would be green with envy."

"Is he still complaining about his lack of a conference room?" Kate asked. "Not that I blame him, after so many meetings with all of us and the dogs crammed into his office."

"And spilling out through the doorway when there wasn't enough room," Brian added. "He won't rest until he gets us some meeting space, but so far it's status quo. Come on, Lacey." He moved down the table, pulled out a chair, and sat down. "Down, girl."

Meg took the chair next to him, and the two dogs lay down against the wall, nose to nose.

Addison studied the dogs for a moment before pulling out his own chair across the table from Kate. "They seem to get along well."

Meg checked the dogs over her shoulder. "They're great together and are a well-matched search team on top of it. They'll do well for you."

"That's what Kate said." Addison clasped his hands and leaned forward onto his forearms. "You'd like more information about what we're trying to do up here?"

"Yes. It doesn't actually affect the searches—we can do that for you even if we don't know anything about the case—but it's good for us to understand the greater scope. Then we can be of more help. The dogs will get us where you need us to be, but if we know what the stakes are, then we can work for you as well."

"Understood. Kate sketched out the idea? Who we're going after and what they're smuggling?"

"Yes."

"Okay, then. Crash course on conflict diamonds so you understand what we're up against. You understand the basic concept, which applies almost solely to African diamonds, where rough diamonds are used by rebel groups or their allies to finance conflict aimed at undermining governments in power?"

Both Meg and Brian nodded.

"Good. The term 'blood diamonds' was first used in the late 1990s, but the actual concept has been around a lot longer than that. I could do a deep historical dive, but let me just sketch out an example. Angola, on the west coast of Southern Africa, was consumed by an on-again, off-again civil war starting in 1975, which was renewed after the failure of their elections in 1992. The war was financed by two main natural resources—oil and diamonds. UNITA—the National Union for the Total Independence of Angola—controlled between sixty to seventy percent of Angola's diamond production. That production generated 3.7 billion dollars in revenue, which funded their war effort, keeping them in the game far longer than they would've been without it. In the end, the civil war continued until 2002 and over five hundred thousand Angolans died."

Meg winced. "That's a horrible loss of life."

"Correct. But not the only loss of life when you take into account the actual mining, which is done in a couple of ways. The safest mining is done by panning, but those workers can work for days in unforgiving conditions before they find anything. No matter the size of the diamond they find, and it could be significant, they earn less than a dollar a day. This is what they're supposed to support their families on. As a result, basic needs, like water and sanitation, can't be met. Hunger, disease, infant mortality, and illiteracy all run rampant.

"Then there's mining by digging. Most of the mines are run without regulation, safety standards, or training, and workers are injured, maimed, or killed every day in mining accidents, cave-ins, and landslides. If they survive, it's at the same low pay. In those areas where there's an established minimum wage, it's rarely enforced, and people simply accept the situation because they're so desperate for any kind of work to help feed their families."

"So the mine owners get rich, while the workers who are putting their lives on the line for pennies are lucky to survive each day." A mixture of disgust and anger underlay Meg's tone.

"Yes." Addison's shuttered expression conveyed he shared

her feelings. "Now all these rough stones have to move into the commercial diamond trade. This is where De Beers comes into the picture. I'm sure you've heard of them, since they control about sixty percent of the global trade in rough diamonds, including conflict diamonds. They'd buy diamonds and channel them through Antwerp in Belgium. Antwerp is the world's largest diamond market, and more than half of the world's rough, polished, and industrial diamonds pass through the city. But they were all turning a blind eye to the origin of those diamonds. And that's when the UN got involved."

"The United Nations?" Brian asked. "They had a stake in it?"

"Not a direct monetary stake. But they were pressured by diamond traders, jewelers, and human rights groups to create a diamond certification process intended to stem the blood diamond trade. That's the Kimberley Process Certification Scheme, or KPCS, as we know it today."

"I've heard of that."

"It's been around since 2003, although it was first proposed in 2000, so I'm not surprised it's familiar. And this is when 'blood diamonds' were redefined as 'conflict diamonds.' The KPCS had certain requirements of the countries that signed on as participants. First of all, any country mining the diamonds had to provide a valid certificate for each shipment and could only make those shipments to another participating country. Meanwhile, any importing participant had to verify the certificate of each shipment, send a confirmation of receipt to the country of origin, and keep a copy of that certificate for three years. Then any country through which the stones traveled had to ensure the shipment left their country in the identical shape to when it entered."

Meg wove her fingers together and rested her chin on

them. "That sounds straightforward. But what compelled any country to join?"

"Any country with an interest in human rights joined immediately. Others were pressured by their own legitimate diamond trade to join. It was fairly successful, onboarding forty-one participants to start. But right out of the gate, there were issues. The World Diamond Council's System of Warranties, which was meant to support the KPCS, relies on written or oral assurances by diamond suppliers, so not the level of independent or transparent processing the system really needs. Then there's the fact the KPCS concentrates on stones mined and sold by rebels to finance a war or an insurgent action against a country's governing body, but they ignored those same practices if carried out by governments in power, state actors, or security firms. Also, it only applied to rough diamonds, allowing fully or partially cut stones to circumvent the initiative."

Brian whistled. "Those are some pretty significant loopholes. Easy to take advantage of."

"Exactly. Also, many diamond shipments that are intended to pass through trading hubs are mixed with diamonds from other countries of export, making the diamonds untraceable to either their initial country or mine of origin."

"That's a problem."

"Those are the requirements," said Meg. "What happens if participants don't comply?"

"That's another issue. The KPCS is supposed to impose sanctions on any country found noncompliant with the minimum requirements. But, so far, it's reticent to do so except in the most egregious and indisputable instances, such as in the war-torn Central African Republic."

"I'm getting the impression the Kimberley Process isn't getting the job done," Brian said.

"It's not, and that's why conflict diamonds are still a problem, and why we're having this conversation. They're still being mined, still financing wars, still being smuggled into the US."

Kate had been quiet, letting Addison take the lead, but now she sat forward. "And that's where we come in. Those stones are still moving. Those forced to mine them are still suffering and dying. International agencies are looking at the larger picture, but we're looking specifically at how they're coming into the US, who's purchasing them, and how they're being distributed. And this effort will deal with those last two."

Meg sat back in her chair and blew out a deep breath. She met Brian's eyes and he gave her a single definitive nod in return. "We're in."

"Excellent." Addison tapped his fist twice on the table in enthusiasm. "One way to stop the trade is for it to become unprofitable. The fewer groups who buy conflict diamonds, the more they'll try to sell legitimately. But if all this seems bleak, there actually is some hope on the horizon coming from another direction entirely."

"What's that?"

"Consumers. Many consumers are pretty savvy, and there are more and more of them every day who are searching for 'ethical' or 'conflict-free' diamonds. There are companies springing up that will only source entirely ethical diamonds, and they're doing big business."

"Vote with your wallet," Brian added dryly.

"Exactly. Also, lab-created diamonds are no longer looked at disparagingly, but are seen as a responsible choice providing the same physical, chemical, and optical characteristics as 'real' diamonds, with none of the mining. And then there's fair trade diamonds."

"Like fair trade coffee?"

"Same idea, different product. It promotes equity in the

diamond trade, with fair pricing and a requirement of accepted human rights practices. It's transforming the artisanal mining sector."

"I had no idea there was such a thing."

"There is. And all of that is good. But it's all small potatoes compared to the illegal diamond trade. We'll have our work cut out for us for many years to come, but I'd like to see us put them out of business eventually." He looked from Brian to Meg and back again. "Any questions?"

Meg pushed away from the table. "Not from me. Thank you for the comprehensive overview. Brian?"

"Nope. I feel like I have a good handle on it." Brian stood. "Thanks."

Kate got to her feet. "Now we just need to wait to hear from Agent Pierce. If he approves our trial run, we'll be ready for action as soon as the stones hit the black market."

CHAPTER 4

Twinning Wisp: A series of optical distortions or inclusions that form along a diamond's growth plate.

Wednesday, July 31, 1:25 PM
Johnson Park
Camden, New Jersey

"He said the statue of a dancing goat?" Meg angled her hand over her eyes and peered into Johnson Park as she, Brian, and Kate stopped for the light at the intersection of Cooper and N Front Streets. All three were dressed in casual clothes, and Hawk and Lacey were both out of their work vests and were working on lead with just their collars to blend in.

Johnson Park was situated near the Benjamin Franklin Bridge, connecting Philadelphia's historic downtown with Camden, New Jersey, just over the Delaware River. The park lay diagonally across the street from where they stood, a walkway cutting toward the early-nineteenth-century library located in the center of the park.

Brian glanced toward the building and then back at Meg. "Uh-oh."

Kate stepped forward, her eyes darting up and down

Front Street, taking in the people, cars, and any movement, her hand automatically lifting toward the holstered firearm under her blazer. "What's wrong?"

"Sorry, stand down. There's no cause for alarm. I just noticed that building"—Brian pointed across the street at the library—"and am anticipating an architecture lesson."

"From?"

"Me." Meg loosened up on Hawk's leash and stepped onto the street as the WALK sign flashed on. "Brian and I jog together a few times a week. He picks parks. I pick the oldest areas of DC so I can gawk at the amazing Classical architecture."

"A lecture usually accompanies said gawking," Brian added.

"I do *not* lecture." She met Kate's eyes and gave a *men . . . what-are-you-going-to-do-with-them?* shrug. "My attempts to school Brian in the finer points of the beauty of old buildings always seem to fall on deaf ears."

"Just do it." Brian's tone was resigned. "You know you want to."

"Want to tell you the library is clearly in the Classical Revival style based on its perfect symmetry, Ionic columns, the pediment over the front door, and its white sandstone construction? Nah, no one wants to hear about that."

Kate chuckled. "Smooth."

Meg sent her a sidelong glance. "It's like hiding vegetables in other foods so kids don't know they're eating healthy. He's learning, he just hasn't recognized it yet."

"It's like you think I can't hear you," Brian grumbled.

"Oh, I know you can hear me. But are you paying attention? That's the real question." Meg stepped up onto the sidewalk. "Do you know where this dancing goat is?"

"He said inside the park, by the rectangular pool. That shouldn't be hard to find." Kate walked briskly down the sidewalk, and Meg, Brian, and the dogs easily kept pace.

They were about to start their trial search and were right on time to meet Finn Pierce. Pierce didn't want to risk being seen with them in Philadelphia and had suggested meeting for the first time across the river in Camden. Kate, Meg, Brian, and the dogs drove in from DC, arriving with just minutes to spare.

They turned into the park entrance. The front walkway ran in two straight lines flanking a long, blue-tiled pool, which stretched toward a semicircular fountain in front of the library steps.

Brian pointed at the midsection of the walkway to a bronze statue of a creature on its back legs. "That might be it there."

They strolled up the walkway, casually chatting as they passed the bronze figure of a young boy with a flute on a pedestal climbed by fairies and squirrels. They continued along the edge of the pool, a group of friends out for a walk on a sunny summer afternoon.

"That's him," Kate said quietly. "Just past the statue, in the shade of that big tree."

Pierce sat on a park bench beside a bronze goat rearing up on its hind legs, its front hooves waving in the air. He held open a copy of the *Philadelphia Inquirer*, his dark head bowed slightly as if reading, but his sharp eyes tracked them over the top of the paper as they approached, taking in first the humans, and then the dogs. He closed and folded the paper, placing it on the seat beside him, his gaze constantly shifting, taking in their entire section of the park. He was a stocky man, with broad shoulders, a thickness that suggested hours spent working weights, and an alertness hinting at instant action, if required. A black leather messenger bag sat at his feet.

Kate strolled directly toward him. "Good to see you." Her voice was pitched high enough so anyone around them would simply see a happy accidental meeting. They wouldn't notice the lack of names or that their voices instantly dropped following the greeting.

"Hey." Pierce's hawkish face was suddenly transformed by a broad smile that would have fooled anyone from a distance who wasn't close enough to see that his flat eyes never sparkled. "It's been too long." He offered his hand to Meg first and then to Brian, careful to address them without using any names. "It's nice to meet you."

He settled back on the bench, draping one arm along the top as he looked up at Meg. The dark eyes that held hers were steady, but the lines around them told a tale of stress and weariness. "You really think this plan will work?"

"Yes." Meg's tone was backed by years of confidence in her dog. "You give them a scent to follow and they'll track it."

"How close behind do they need to be?"

"For this, a three- to five-minute lag essentially makes them invisible. But we've followed trails that are hours old. Occasionally days old, depending on the conditions."

Brian dropped a gentle hand onto Lacey's head and stroked. "They won't let you down. They're great separately; they're unbeatable as a team. We'll do a test search to show you, but you won't be disappointed."

"They can follow a scent both inside and outside? This would have to be a combination of the two."

"Yes."

"Then let's test the system. This is how it would go: I'll send you a text containing the GPS coordinates of the start site; then you'll have to track me through town from there to the final destination."

"Isn't that—"

"But that's—"

Kate and Meg both jerked to a halt, and Meg motioned to Kate to go first.

"Isn't that dangerous?" Kate said. "You can't afford to have anything to tie you to a bust."

"I'm not going to sit there and text you out in the open. I had a friend hire an app developer so there was less chance it could be traced back to me. The guy wrote code to pick up my exact GPS location and send it to a single phone number. One press of a button does the entire job and then automatically uninstalls the app in case anyone tries to tie my phone to anything. And I'll use a burner phone and dispose of it as soon as possible afterward. That's standard practice for us anyway, so it won't be suspicious. We don't trust any communication device for business not to be hacked, so we don't keep it long enough for that to happen." He looked up at Meg expectantly.

"Is that scenario realistic? You're not going to park in front of a building somewhere? Why would you walk any distance without it appearing like you're leaving a trail?"

"Because it's what we already do. The city is covered with closed-circuit TV. There are almost six hundred cameras in the downtown core alone." He sat back on the bench, crossing his arms over his chest. "We don't get caught on CCTV."

Meg nodded in understanding of what he didn't say. "You make sure anything that could ID you, like a license plate, is kept far away from a buy site. Do you have the camera sites memorized?"

"For the downtown core, sure."

"Makes sense," Brian said. "It's a low-tech way to foil their high-tech system. How far do you typically walk?"

"Four or five blocks. Depends on the location. We stay out of sight as much as possible because of facial recognition software. Okay, prove to me this will work. Go grab a coffee for a half hour. I'll go back and will let you know where the starting point is."

"We don't need to be that far behind you. It actually won't work if we're that far behind you, not if you want us to catch the hand-off in progress."

"I know. Just satisfy me this will work, and I'm in."

"Did you bring the clothing?" Kate asked.

"Yeah." Pierce bent down and pulled an opaque plastic bag from his messenger bag and handed it to Kate.

Meg slipped off her backpack, opened it, and Kate dropped the bag inside. "Thanks."

"Go. I'll text you in thirty."

With cheerful waves and a call of "Tell Marie we need to get together sometime" the FBI team moved on, circling the library, and then leaving the park on the far side before heading back to their vehicles.

Meg and Brian loaded the dogs into Meg's SUV and then popped the back hatch. As Kate and Brian crowded in, Meg opened up her backpack and pulled out Pierce's plastic bag. She dumped out the contents and then picked up one of the two clear zippered bags, each with a crumpled sock in it. "Perfect."

Kate leaned in and wrinkled her nose. "They look well used, all right. It'll do for the dogs?"

"It'll be great. And we have two separate bags, so if we get split up, we've each still got his scent." Meg looked sideways at Brian. "We need to clue the dogs into a key word right away with this, but I think we need a code word for Special Agent Pierce. In case we're overheard and anyone connects us to him, we don't want to use a name someone might be able to trace back to him, and then to the Bureau."

"Agreed. What should we call him?"

"How about Jameson?" suggested Kate.

"Like the whiskey?"

"Sure. With a name like Finn Pierce, you think he's not Irish? He just looks Italian enough for them to accept him as Angelo Marzano."

"You have a point. That works for me."

"Me too," said Meg. "I assume you're coming with us as part of this trial?"

"You bet," Kate said. "Doug couldn't make it today, but otherwise this is essentially a dry run of how these searches will go."

Meg considered Kate's loose khakis and sneakers. "You may find that's not athletic enough if we're going to be running miles. Today won't be a sprint search, but, overall, we're always prepared that there may be times when we're running for our lives. There are risks involved. It's not just our search for them, it may be their search for us. We have to be ready for things to go sideways."

Kate quickly scanned Meg, from her expensive hiking boots to her yoga pants to her moisture-wicking athletic T-shirt. "Understood. Thanks. So, then, this will also be a test of how well I can keep up. If I can't, this won't work."

Brian slid off his backpack and tossed it beside Meg's as she zipped hers up. "It'll be a test all around." He grinned. "I have faith. We can do this. But you're sure this won't look suspicious? I mean, a couple out for a walk with their dogs is never suspicious, but if all of us show up . . ."

"We're not going to be anywhere near Pierce," Kate said. "When we find him, we won't even make contact with him again. No one is going to be watching for someone to pick up his trail a full half hour after he was there. Not to mention that we're in civvies. This time it'll be fine. But you're right. When you're five minutes behind him, no way can we all be seen together."

"Okay, just checking." Brian pulled out his phone and checked the time. "Fifteen minutes to go. Then we need to be ready to run."

CHAPTER 5

Solitaire: A piece of jewelry containing just one gemstone.

Wednesday, July 31, 2:28 PM
Penn's Landing
Philadelphia, Pennsylvania

"It's right here." Brian pointed to the upcoming turn-off and glanced again at the piece of paper standing in the cup holder between himself and Meg. "39.9428 north by -75.1417 west," he mumbled to himself for about the sixth time.

"Where are we now?" Meg took the corner into the parking lot carefully, conscious of the two dogs in the K-9 compartment taking up the entire space where a second seat would normally be in her SUV. Separated by mesh, the dogs were visible in the back, lying side by side, relaxed with their heads on their paws. They knew the routine, and knew to rest while they could, before they had to go to work.

Behind them, Kate's silver sedan pulled into the parking lot.

Brian studied the app on his phone that displayed a large compass surrounded by neat boxes of information, including latitude, longitude, altitude, speed, and time. "39.9430 north by -75.1419 west."

"That sounds like the same set of numbers."

"They're off by a fraction of a degree. We're close."

"That's an understatement."

"We have to get the starting location right or the whole thing is off. Notice he didn't tell us what he's driving?"

"Yes. I think that may be because he won't always be in the same vehicle. That way we can't get hung up on the starting point."

"He doesn't know the dogs are the starting point. Right, Lacey, my girl?"

At the sound of her name, the German shepherd scrambled to her feet to stick her head through the open compartment window over the console. She butted her nose against Brian's arm until he reached back, without looking, to scratch her behind the ears. "Good girl, almost there." He was silent for a moment, his eyes fixed on his phone. "Slow . . . slow . . . here!"

Meg flicked a glance in her rearview mirror to make sure Kate was far enough behind her and gently braked to a stop. "Here?"

Brian craned around in his seat. "Slightly past, but good enough. Find a place to park. We want to come back to the navy Honda just behind us. We'll let the dogs find the scent and really get us moving." Straightening and bracing a hand on the dash, he leaned forward to peer through the windshield. "This place is packed. Find any open spot, even if we have to jog back."

Meg finally found two nearly adjacent spots at the far end of the lot, one aisle over, and pulled in. "Think he picked this as a starting point to lose us time right out of the gate?"

"You bet. He wants to test the dogs' abilities and will likely make this as hard as would be realistic."

"Downtown historic Philly in the middle of the summer? That's peak tourist season. This place is going to be wall-to-wall bodies." Meg climbed out and circled around to the rear of the SUV to grab her go bag while Brian did the same. Then they opened the compartment doors and leashed their dogs.

Kate appeared from behind her vehicle. "You have the location?"

"Brian does. It's back where we stopped briefly." Meg glanced at her fitness tracker. "I'm sure it's what he intended, but we're definitely losing time. You ready?"

"Yes, ma'am."

"Then let's go."

They jogged back to the vehicle Brian had marked as the starting location. Meg pulled the plastic-wrapped dirty sock out of her backpack, opened the bag, and offered it to both dogs to take the scent. "Lacey, Hawk, this is Jameson. Find Jameson." She resealed the bag, tucked it into an external pocket for easy access if they needed to refresh the dogs' memory of the scent, and reseated her backpack.

The dogs were already scenting the ground, noses down, moving around the Honda toward the surrounding cars. Hawk found the scent first, his posture quickly morphing from relaxed and alert to intense concentration. Every cue from the pull on the leash to the proud upward wave of his tail told Meg he had the trail. "Brian, Hawk has it. Hawk, find Jameson."

"Coming." Brian and Lacey slipped between the Honda and the black sedan behind it. Lacey moved toward Hawk and instantly alerted on the scent. "She has it too. Lacey, find Jameson."

They let the dogs set the pace, jogging lightly through the parking lot toward the walkway running alongside the Delaware River.

Part of Philadelphia's bustling waterfront, Penn's Landing was part historical site, part commercial enterprise. As they jogged by the bow of the century-old four-masted *Moshulu*, a well-lit sign displayed the menu of the restaurant within. Heavy foot traffic slowed them down to a fast walk as they passed the twinned submarine *USS Becuna* and the Spanish-American War cruiser *USS Olympia*, both swarming with tourists. Past the historic ships, they picked up the pace, following the waterfront walkway as it wound its way between the river and a line of gourmet food trucks doing brisk business.

The dogs were sure of their path and trotted along the walkway, noses down. Normally in an outdoor search with a delayed start, the dogs kept their heads high as they tried to find and then stay within the scent cone pushed along with the wind in an ever-widening angle from the point of origin. But with a known scent this fresh, especially on a day like today when the flags flanking the river only swayed gently in the low breeze, the dogs could employ the more efficient head-down trailing technique to follow a narrow path.

Meg and Brian jogged behind them, leashes fully extended, keeping an easy pace. Meg's gaze dropped to Hawk, who ran comfortably about eight feet ahead at the end of his leash, and then to Lacey beside him. She studied her critically, noting her fluid gait, as well as her scenting technique. "Brian, she looks really good. She moves comfortably, and, clearly, her nose hasn't gotten rusty."

Brian didn't glance at her, but his smile told her everything about how worried he'd been. "My girl is kick-ass, no doubt about it."

Meg understood his worry. It wasn't just about his dog, though that was certainly at the top of the list, but it was also about their careers. They were a part of the Human Scent Evidence Team, as much as it was a part of them. To not be part of the team, to not contribute to the greater good they did, would have been an emotional blow to both of them. K-9 handlers were realistic about the working lives of their dogs. Hawk was four now, and while he should have another three or four years left as a working dog, the strenuous nature of their calling meant any injury or illness could retire them permanently at any time. It was one thing to prepare to retire gracefully at an expected time. It was something else to crash out of the Bureau without warning. She knew Brian's fear that they'd never be back, had shared it, but seeing Lacey in action again only three months after nearly dying at the claws and teeth of a cougar gave her a real boost. And from the spring in Brian's step, he clearly felt it too.

The dogs turned left off the walkway and onto a narrow path that led to a round, red-bricked patio, a giant compass encircled by folding wooden picnic tables and chairs beside a painted chess board with four-foot-tall pieces. Meg followed Hawk as he darted around a little girl hopping along a line of bricks and then they were through, up a short flight of six steps to the upper walkway, and out to the intersection of Dock Street and Christopher Columbus Boulevard.

Forced to stop at the light, they stood breathing heavily. Meg took the brief break to pull the bag out again and refresh the scent with the dogs.

Bent over, offering the bag to Lacey, she looked up over her shoulder at Kate. "How are you doing?"

Kate was breathing hard, with her face flushed pink and

a sheen of perspiration across her forehead. "Fine. Though I'm thinking it might not be a bad idea to mix more cardio and less weight training into my exercise regimen."

"You won't need to while we're on this case if all the searches are like this. There's our light. Hawk, find Jameson."

Brian echoed the command to Lacey and they were off again, weaving through pedestrians flooding the intersection. Halfway through the intersection, the dogs took a hard right through a gap in traffic and ran between the neglected tracks of an old trolley line set into packed dirt. Brian dropped back slightly so Hawk could go first, followed by Meg. Then Kate followed in the rear.

Kate turned to look behind them down the track. "I don't see any trains," she called. "Y'all think this line is still being used?"

"Don't think so." Brian sounded a tiny bit breathless. "Look at the dirt and rust on the track. If they were being used, they'd be grimy and oily. I think it's been a while since they've seen traffic."

Meg tightened up on the leash slightly. Hawk wasn't wavering in his path down the track, but cars were driving by at forty miles per hour, and it would only take one slip of the foot to put them off the track and into traffic. "He probably used this line because it's decommissioned. Helped him avoid the foot traffic."

"Helps us too."

They had to wait for traffic to clear below an overpass, and then sprinted across the road and around to mirrored circular staircases leading up to Walnut Street. Up the stairs they found a redbrick herringbone footpath nearly devoid of people, and the dogs picked up their pace as they jogged over I-95 and then cut right onto Front Street.

Meg checked the time—they'd been at it for ten minutes. The tightness in her legs from the cold start had loosened into a pleasant warmth and her breath was even and measured. Hawk's stride had lengthened and he moved with an easy grace, his head occasionally dipping to sample the scent. He loved working a search, and loved it even more when paired with Lacey. A quick glance at Lacey reassured her the German shepherd was managing the exercise well. If anything, it was Brian who looked a little out of practice, color brightening his cheekbones a little more than usual. She was tempted to give him a little good-natured poke, but she suspected Brian hadn't jogged on his own quite as much as he'd implied while Lacey was recovering. He'd go out with her at a moment's notice to make sure she was fit and ready for duty, but he'd never liked jogging for its own sake. Meg suspected he was kicking himself for that now.

They cut into a park, and down a path between wooden benches and trees in full leaf, then past the sprawling Irish Memorial, complete with gravestones, starving children, and immigrants disembarking from a boat in the New World, all set against the backdrop of the modern tower and heavy cables of the Benjamin Franklin suspension bridge. Heavy tourist foot traffic forced them to slow down to a fast walk as the dogs led them into the heart of historic Philadelphia: past the Museum of the American Revolution, down 3rd Street, through the eighteenth-century garden around the historic Todd House and Carpenters' Hall, out onto Chestnut Street, then up toward Independence Hall, before crossing over to the far side and taking a diagonal path toward a long, low building running for an entire block.

Meg glanced across the street toward Independence Hall. She'd never been inside the two-story Georgian structure, but knew it was where the Declaration of Independence was signed on July 4, 1776, and the Constitution was completed there in September 1787. She gave herself a few seconds to take in the bell tower where the famous cracked Liberty Bell first hung, the steeple, the eighteenth-century clock, and the statue of George Washington on the front walk, before turning her attention back to the search.

Brian caught her eye and grinned at her. *Caught you gawking.*

Meg ignored him. "What's the building up ahead?"

"Unless I miss my guess, that's the Liberty Bell Center," Kate puffed.

Meg scanned the group of people streaming into the building. "You don't think he actually went through there, do you?"

"I bet he did. He said there'd be indoor and outdoor searches."

They knew for certain when the dogs took them right up to the front door.

"Wait here," Kate said. "I'm going to get us in." She strode away from them, already pulling her FBI flip case out of her pants pocket. She approached the nearest security guard, extended the ID, and had a quiet conversation before waving them over. "I've explained to"—her eyes cut quickly to the nameplate on the man's breast pocket—"Officer Chopra why we're here, and he's offered to take one of you through the building and will stay with you while you're inside." She indicated Hawk. "Meg, you go, and Brian and I will wait out here."

"Better idea," said Brian, "while she's inside, Lacey and I will check the exits to track how he left the building. Assuming he's not still inside. If he is, we'll come back here."

"I'm with you then."

Meg followed the officer inside, winding through the

gallery of exhibits filling the main hall and down to the far end to where the Liberty Bell hung inside, cordoned off from the public by a steel railing. She tried her best to politely move through the tourists packing the space, deftly avoiding the small hands reaching for her dog—*Sorry, he's a working dog and he's on duty right now*—and meeting pointed and sometimes curious gazes at the animal in the midst of a museum. Officer Chopra helped clear her way as she and Hawk wove through the crowd, as she let Hawk lead her all the way to the special alcove built to house the bell.

Definitely trying to make this hard on the dogs.

Their path circled the bell and then right to the exit. Meg thanked Chopra for his help, and then she and Hawk stepped out into fresh air, where she found Brian, Lacey, and Kate.

"Lacey picked up his scent right outside this door," Brian said.

"Yeah, he passed through a busy indoor museum to see if he could lose us." Meg checked the time again. "This is taking too long. We're constantly losing time because of all the people."

"He likely had all the same slowdowns," Kate reasoned. "Do the dogs need the scent again?"

Meg studied Hawk's posture as he put his nose down and kept moving smoothly forward. "Doesn't look like it."

They followed the dogs back toward Independence Hall, and then looped around to 6th Street to go north.

Meg noticed that while Hawk was head down, pushing hard, Lacey was alert, but was now staying several paces behind Hawk instead of being shoulder to shoulder with him as she normally would. But her gait was steady and her nose work was solid. *Her first long search in months. Is she beginning to tire?*

Hawk led them down 6th Street to a glass-and-concrete

office building, where they climbed the short flight of steps under large block letters reading 100 INDEPENDENCE MALL WEST. Hawk immediately turned toward a chalkboard reading WELCOME TO THE INDEPENDENCE BEER GARDEN and the patio beyond. Rows of tables, surrounded by benches and bar stools, were lined up in neat rows under an iron I-beam frame running with heavy chains, from which dripped miniature incandescent Edison bulbs. The patio lived up to its name and lush greenery, flowers, and grasses burst from massive pots, tumbled from hanging planters, or climbed wooden trellises. The patio was packed, mostly with young people in shorts, sundresses, and sandals, escaping the heat with a cold drink. A heavy, rhythmic beat and laughter spilled out onto the sidewalk.

Hawk pulled again on his leash, sensing the end of the search, but just at that moment, Meg caught Pierce's eye. He sat alone in a corner near the entrance, perched on a stool at a table for two, nursing a beer and scrolling his phone. His head was bent, but his eyes watched the entrance and she realized he'd seen her long before she'd spotted him.

He gave a barely noticeable shake of his head. *That's far enough.* Then his eyes dropped to his phone.

"Hawk, stop. Sit." Ignoring Brian's questioning expression, Meg dropped her backpack to the ground, dug in it for a moment, and pulled out a map. Snapping it open, she held the map of Philadelphia out toward Brian and Kate. "Don't look into the bar." She kept her voice down and then pressed close. "Pierce is there, near the door, but he knows we're here and has warned us off."

"Doesn't want to be seen near us in town," Kate murmured. "Dogs did a great job, though. Took us right to him."

"Or would have if we'd let them." Brian also took off his backpack, squatted down, and pulled out a bag of treats for Lacey. "Good girl." He looked up at Kate as Meg folded up the map, slipped it away, and pulled out treats for Hawk. "She's confused as to why we're breaking off the search. She knows we're practically on top of the target. Why stop now?"

Meg poured a half-dozen treats into her hand and offered them to Hawk, who swooped in and emptied her palm with a simple swipe of his tongue. "I wish I could explain it to them. They'll think the search isn't done." She swung her pack on and tightened up the lead. "Hawk, come." She could feel his reluctance, but gentle pressure on the lead brought him to heel as they went down the steps and continued on toward Market Street. Catching the light, they crossed back toward the Liberty Bell Center and the Delaware River, the dogs trotting easily at their sides on a loose leash.

Meg studied Kate, who pulled at the front of her T-shirt. "Hot?"

Kate swiped some of the sweat off her brow with the back of her hand. "I'm sweating like a whore in church."

"You're . . . what?" The word came out as half question, half laughter.

"Sorry, we Southerners love a colorful phrase. The answer to your question is yes, I'm hot. And not in as good shape as I thought."

"That's not even a long search."

"I was afraid you'd say that. How do you guys do it?"

"Jogging," Brian replied. "A *lot* of jogging." He scowled. "Have I ever mentioned to you how much I hate jogging?"

"Until you're out on a search," Meg countered, "then you remember how useful it is because it allows you to keep going."

"Yeah, yeah, I know. It's why I keep doing it. Why *we*

keep doing it." He looked past Meg to Kate. "Do you think that was enough to green-light us?"

"I think so, but he'll get in touch with me when he can. Then it's just a matter of waiting for Pierce to let us know and for us to be ready to jump at it. The shipment of diamonds is expected soon, so we could easily start for real inside of the next few days. Be ready."

CHAPTER 6

Cleavage: A weak spot where a diamond may fracture if struck in a certain direction.

Thursday, August 1, 5:46 AM
Jennings/Webb residence
Washington, DC

Light and sound exploded into the quiet dark. Meg pulled away from Webb, rolling over to flail blindly for the cacophony until her fingers closed over her phone. Only then, did she crack open her eyelids to peer blearily at Brian's name on the screen and the time. She answered the call. "I'm getting up. You don't have to nag."

"I'm not nagging. I'm canceling our jog."

The flatness of Brian's tone jolted Meg out of her sleepiness. "What's wrong?"

Webb pushed up on one elbow, his sharp gaze locked on Meg in the dim light thrown by the cell phone pressed to her cheek. He had a pillowcase crease along one cheek and his short hair was mussed, but his dark eyes were clear and assessing.

"I don't like the way Lacey looks this morning."

"What does that mean?"

"Maybe she's not really ready for this."

Meg dragged herself upright, pulling her knees up to her chest. "Brian, you're not making sense. What's going on? What don't you like about the way she looks?"

"I can tell yesterday really took it out of her. She's game to do what I need her to do, but I think she's pushing. She's stiff and not moving smoothly."

A vision of Lacey near the end of yesterday's search filled Meg's mind. The shepherd had begun to flag toward the end, but hadn't seemed to be in pain. "Dogs have the same muscular system we do. She pushed it a bit and now she's stiff and a bit sore. You need to work her through it, not let her sit until it wears off. And then we need to keep her active. She'll get back up to speed. Think of where she was three months ago. In some ways it's a miracle she pulled through that, so give her a bit of a break if the rest of her recovery has been pretty run-of-the-mill."

"I wish I could get her into her therapist because the water tank there would be perfect right now. But you have to book weeks out to get onto their schedule."

"Maybe jogging with her is too much, but why don't we take her on a long walk to keep her muscles warm and active. That would . . . Wait . . ."

"What?"

"I can get you a water workout if you really want it."

"I'm not tossing her into the Potomac."

"Ugh. We want to get her better, not actually make her sick. No, I'm thinking of my parents' rescue. Dad does a ton of rehab with the animals, so they put in a small, heated rehab pool in the barn so he could work with them year-round. It's not super fancy, no treadmill or anything, which would have been prohibitively expensive, but she could do some swimming. Non–weight bearing exercise would be just what Lacey needs to work those sore mus-

cles. It would do her some good. And it would do you some good to be doing something proactive for her. Interested? I'll call Craig and clear it with him and tell him we're still available if something comes up."

"Think your parents would mind?"

Meg laughed. "Mind their daughter, who hasn't seen them in over a month, by the way, dropping in to visit? I'm pretty sure they'll be fine with it. Come over at eight, and we'll leave then. If you're not going to torture me with a jog, I'm going back to bed for an hour."

"See you at eight." His voice sounding considerably lighter, Brian ended the call.

Meg lay her phone facedown on her bedside table, the room sinking into darkness again as she slid down in bed with a sigh.

Webb tucked her in close against him. "Is Lacey okay?"

"I think so. She did great yesterday during the search, until the very end when she started to slow down a bit. The spirit is willing, but the body is a little out of practice. Nothing serious, I think; she just needs to get back in the game. And so does Brian. He's spent months being totally focused on her; he needs to take a step back now and let her prove herself."

"The best way to get back in the game is to actually be in the game."

"There we go, being on the same wavelength again." She curled closer. "And now I get an extra hour of sleep with you and get to skip out on an activity I loathe. It's going to be a good day." She closed her eyes and let her body go boneless. "You're not on shift today. Want to come?"

"I thought you'd never ask. I noticed you planned your arrival in time for lunch. Your mom sure does put up a good meal." She could hear his smile in the dark. "It's going to be a good day."

She chuckled. "Especially when she knows we're coming . . . which she will in about an hour." Meg stifled a huge yawn against Webb's shoulder. She needed to call her mother, she should see if Cara was free to come, and if Todd would drive, they could bring all the dogs . . .

In two more breaths she was out.

CHAPTER 7

Artisanal Mining: Artisanal mining is done by independent subsistence miners. Diamonds are extracted from riverbed deposits by artisanal miners who pan manually to separate diamonds and gold from the gravel they haul up from the river bottom.

Thursday, August 1, 10:51 AM
Cold Spring Haven Animal Rescue
Cold Spring Hollow, Virginia

Meg had rolled out of bed at seven and promptly called Cara, who was happy to join the trip to Cold Spring Haven, as long as they could return in time for her to prepare for the advanced group training class at her dog school, scheduled for seven that evening. They'd set off for Virginia at eight fifteen, Brian riding with Meg in her SUV with Lacey and Hawk in the K-9 compartment, and Webb driving Cara, Saki, Blink, and Cody. She'd caught his expression when Cara came out with all three dogs, a look that said *Why me?* but he good-naturedly loaded all the dogs into his truck.

McCord had his head in a story and was out of the house even before Meg called Cara.

Traffic was steady, and it took a little over two and a

half hours to get there. But it was a beautiful, sunny day, so they rolled down the windows, cranked up the music—as loud as possible without bothering the dogs snoozing in the back—and enjoyed a day out of the office with the boss's approval.

Brian had never been to the rescue before, and he leaned forward eagerly as they drove up the long, winding driveway. Cresting a rise, they broke out of the trees to find the rescue spread out before them. Open fields stretched out to their right, while a white wooden pasture fence sped past in a blur on their left. Down the hill a long, rambling ranch house, with a wraparound porch, stood at the end of the driveway. Behind the house sat a freshly painted red barn, with bright white trim, and several outbuildings surrounded by fields and fenced pastures to help manage the varied livestock, wildlife, smaller animals, reptiles, and birds.

"Wait for it . . . ," Meg said.

Brian looked at her quizzically, then toward the approaching house. "Wait for what?"

"Give him a second . . ."

Hawk shot up from where he'd been napping, pressed his nose against the screen of the K-9 compartment, and whined.

"Almost there, Hawk. Hang on. I love this part. He's so excited every time we come here. He knows the smell of the rescue, knows when we're coming up the driveway. Knows she's here."

"Who?"

"Auria, our old bay mare. She came to the rescue around the same time as Hawk." Her smile widened when Hawk whined again. "Hang on, buddy. Here we are." She slowed to a stop at the end of the driveway, directly in front of the house. "Watch this."

She climbed out of the SUV and opened the door to the K-9 compartment. "Hawk, down."

Hawk jumped down, but stood by the vehicle, unmoving but clearly tense, his head high, eyes bright and fixed on something behind Meg while his tail wagged furiously.

Brian watched from the front seat. "What's he waiting for?"

"Me. Hawk?"

The dog's head eagerly swung up.

Meg pointed in the direction of the barn. "Go get Auria!"

The Labrador took off, sprinting in the direction of the barn. He streaked by the older couple coming down the porch steps who watched him go with matching grins, and then he shot past the end of the house and through the open barn door behind it. There were several seconds of silence, followed by a single bark and a long whinny of greeting.

Meg peered in through the compartment door. "They're totally attached and have been since he was a puppy. It makes his day to come to see her. Makes her day too." She glanced at the approaching couple. "Come say hi to my parents."

Meg walked into her father's arms for a hug and a kiss and then her mother's. By that time Cara, Webb, and the other dogs had joined them. There were hugs, and handshakes between the men, and then Meg grabbed Brian's arm to pull him forward.

"Mom, Dad, you remember Brian."

Jake Jennings stepped forward, warmly extending his hand. "Of course we do. We met at Meg and Cara's after the close of the Garber case. Good to see you again." Letting go of Brian's hand, he stepped toward the German shepherd, extending his hand for Lacey to scent before getting closer. "Hi, Lacey. Good to see you again too." He didn't move, but his eyes shot sideways to Brian. "May I pet her?"

"Oh yeah, she's great with people."

"She was friendly when I met her before, but it's always good to ask." He bent down and ran a hand over Lacey's head and down her back. Lacey gazed up at him, tongue lolling, tail wagging in pleasure. He ran quick, experienced hands over the dog, pausing briefly at the ridges of scar tissue under her fur before straightening. "She's healed up nicely. Meg told us what happened. We were so relieved when she came through the surgery successfully and then her recovery was smooth. I hope it's okay that Meg's been keeping us up to date."

Eda Jennings laid a hand warmly on Brian's arm and gave it a gentle squeeze. "Even though we only met briefly last year, we've heard so much about both of you over the years, you've always felt like family. We kept pestering Meg for updates and were thrilled to hear you were back on the team."

Brian's smile melted away. "Actually, that's why we're here. Lacey went on her first search yesterday since the attack and I could tell this morning she was sore."

"Gotta ease her back into it." Jake moved several paces away. "Lacey, come here, girl." He studied the dog critically as she trotted over to him. "Looks good to me, but Meg said you want to take her swimming. That's a good idea. Loosen her up without weight bearing."

"That was my thought."

"I'd be happy to work with her if you like," Jake offered. "I've rehabilitated a lot of animals through both injury and illness." He threw an arm wide. "Kind of what we do here."

Brian's shoulders sagged with relief. "I'd appreciate that, Mr. Jennings."

"Just Jake will do. We're not formal with family around here."

"Brunch first," Eda said. "Cara, come in and give me a hand?" She considered the dog who pressed against her legs. "You coming too, Blinky?" She ran a hand over his long, slender back. "He's getting so much better now. Not that long ago, he didn't want to get out of the car."

"Notice he still clings to you like Velcro?"

"I've never minded. All our animals have their own set of needs."

"Hello!"

The group turned toward the barn at the sound of a female voice. Coming out of the barn door was a young woman, slender and blond, in cutoff denim shorts and an aqua tank top, leading a horse on a head rope and waving one arm over her head. Hawk trotted on the other side of the mare, staying close, but out of reach of her sturdy hooves.

"Is that Emma?" Webb squinted at the approaching group. "I haven't seen her since Christmas. She's really settled in."

Meg could picture the girl as she'd first seen her—in a black sheath dress, too tight and too short, and overly bright makeup. She'd been shimmied halfway up a fallen tree in a swamp, pursued by the largest alligator Meg had ever seen. She and Hawk had rescued Emma that day. First from the alligator, who'd died under the blade of Meg's search-and-rescue knife, and then from a sex-trafficking ring they'd subsequently identified and blown wide open. All alone in the world, without even a last name she'd admit to. Meg had brought Emma home to her parents. The Jenningses had experience raising two teenage daughters, and had agreed to take the exhausted, abused, and frightened girl into their home. They'd put her to work at the rescue, and just as Meg had found healing working with the animals after the death of her first K-9, Deuce, so had Emma. For the past year, Meg and Cara had heard stories about how Emma had slowly melded into the life of the rescue, learning how to mend a broken wing, bottle-feed newborns every two hours through the night, feed the resident emu, Jeeves, shovel horse manure, and mend fences.

When she'd first come to the rescue, Meg had high hopes Emma would mesh with her parents and the rescue, but was realistic about their chances. Sex-trafficked since she was thirteen, Emma had been locked in a room with a constant stream of girls except for the times she was let out to service whoever paid for her. She trusted no one, and with good reason. But the Jenningses had treated her like any creature under their care—with love and respect and empathy. There'd been some definite bumps along the way, but Jake and Eda had dug in their heels for the long haul and, slowly, Emma had come out of her brittle shell and started to shine.

The woman before them now, strong and self-confident, was the antithesis of the terrified girl transplanted here a year before.

Meg met her halfway to the paddock and folded her into a tight hug, which was enthusiastically returned. Emma sported the sun-bleached hair and slightly tanned skin Meg knew came from long hours outside even with SPF 30, and a newly fit build, the natural result of regularly handling animals sometimes ten times her own weight. She'd lost the gauntness of the previous year and was filling out with the natural curves that came from regular meals at Eda's table. Meg took a step away, giving her the once-over. "Looking good!" She gave the girl's biceps a squeeze. "You've been working out."

High color suffused Emma's cheeks. "Only if working out involves hefting hay bales and dragging this one around." Contradicting her words, she leaned in and placed a smacking kiss on Auria's jaw. The horse blew out a breath, her lips flapping, and everyone laughed. "Let me put her in the paddock."

"I'll get the gate for you." Meg ran a hand down Auria's nose and Auria playfully butted her head against Meg's chest, sending her staggering. "Good to see you too, old girl. Hawk obviously agrees. Now go play."

Meg unlatched the gate and dragged it open, and Emma led the mare into the paddock. Emma slipped off the head rope and slapped Auria on the rump. "Off you go."

The mare took off at a trot with Hawk at her side, and Emma moved to close the gate.

"Hang on," Meg called. "Lacey? Cody? Saki? Blink?"

Cody didn't wait for any additional invitation and streaked through the gate, barking, arrowing after Hawk. Saki and Lacey trotted through at a more sedate pace.

Everyone turned to look at Blink.

Cara met Meg's eyes. "He wants to go, he's just scared."

"Bring him over, let him run. It would do him good to work off some of that anxiety."

"Agreed. Blink, come." Even though mostly terrified, the dog still knew to obey Cara's command. She walked him over to the gate. "Go get Hawk. Go on. Get Hawk!"

The dog quivered for a moment, and then took off like a runner exploding out of the starting blocks.

Brian walked over to prop his arms on the top of the fence as Meg shut the gate. "That dog can run."

"We took Blink off the racetrack, but part of the racetrack will always be with him. He can move like the wind." Meg pointed down pasture. "But look at Lacey go. She looks good. Maybe she was a little stiff this morning, but she's letting it rip now."

"I should call her back; she's pushing too hard." He drew breath to shout his dog's name, but Meg's elbow in

his ribs had him expelling everything from his lungs. "What?"

"Take a breath. She's fine. Watch her—she's having a ball. She's under her own command. If something hurts, or if she tires, she can slow down. It's good for her to play like this."

Twenty minutes later, everyone gathered around the kitchen table for brunch, and an hour after that, Meg, Brian, Webb, Jake, Lacey, and Hawk headed for the barn.

They entered through the open double doors at one end. The doors on the far side were also open to let the warm summer air sweep through. Inside the barn was a run of six stalls in a line down one side, and a small tack-and-equipment room beside stacks of hay bales on the other. As they entered, a pair of songbirds took flight from the upper rafters and soared out the far door. A black-and-white barn cat looked up at them from where he curled on top of a bale of hay.

"Pool's down at the far end," said Jake, leading them past the stalls, their half-grilled pine doors rolled open.

"What do you keep in here?" Brian asked. "Just Auria?"

"Her stall is here, but our other permanent resident is Jeeves, our emu. He's out in the back pasture. Otherwise, animals rotate through as they come in for healing, rehab, or rehoming. Some sheep, a few goats, a donkey or two, or the odd llama." They passed a stall in the middle of the building lined with large grilled double boxes, each with a litter box, some toys, and a bed. "This is our 'cat room.' Kitten season was busy, but we got them all placed successfully. We only have one senior bonded pair right now, but we have some interest in them, so we're hoping they'll go out in the next few weeks. And here we are."

They stopped at the last stall, but instead of a stall front, sliding door, and hayrack, there was a four-foot-tall tank that looked like a miniature aboveground pool, with steps

marching up to it and then steps leading down and under the water.

Brian peered into the pool. "Nice setup."

"It's not big, but it works for us. We can adjust the water level for the animal we're working with and heat it in the winter. When it's this hot outside, we just let the water warm up to ambient. Let's get Lacey in and get her working."

Both Jake and Brian, in swim trunks and T-shirts, walked down the steps into the waist-high water, Brian calling Lacey after him. Lacey only hesitated momentarily and launched herself into the pool.

Meg leaned against the raised edge, with Webb beside her. Hawk climbed the first couple of steps and watched forlornly as Lacey swam the few feet toward Brian and then paddled around him.

Webb nudged Meg. "It's killing him."

"He's a water dog, what did you expect? But the pool isn't that big and there's already three of them in there."

"We're wet anyway," said Brian. "What's one more dog?"

"You're sure?"

"Absolutely."

"Okay. Hawk, go on in. Get Lacey."

Hawk's ears perked with enthusiasm as he bolted up the rest of the steps to leap into the water before Meg could change her mind. He landed near Jake, sending a spray of water into his face before he could raise an arm to block it.

Jake eyed his eldest daughter with raised brows as he wiped the water dripping into his eyes. She grinned back at him, utterly unrepentant.

"How are they doing?"

Meg turned to see her mother, her arms full of towels, with Emma, Cara, Blink, Saki, and Cody entering the barn. Cara joined Webb while Eda set the towels down on

the bench against the wall. Emma leaned on the pool edge next to Meg. Saki sat down beside Cara, while Cody wandered off, his nose to the ground, clearly intent on investigating every corner in the barn. Blink wandered into the next stall, turned around three times, and curled up in the hay to nap.

Webb nodded at Blink in approval. "That dog's no dummy, especially after a meal like we just had. Outstanding as always, Eda. I'm tempted to join him."

"Feel free to stretch out on the porch when we get back." Eda's eyes twinkled as she met Meg's. "No greater compliment than the need for a nap after a good meal. Must have been his third helping of Farmer's Casserole."

"Could have been the second slice of apple pie," Meg countered.

"Might have been the three or four slices of freshly baked bread," Cara added.

Webb didn't take his eyes off the men and dogs in the pool. "It was all of it and I feel zero guilt. I carried two people out of an apartment fire two days ago and must have lost ten pounds just in sweat at that one incident. I don't eat like that often, but I think of it as getting back in shape for tomorrow's shift."

Meg patted him on the arm. "You tell yourself that if it makes you feel better."

Webb gave her a sideways stink eye. "You're just jealous."

"That you can eat like that and not gain an ounce? Madly jealous." Meg returned her attention to the water, where Jake took Lacey through a series of exercises, studying her movement and judging her endurance. Hawk duly followed Lacey through every step, as if it was a team sport.

Feeling the edge of the pool vibrate, Meg glanced at Emma, who stood jiggling her leg at almost light speed beside her. "What's up with you?"

Emma looked imploringly at Eda. "Can we tell them?"

"Do you want to? You don't want to wait until it's a little more official?"

"No, I want to tell them now, while they're here."

Meg met her mother's eyes over Emma's shoulder, her head tilting in question. She could read her mother's reluctance. "Is it bad news?"

"We don't think so. We hope you two don't either. I was going to call you next week, once we had more information and really got things settled."

Meg exchanged a glance with Cara, reading confusion there as well. "Why don't you tell us about it."

"Very well." Eda laid a hand on Emma's arm. "Take a breath, honey. I know my girls. It's going to be okay."

The jiggling stopped.

Eda met first Meg's eyes, then Cara's. "Emma's been here for a year and a day now. She's nineteen. There are things she's going to need to do as an adult. Get a job. File her taxes. Apply for a credit card. All of those things need a full identity. They definitely need a last name."

Meg's gaze slid to Emma, but the girl's eyes were downcast as she nibbled on her lower lip. "They do."

"Dad and I talked it over, and then we talked to Emma about it. We'd like to give her our name. And we'd like to make it official. Virginia allows adult adoption of anyone unrelated, as long as good cause is shown, and as long as the adoptee is more than fifteen years the adopters' junior. Emma is all those things." Eda met Meg's eyes, and then Cara's. "We'd like to adopt Emma. And Emma would like to join our family."

There was a second of silence and then Meg whooped and wrapped Emma, who let out a squeal, in a hug. Then Cara joined in, wrapping one arm around both of them, and the other around her mother.

All motion in the pool stopped and then Jake smiled

widely and murmured something to Brian, who thumped Jake on the shoulder in congratulations.

"You're sure you don't mind?" Emma's voice was muffled against Meg's shoulder.

Meg released her and stepped back a pace to give her room to breathe. "Mind? Why would I mind? There's plenty of love to go around. And you've found your place here. I'm glad it will be permanent, even if like Cara and me, you eventually move away. Your roots will always lead you back." She held out her hand and her mother grasped it, holding tight. "Ours do."

"I don't think I want to move away. I love the rescue. I love what we do here. Sometimes it's hard, like when you lose an animal you've been fighting to save. Or when you heal one and have to say goodbye as it moves on to its new life, but it's good work. It's work that matters. And I've had enough dealings with people to last a lifetime. I think I like animals better than people anyway."

"I knew there was a reason I clicked with you." Cara held up a hand and Emma high-fived her. "Sister."

Emma blushed, but looked immeasurably pleased.

Webb glanced from Eda's shining eyes as she held Meg's hand, to Cara and Emma standing close together, gauging the speed of Emma's blinking. "Now don't you all go weepy on me. I'm the only guy here. At least wait until Brian and Jake are out of the pool."

"Stop it." Meg gave him an affectionate *thwack* on the arm, but appreciated his poke at humor to keep things light. "Would serve you right if we did all go weepy on you."

"We've still got some work to do on this," Eda said. "Emma's not a minor, so we don't need to get anyone else's permission, but we have to demonstrate good cause—"

"That's a no-brainer," Meg said. "After what she survived?"

"I know, but we still have to go through the process."

"Well, if you have any trouble, you let me know." Meg let go of her mother's hand to drape her arm over Emma's shoulders. "Most of my current contacts are federal, but there are people I knew back in my days on the Richmond PD, so I can pull some strings if needed." She smiled down into Emma's blue eyes. "Because you're a part of the family already, but we'd like to make it official. Emma Jennings . . . I like the sound of that."

As Emma blinked back tears, Webb murmured into Meg's ear, "See? Told you it was going to be a good day."

CHAPTER 8

Bruise: An imperfection or break in a diamond's exterior, usually the result of hitting a hard surface.

Saturday, August 3, 10:05 AM
Philadelphia FBI field office
Philadelphia, Pennsylvania

The first message from Pierce came on Thursday. **Diamonds incoming today. Be ready for Saturday morning after inventory Friday.**

Brian and Meg talked it over and decided they'd both rather sleep in their own beds and get up when they normally would to jog, only this time they'd hit the shower, grab breakfast at a drive-through, and be on the road to Philadelphia by seven in the morning. Kate agreed and they made plans to meet at the Philadelphia FBI field office with Addison. A mere block away from the Liberty Bell Center and the Independence Beer Garden, it was in the middle of downtown and would be their best bet as a starting location for the search.

Sensitive to the possibility of being identified as law enforcement, now the searches were official, Meg and Brian made some changes. As both their SUVs were official unmarked FBI vehicles with a proper K-9 compartment for their dogs that could give them away as professionals, Meg and Webb exchanged vehicles. A charcoal-gray king cab, instead of a black tricked-out SUV, Webb's truck was the kind of vehicle any civilian might drive. Recognizing the same issue, Kate requisitioned a hunter-green hatchback for herself and Addison. For this search they would pair up, but put distance between the pairs so they appeared to be two couples who just happened to be taking a walk in the same direction, one couple with their dogs. They'd discussed pairing an agent with a handler and going in mixed couples, but Meg and Brian advised that the best way to protect against diverging paths was to keep the dogs together, or else they might inadvertently follow the same path at a fork when they should take separate trails.

All wore civilian clothes for easy movement, but in light layers to camouflage their weapons. They were tracking and trailing the Mob—no one went alone or unarmed.

The Philadelphia field office was a bustling hub, but Kate found them a conference room where they could relax and wait for word to come in. They only had to wait just over an hour before the text came in to Kate's phone: **=39.955398-75.145685**

"Clever," Kate said, turning around her phone to show the rest of the group.

Meg leaned in for a closer look. "I'll say. He changed the message format so there are no directions or spaces, and added an equals sign so it appears to be a mathematical or spreadsheet equation. He's going to toss the phone, but just in case, he doesn't want anything that can track back to him." She pushed back her chair. "We need to move now."

"Hang on . . . 39.955398 north, -75.145685 west . . . got it." Brian stood. "On New Street. It's right by some old

historic church only five minutes away by car. St. George's."
A few more taps on his phone. "Kate, you should have the
directions now."

As if on cue Kate's phone beeped and she pulled up
Brian's directions. "Let's go. We'll stay at least a few hundred feet behind you."

Meg patted the rectangular lump in the pocket in her
yoga pants—an electronic tracker with an emergency call
button. Kate had given one to each handler so they could
be followed in any situation and could call for help if required. "If you lose sight of us, track us."

In minutes they were racing up N 7th Street, trying to
make up as much time as traffic and discretion would
allow. A tall condo building, all curves and glinting glass,
whizzed by on their left; a park with a busy playground
was a blur on the opposite side. Through Brian's open
window music thumped and the babble of voices filtered
into the truck.

Meg tossed a lightning-fast glance toward the playground and got a vague impression of packed spaces and
moving bodies. "What's going on there?"

"Maybe some kind of kids' festival?" Brian peered out
the window at the cloudless blue sky. "If so, they have a
good day for it. Okay, follow this road under I-676 and
it'll curve around and back down North 6th Street. Take a
left onto Wood, a right onto North 4th Street, a left onto
New Street, and we're there."

"Check." Meg checked the clock on the dash and made
a low sound in the back of her throat.

"What?"

"Look at the time. We lost time getting to our vehicles.
The starting point may be only five minutes away, but we
should have been quicker off the mark. We should have
stayed in the truck." A check of the rearview mirror

showed both dogs sitting on the backseat, heads alert, noses scenting the incoming air. "The dogs could manage it. They'd just nap until we were ready to go."

Brian grabbed his door handle as Meg cut under the highway and took the loop to N 6th Street at ten miles per hour over the limit. "Something to consider for next time."

N 6th Street brought them down along the other side of the park; then they turned down a street lined with apartment buildings.

"Uh-oh." Brian pointed to unbroken lines of cars stretching down both sides of the street. "That festival, or whatever it is, may complicate this. Check out all the cars."

"It's Saturday and this area is one apartment building after another. It may just be resident parking. Either way, it's not going to help us if it's like this near the starting point."

Brian checked his map. "We're not far now. Finding a parking spot, especially for this beast, may be a problem."

"I'll remind you that you liked this beast this morning."

"With all this legroom and about a dozen cup holders? Sure. But it's still a beast."

N 4th Street brought more apartment buildings and more cars. In the distance a square redbrick bell tower, topped by a narrow white spire, speared into the blue sky.

"That's it up there?" Meg asked.

"Actually, no." Brian expanded his map. "That's across the street from St. George's, which we can't see behind all the trees. That spire belongs to St. Augustine's Catholic Church."

They stopped at an intersection and Meg checked up and down both sides of the cross street. "No parking. This place is jammed. It's going to be like the first search, as far as people are concerned." She scanned the parking lot to her left—clearly marked PRIVATE PARKING for the adjacent apartment building—and to her right—full—and proceeded through the intersection.

"We have to take the next left onto New Street anyway, so—" Brian cut off abruptly as Meg made a sudden turn to the right into the parking lot next to St. Augustine's. "What are you doing?"

"Check out the sign and get out your wallet." Meg pointed to the young woman standing just inside the sidewalk holding a large neon Bristol board sign—ST. AUGUSTINE ART IN THE PARK PARKING $40.

"Forty dollars? That's highway robbery."

"Do we want to get in on this search or not? They have one space left and we'll fit. Now get out your wallet. I'm sure you can expense it."

"Like I'm going to get a receipt for this," Brian grumbled, but pulled his wallet out of his back pocket, extracted two 20-dollar bills, and handed them to Meg.

Meg handed the money to the young woman, who pointed them at the only free spot. As they drove through, Meg looked in her rearview mirror to see her drag a bright orange wooden A-frame traffic barricade across the driveway. A few seconds later, Kate's hatchback streaked by.

They quickly got out of the truck, leashed the dogs, and set out. They walked down N 4th Street to the intersection with New Street across from St. George's, a sturdy three-story structure with even-spaced, large, mullioned casement windows below a steep-pitched black-shingle roof.

"As churches go, that one's pretty plain," Brian commented. "Does it hurt your architecture-loving heart?"

"Not at all. That's classic Colonial Georgian architecture if I've ever seen it. Now stop trying to trip me up. It's not going to happen and we need to get our heads in the game. How close are we?"

"Very. It's just up the block."

They continued down the sidewalk, between tightly packed cars and St. George's.

"Hang on." Eyes fixed on his phone, Brian stopped opposite stairs leading up to a door marked as the entrance to St. George's office and museum. "Here." He looked sideways to the line of cars. They stood at the front wheel of a red sports coupe.

"Let's get them moving. Hopefully, Kate has found a place to park." Meg pulled the bag of dirty laundry from her pack. "Hawk, Lacey, remember Jameson? Find Jameson."

The dogs' heads went up, scenting the air.

They had hardly walked past the steps leading up to the office door when Lacey suddenly cut left, Hawk instantly following her. They both sniffed around the passenger door of a white sedan and sat.

"They have it," Meg said. "And just like we thought last week, it's a different vehicle. Pierce was the passenger. Hawk, good boy. Now find Jameson."

The dogs circled the car, crossed the street in the middle of the block, and started back up New Street toward St. Augustine's, and then up N 4th Street.

They kept up the appearance of simply being a couple out for a walk with their dogs. No go bags to shoulder, a brisk pace, but not one to raise eyebrows or questions; and while anyone who actually knew how they would really walk the dogs—heeling perfectly at their owner's knee—would question the dogs being so far out in front, most observers would think they were simply untrained dogs dragging their owners behind them.

Just the look they were going for.

They rapidly covered a two-block stretch of Vine Street, passing commercial and apartment buildings alike, until Vine banked to the right at I-676 and their trail took them forward onto a narrow footpath. They passed under the *whoosh* and roar of I-676 and then were back onto N 6th Street. Pedestrians flowed down the sidewalks, turning into the green space across from them.

"Isn't that—"

"The park we went past?" Meg finished for him. "Yes. Remember the sign where we parked? Art in the Park. It's an art festival." She glanced at her watch. "I still don't like how long this is taking."

Brian eyed the traffic zipping by. "I know, but we can't walk into traffic. And if we let the dogs take it at the speed they'd like, we're giving away the game."

"We may lose the game otherwise. I'm not sure this setup is going to work as well as Kate thinks it is." Meg casually looked over her shoulder and then faced forward again. "Kate and Doug are about a block back."

"They seem casual?"

"They're holding hands, does that count? They look like they're headed for the festival too. There's our break in the traffic. Hawk, find Jameson."

They crossed N 6th and then yet another on-ramp to I-676 before entering the park. A long herringbone red-brick path stretched toward the middle of the park. Flanking the path on both sides were two rows of white tents—most of them spindly white metal legs supporting just a cap of nylon to shield the artisans and their wares below, with a few full-sized tents in brilliant shots of color sprinkled through.

The dogs trotted down the walkway, weaving through heavy foot traffic going in all directions. When two young children almost plowed into Lacey, both handlers pulled the dogs in slightly, shortening their leashes so the dogs were just in front of them, still leading the search, but decreasing the chance of an accidental collision to slow them further.

Not able to use the weaving back-and-forth pattern

they normally worked while tracking because of the festival crowd, the dogs stayed steady in the middle of the footpath where there were the fewest people. Meg scanned the exhibitors as they went by, knowing Pierce and his colleague were here to meet one of them. There was a stall for everything one could imagine finding at an art festival: the works of a local organization of children's authors, knitting and crocheting, watercolors of local landmarks, carpentry, gourmet chocolates, hand-thrown pottery, stained glass, and even a stall selling lawn ornaments constructed out of a jumble of metal junk pieces.

Coming to the end of this row of tents, Hawk rounded the outer edge of a tent where a woman sketched caricatures while people waited, when he suddenly stopped, his tail shooting into the air, his dark head high. Close behind, Meg almost ran into him. She opened her mouth to order him to continue when she realized his confusion.

The source of the scent trail he'd been following was right in front of him.

Pierce was only about three feet away, partially blocked behind the man he followed as he impatiently shoved through the crowd, a man who was practically on top of her dog as Hawk appeared in front of him around the corner.

Meg saw the man's intent a split second before he acted and moved fast. She threw a low spread hand behind her to warn Brian away, while yanking hard on Hawk's leash with the other, harshly dragging him back with a force she would normally never use. She stepped between man and dog just as the man pulled back to land a brutal kick to Hawk's chest. Instead, his boot made contact with Meg with breathtaking force.

Searing pain shot through her left shin and she couldn't hold back a yelp of pain.

She had a brief impression of size, bulk, sour breath, and cold eyes, and then the man shouldered past her, nearly knocking her off balance. Pierce strode past them, acting as if he'd seen nothing, his eyes locked straight ahead, his manner intent.

They disappeared into the crowd.

"Meg! Are you okay?" Brian grabbed her arm, steadying her until she had her balance.

She sucked in a breath between clenched teeth and then let out a low, vicious curse. "Not really. That bastard was wearing steel toes."

"No doubt a handy tool if he needed to rough someone up."

"Mission accomplished. Come on. We've already blown this one because we've missed the pass-off. The best we can do at this point is to try to track the gems based on the trail."

"Which now goes in two directions, with the stronger trail going the wrong way. But they're pros, they can do it. Lacey, find Jameson."

When Lacey immediately tried to follow the freshest trail, Brian simply pointed her in the correct direction, continuing along the path Hawk had tried to take into a new line of vendors. Lacey went forward, passing tents with little interest, Hawk immediately behind her, and Meg limping along in the rear. Lacey turned a corner leading to another long run of tents, and passed five before she slowed, then stopped. She looked up at Brian and whined.

"She's lost it." He spun her around. "Lacey, find Jameson."

The German shepherd retraced her steps, Brian holding her back to slow her; then she abruptly cut left between two tents. She stopped between the tents and sat down. Hawk, following her, did the same.

"I'll do it," Meg said, and reached into her pocket to hit the emergency call button on her tracker. "They can't be far behind, but let's step out."

Once again in the path between the rows of vendors, Meg positioned herself so she could see over Brian's shoulder. "Stand so you're facing me like we're having a conversation."

Brian did so without question. "Can you see in?"

"Yes." Meg took a moment to study the tent, knowing that to the casual passerby it would appear she was staring at Brian. Unlike the majority of the tents, which were clearly temporary rentals for vendors who did shows occasionally, this was a full tent with heavy side panels all the way to the ground, and the name HOUSE OF BARTHOLOMEW in flowing gold script on the tent cap on all visible sides.

"And . . . ? You have me standing so I can give you cover, but I can't see anything."

"They've set up tables across the front of the stall, with shorter ones on the sides. Tons of jewelry, all under suspended lights."

"They're selling expensive jewelry at an art fair?"

"I don't think so. This looks more artistic and flashy than quiet and pricey. Probably custom crafted in-store, but this is mostly gold and silver, not much in the way of stones. One girl at the front table currently talking to a couple of twentysomethings going through a tray of necklaces. But there's a table separating the front of the tent from the back, where there's an older man. He's turned away, bent over something, and . . . wait . . . he's holding something in his hand."

"What?"

"I think it's a jeweler's loupe. He's studying something under a light. Putting it down, picking up another." She squinted, trying to visualize the tiny pieces he was examining. "Brian, I'm pretty sure he's checking out the rough diamonds. Where's Kate?"

"Coming around the corner."

"Just in time. We're not going to get anyone from the family, but we're going to nab this jeweler. If he'd put them away before we got here, we wouldn't be able to grab him. But the gems are visible. Kate can do a warrantless search if they're out in plain sight and in view from a public space."

"Sure she'll have a leg to stand on? It's a jewelry tent. Of course they'll have jewelry."

"They're only selling completed pieces at this show. I'm no expert, but what he's holding looks too big to have been cut already. There's no logical reason for him to have brought a fortune in rough gems to an art show just to . . . store them in back?"

"Well, when you put it that way. Come on. Let's not give the guy the heads-up."

They met Kate two tents down.

"You know where the buy went down?" Kate scanned the tents over Meg's shoulder.

"Yes. See the tent on your right? The one labeled 'House of Bartholomew'? That's it. Two vendors present. A female, midtwenties in the front. I'd guess she's a salesgirl. But I think the older man, midfifties, in the back, is actively examining the rough diamonds as we speak."

Kate and Addison quickly circled the handlers and dogs and headed for the tent. They paused for only a moment in front of it, then, taking out their badges, pulled back the side panel to step inside. The panel fell closed behind them and they disappeared from view.

Not wanting to go far, in case they were needed, Meg sidestepped toward a rack of bath salts and dropped down to one knee. A jagged tear split the left leg of her yoga pants and blood welled and flowed down her shin to pool at the top of her tightly laced hiking boot. She pulled the snug fabric aside to examine a bloody gash already starting to discolor and swell. Hawk bumped his head against her and tried to nose in to see what she was doing. "Hawk, buddy, I'm okay. I'm trying to see what that bastard really wanted to do to you."

"You blocked my view. You really think he wanted to kick Hawk?"

Meg resettled the fabric, trying to keep the wound clear, and straightened to face Brian. "I'm one hundred percent sure. Hawk stepped into his path and he wasn't even going to stop. Just kick him out of his way and keep going." She ran her fingers under Hawk's collar, examining him for any tenderness from her rough handling. "I didn't dare use his 'don't mess with me' name," she said, referring to "Talon," the name she used for Hawk whenever instant and unquestioning obedience was required. "I didn't want any recognizable name dropped inside his hearing in case I ever need voice commands with Hawk later and he's paired with Pierce again. Barring communication, the only thing I could do was pull him out of the way and take the blow myself." She frowned down at Hawk. "I must have hurt him, yanking him away like that. He wouldn't have expected that kind of rough handling from me."

Brian studied the dog standing at ease under Meg's touch. "He's not showing any signs of pain, so no harm done. And he trusts you implicitly. You were pulling him out of harm's way so you could put yourself into it; he knows that."

"I guess. But you know who did great today? Lacey. On point the whole time and led us right to him."

"That's my Lacey-girl." At the sound of her name, the dog looked up at Brian with bright eyes, and he ran his hand over her head and down to her back. "I guess she *is* ready."

"Damn straight she is." Meg flicked a glance toward the tent. "Let's get a little closer and make sure they don't need anything."

One look told them everything they needed to know: the salesgirl stood near the front, her eyes wide and her hands cupped over her mouth as her boss was handcuffed by Addison while Kate trickled the diamonds from her palm into a small velvet drawstring bag. When she noticed Brian and Meg, Kate held up the bag.

They hadn't arrested anyone from the Philadelphia crime family, but they'd taken one illegal gem dealer off the street.

It was a start.

CHAPTER 9

Bearded Girdle: An area of hairline chips or fractures along the outside edge, or circumference, of a polished diamond.

Saturday, August 3, 1:22 PM
Philadelphia FBI field office
Philadelphia, Pennsylvania

When Kate entered with Addison on her heels, Meg looked up from the sub sandwich she and Brian had picked up on the way back to the field office. Meg wiped her mouth with her napkin and pointed to the two wrapped rolls on the conference room table. "Yours are there. Is Bartholomew booked?"

"Yes." Kate pulled the sandwich and fountain drink with her name on it toward her and sat down. "And singing like a canary."

Addison grabbed the last sandwich and took the chair next to Kate. "This is the advantage of working with the jeweler end of this equation. By and large, these aren't hardened criminals. When you catch them in the act, they spill their guts immediately, anything to make us go easier on them."

Kate unwrapped one end of her sandwich and took a

big bite, sitting back in her chair with a satisfied sigh as she chewed and swallowed. "Thanks for this, by the way. Who do I owe?"

Brian waved the offer away. "I bought, but we'll do this again. You can take your turn one of those times. Is the DA cutting him a deal?"

"Assistant US Attorney Jacobs knows exactly what we're up against and is willing to work with us to get the upper-level players. She's in with Mr. Bartholomew right now. I would assume they're exchanging information for a reduced sentence. Or maybe no sentence. Depends on what he has to offer."

"Bartholomew was buying rough gems himself and not using a broker?"

"Some jewelers buy their own gems if they have the right contacts. Saves them from paying the middleman. But not many do it. Bartholomew has been in this business since his teen years when he worked in his father's jewelry store."

"It's a family business?" Meg asked.

"It was Bartholomew's Jewelers back then, run by Aaron Bartholomew. When this Bartholomew, Ezra, took over, he thought the company image needed a boost and thought a couture-ish name would make the store seem exotic. And House of Bartholomew was born. They became the biggest jeweler in Philadelphia. That gave them the status to make the contacts and have the buying power to bypass always using a broker. He does use a broker for some transactions, but depending on what and how much he's buying, he'll go around the broker. He says it lets him set a lower price point."

"Did Bartholomew reach out to them, or did they contact him once they knew a shipment was coming or was in hand?"

"They always contact him. He says it's always the same

voice on the end of the line, but the calls come from different numbers."

"Disposable burner phones," Brian said.

"That's my take on it. These are experienced criminals. They know how long it takes for law enforcement to figure out their new number and get a warrant for it. By that time they've tossed it and have a new burner phone."

"It's simply the cost of doing business." Meg set her sandwich down. "The guys he met with today—Pierce and the other man—is either one the voice on the line?"

"No. He says the runners are always different. There are always two, but each time they've been different."

"How many shipments has he received?"

"This was his third shipment in four years. He's only one store, so that cache of gems is enough to tide him over for a year or more."

"That might explain the different faces," Brian suggested. "I wonder what kind of turnover happens inside the family?"

"It may not even be turnover," Meg interjected. "It could just be they move guys around in different positions so neither law enforcement nor the customer sees a pattern. Or maybe if they feel law enforcement was watching a specific incident, they need them to stay in-house until the pressure is off. Had Bartholomew ever seen either of them before?"

"No. I was hoping we'd be able to get something from Bartholomew on the other guy, but he didn't have anything. The payment is set up by wire transfer to an offshore account before the drop. When the stones are delivered, they only stay long enough for Bartholomew to do a quick general check, and then they leave."

"He doesn't examine all the goods before they go?" Brian asked. "That seems like a sure-fire way to get swindled."

"It sounds like that kind of examination of so many stones takes time, so he knows it's not really possible. But it's business. They know if they deliver inferior goods, he'll never buy from them again. And he could spread the word that their product is garbage, and then they'll lose customers. Yes, they're the Mob; yes, they can strong-arm people—but they're also running a business and they don't want to be stuck with a fortune in uncut stones they can't move."

"When we got there, Bartholomew was examining the rough stones," Meg said. "Guess he just couldn't wait to check out his new toys, so to speak."

"That was his big mistake. If he hadn't had them out where we could see them, he wouldn't be in custody." Kate sat back in her chair, a satisfied smile curving her lips. "Works for me."

"We need to figure out how to make this work better." Realizing she was worrying the edge of the sandwich wrapper with both hands, Meg smoothed it flat on the table and laced her fingers together. "We missed the drop altogether because the whole thing moved so fast and we were so far behind."

Addison leaned in and pinned first Meg and then Brian with his gaze. "You guys are the experts. How do we fix it?"

Brian turned to Meg. "You already suggested waiting in the truck so we can start faster."

"If Pierce can ballpark a neighborhood, we'll be closer. Then we wait in the truck there," Meg countered. "He can send the specific coordinates after."

"Pierce can try to slow down their pace, though that may be impossible."

"We also need to ditch the casual wear and go athletic. We're a couple on a jog, not a brisk walk. You guys may need to do the same."

"If there's any way to get advance information on who

the drop is with, that would be useful. Tells us who we're dealing with."

"That's good." Kate toasted them with her drink. "All things we can work on. Pierce will touch base when it's safe, and I'll tell him how he can help us file down the edges."

"Good." Meg's tone went dark. "I really want the guy who accompanied Pierce."

"Because of his role in the whole operation?"

"Because he kicked my dog." Meg's voice cracked like a whip.

"Well, he didn't actually—" Addison interjected.

"If I hadn't gotten in the way, he would have succeeded." Meg ruthlessly cut him off. "All that matters to me is the intent. *He kicked my dog.*"

Addison held up both hands in surrender. "Okay, okay, I agree with you about the intent. He definitely wanted to take a chunk out of Hawk."

"I'm with Meg," Kate said. "If someone had tried to kick one of my dogs for just walking down a path, I'd be madder than a wet hen. And I'd want a piece of him." She bent sideways in her chair and peered under the table. "Instead, he got a piece of you. How's the leg?"

Meg studied the lump of bandage bulging through the slice in her pant leg. "Better. It's swollen and throbbing and could use an ice pack, which I'll do when I get home, but I'll live."

"Handy that you live with a paramedic."

"Not that there's much he'll need to do. It's just bruised and swollen. There's nothing broken or that needs stitches."

"This time," Brian quipped, earning a cocked eyebrow glare from Meg. "Hey, you know you tend to throw yourself whole hog into investigations. The result is you tend to get banged up. Todd's used to it. He'll just pull out his med pack and get to work."

"Which is overkill, but yeah, that's probably what he'll do." Meg turned back to Kate. "So, what's next?"

"Next up is doing a quick debrief with Pierce. I'll find out if he has any suggestions on how to narrow the time gap between us during the drop. After that, we wait. They have a full load of stones. They're not going to want to sit on them. And when they move again, we'll be ready."

CHAPTER 10

Abrasion: A small scratch on the surface of a gemstone.

Saturday, August 3, 6:38 PM
Jennings/Webb residence
Washington, DC

The wind ripped the doorknob from Meg's wet fingers, crashing it against the doorstop as she and Hawk stepped inside and out of the driving rain. Meg wrestled the front door shut around Hawk, who knew not to move off the mat when he had wet feet.

Wet feet didn't really cover it. They were both drenched to the skin.

Meg loved the house she shared with Webb. When Webb suggested they move in together, Meg had initially dragged her feet, guilt-ridden at the thought of leaving Cara high and dry, all alone in the house they'd purchased together because they couldn't afford to live separately. Webb had doggedly searched for their ideal arrangement, and had found the perfect compromise when one of the guys at the firehouse offered him the duplex he was renovating. One half for himself and Meg, the other for Cara and McCord.

The one negative to living in old Washington, DC, in a

house over a century old, was the lack of parking. Their street was one way only, with parking on both sides of the road, but still there were nights when Meg came home late and would have to park two or three streets over. Webb was off shift today, so, of course, her own SUV was in front of the house, while she'd had to park Webb's truck nearly three blocks away. And where was her emergency rain gear? In her own vehicle. Which was why she and Hawk were dripping on the front mat.

In the kitchen the water running into the sink shut off.

"You're back." Webb's voice preceded him out of the kitchen. He stepped into view in the hallway, still drying his hands on a towel. "I was just holding dinner . . ." His voice trailed off at the sight of her, and while his lips twitched, he kept the smile off his face. "Raining, is it?"

"You're always so observant. Can you go grab Hawk's towel from the mudroom?"

"Give me a sec."

As he disappeared down the hall, Meg shimmied out of her backpack and left it on a corner of the mat to dry out. "Hang on, boy. He's coming." She'd trained Hawk not to shake off in the house, but she knew he had to be fighting the instinct. In a minute Webb returned with a large microfiber towel and she gave Hawk a good rubdown. "Can you hold dinner a little longer? I need to get out of these clothes."

"Sure. How did it go today?"

Meg threw him a disgruntled look.

"That bad?"

"It wasn't a total washout, but it wasn't entirely successful." She wiped each of Hawk's paws and then released him. "Okay, Hawk, good boy." She straightened and handed Webb the sopping towel. "Can you please hang this up and then feed him? He must be starving. I'll go up and change and then we can eat."

"Sure. Come on, Hawk. Dinnertime."

The Labrador's ears perked up and he trotted down the hall after Webb.

Meg knelt down, unlaced and stepped out of her hiking boots, thankful Webb had been so focused on her wet face and dripping hair that he hadn't noticed the bandage under her pants. He was well within his rights to question her about it, but she wanted to be dry while he did.

She trudged up the stairs in dry socks, though one was noticeably bloody, and went straight to the master bathroom, where she stripped off her athletic jacket and dropped it in the tub. Returning to the bedroom, she took off her shoulder holster and secured her Glock in the gun safe tucked out of sight inside her wardrobe. As she walked back to the bathroom, she pulled her T-shirt over her head and tossed it into the tub as well. After tugging the elastic out of her ponytail, she twisted her long hair into a tail and wrung it out into the sink before finger-combing it out over her shoulders to dry. Peeling off her socks and then pulling down her yoga pants, she sat on the edge of the tub to work the pant leg down around her injury.

Webb found her muttering under her breath at material glued in place by dried blood.

He stopped dead in the doorway. "What happened this time? And how bad is it?"

"Steel-toed boot to my shin."

"How'd that happen?" He dropped to his knees in front of her and pushed her hands away. "Let me."

"I don't need treatment. It's not that bad."

"That's what you always say." He slipped her right leg free and then went to work on her left, sliding his fingers up the leg and slowly easing the material free. "Good thing you got wet. Saves me having to soak it off."

"Small favors." When Webb looked up and pinned her

with a silent stare, she answered his question. "We were tracking Pierce through an art festival. We were trying to be casual, you know? Just a couple out for a walk with their dogs."

"A couple, huh? Do Brian and I need to have words?" Webb's head was down, but Meg could hear the smile in his voice.

"Ha-ha. If you do, then so does his husband. Anyway, we had the dogs out in front, but still close. Hawk took the corner first and then stopped dead because Pierce was only feet away and headed right for us. But it was the guy Pierce was following. He tried to kick Hawk out of his way. I got between them."

Webb's fingers twitched, yanking the material free with more force than intended, and Meg's breath caught on a quick gasp. "Sorry. He tried to kick Hawk?" His voice was a low growl as he drew her pants off and added them to the pile of wet clothes in the bathtub, and turned his attention to the bandage Meg had applied earlier.

"He's a real sterling guy. I pulled Hawk back and stepped in front of him, so I took the kick."

Webb pulled the tape off and peeled the dressing away. He was careful, but it still stuck at the edges, dragging an accompanying hiss from Meg. "Trying to do this carefully, but some of the blood is stuck."

"Don't apologize. You did it more gently than I would have." She took in the swollen purple-and-black contusion radiating out from the two-inch gash. "See? It's not that bad. Nothing to glue together this time."

Webb's gaze shot to the scar over her right eyebrow. "That's a nice change. I do want to give this a good cleaning, though." Standing, he pulled first-aid supplies out of a drawer in the cabinet and then washed his hands.

"This isn't surgery, you know."

"I get that. But let's not add anything to the injury. We

have no idea what was on the sole of his boot when he rammed it into your shin. He could have just stepped in dog poop." He rapped his knuckles on the granite countertop. "Hop up and stretch your leg out. Better lighting here."

He stepped away as she shimmied up onto the counter, slid back, and swung her injured leg up so only her foot hung over the edge. Slipping her hands under her knee, she bent forward to examine her wound. "I guess it doesn't look so good. He really hammered me."

"Hold on to the counter. This is going to sting." Wetting a sterile square of gauze with antiseptic, Webb began cleaning the wound. "Do you think the son of a bitch was pissed you stepped in his way, or was it his intention to nail Hawk?" His fingers were gentle, but there was a backbone of steel behind his words.

"Without a doubt, he intended to nail Hawk with that amount of force. And from the trajectory, if I hadn't moved him, Hawk would have taken it right in the chest." As if on cue Hawk wandered into the bathroom. "Hey, buddy." The anger was instantly gone from her voice. Hawk was smart, but if he heard anger in her tone, he would assume it was for him. "How's my guy? Did you eat?" She reached out a hand and Hawk circled Webb to stand under her touch, tail wagging and tongue lolling. "Good boy. I wouldn't let the nasty man hurt you."

Webb tossed the bloody gauze into the garbage and then gently palpated the puffy purple skin around the gash, even as she drew in a sharp breath through gritted teeth. "Any difficulty walking?"

"I limped through the last part of the search, but other than that, it was fine."

"From the contusions you've bruised the bone nicely. It will heal, but it will take a few weeks. Is this going to interfere with your ability to do the job?"

"No. I'll just bandage it and take painkillers if I need them."

"You will. We'll make sure they're also anti-inflammatories and you'll be much better. And we'll check it on a regular basis." He applied an antibacterial ointment to the gash and then applied a fresh dressing. "So . . . this guy. You realize there's a problem, right?"

Meg looked away from her leg to meet his eyes. "Yes, he's seen me. More than that, he kicked me. Not that he knew he was assaulting someone from the FBI, but just nailing an innocent bystander in a crowd means I'm going to stick in his memory. Hawk too."

"Exactly. Should you and Hawk be taken off this case?"

"There's no guarantee it's going to be the same guy next time. We've proven to Pierce we can do this. Besides, Lauren and Scott are both on separate short-term deployments. We'd have to wait for one or both of them to be free. Brian and I are right here. We'll stay on, but I admit we're going to need to take extra care now."

"What if you tried to hide your identity? Not a TV detective drama hat-and-sunglasses disguise that any mob professional would see straight through, but what if you lightened your hair? Or wore a wig?"

"You're missing the most obvious flaw in your plan. Hawk is the linchpin of the team and remains a constant. If anyone from the Mob figures out they're being trailed by the same dog or dogs, forget about which human is with them, it's game over. The key here is not to be seen. That's the point of the dogs. They can be out of sight tracking the scent."

"Until you close in."

"We're never supposed to close in. When we know we're near the drop point, that's when we call in Kate and Doug."

Webb smoothed the outer edges of the dressing down

and tugged her leg down so she sat facing him, eye to eye, as he stepped into the V of her legs. "These aren't the type of guys to fool around with. You need to be ready to defend yourself if something goes sideways in your plan."

"I am. This is the Mob. They execute first and ask questions later. Everyone is carrying. I have my Glock 43 in my concealment shoulder holster so I can move easily with it."

"Good."

"And don't forget I have Hawk." She studied the dog curled up on the bath mat to wait for her. "He looks like a family pet, but never forget how he went after Daniel Mannew and drove him off the edge of that cliff. At my command he's a weapon."

"I know. But I don't want you to have to deploy him because that means your life is in danger. Seriously, Meg, I want you to be careful. It was nothing more than bad timing today, but it dials up your risk in a big way. If he figures out you're law enforcement, he won't just injure you. He'll end you."

Webb usually was extremely good at hiding the worry he carried about the risks inherent with her job; she understood that worry because she carried the same concern for him every time he voluntarily walked into an inferno. But tonight the furrow between his brows wordlessly gave away his concern. "I know. I'm taking it seriously. And so will Brian." Grasping his tightly set shoulders, she tugged him in and kissed him, his unease telegraphed in the brief press of his lips. "Thank you for patching me up. Again."

"You're welcome. I look forward to the case where I don't have to set your shoulder, patch up the knee you sliced open on broken glass, or glue your forehead together."

"Me too." She went for humor to lighten the mood. "But you know me—I only make a particular mistake once. I'll

CHAPTER 11

Knot: A type of inclusion where one diamond crystal is entirely lodged within a larger diamond crystal.

Tuesday, August 6, 7:44 PM
Callowhill Street
Philadelphia, Pennsylvania

Meg checked the clock on the truck dash for the third time in ten minutes.

"Staring at the clock isn't going to make this go any faster," Brian commented. "Sit back and relax. There's nothing we can do until we get the coordinates."

Meg threw Brian an aggrieved look, but tipped her head back against the seat rest, forcing herself to loosen her tight shoulders as she tried not to count off the seconds.

Kate had received a text that morning specifying the intersection of Callowhill and N Broad Streets at seven thirty at night. They'd come into town in the late afternoon, not wanting to take any chances with traffic, preferring to kill several hours at the field office rather than miss the drop. Arriving at the designated intersection at seven fifteen, they lucked into street parking, since most of the city's workers were already done for the day and safely on their way home.

always find a new way to get injured. Guess now I can take steel-toed boots off the list." She hopped off the counter and held out her hand to him. "Come on, I've made you leave dinner sitting long enough. Let me grab some dry clothes, then let's go eat."

She led him into their bedroom, and then a few minutes later downstairs to the kitchen where dinner waited for them.

But the furrow of worry never eased from his expression.

Since then, they'd waited.

"This is taking so long, I have to wonder if the deal's fallen through," Meg said.

"Maybe. Or maybe he wanted us here early so there was no risk of being seen coming into the area. You're wound up today. What's up?" He looked over his shoulder into the back where the dogs lay peacefully dozing. "It's not Hawk. He seems perfectly fine."

"It's Todd."

"Is everything okay between you guys? Is the honeymoon over?"

That brought a smile to her lips. "No, we're fine. He's not saying much, but I know he's worried."

"About this case?"

"About Giraldi."

Kate had made sure to touch base with Pierce following the arrest of Ezra Bartholomew. They'd learned the name of the man Pierce had been with that day—Lou Giraldi—and about his role as an enforcer.

"Todd had misgivings that Giraldi not only saw me on Saturday, but assaulted me. He thinks I'm going to stick in his brain for that alone, as will Hawk. When he found out the guy was an enforcer, it only jacked up his concern."

"Did he ask you to step out of the case?"

"While he was bandaging me, he sounded me out." Meg absently ran her fingertips over the layer of bandage on her shin. It was healing nicely and the swelling had gone down, though it was now bruised an intense black. "He hasn't brought it up since, but I know he'd like me to think about stepping aside."

"I'm sure there are times when you wish he'd work more as a paramedic and less as the guy running into burning buildings when everyone else is running out. But it's what he does. Just like this is what you do. When you two stuck, you did it knowing what you were getting into with each other. You don't ask him to hold back, and he's not asking you to. Seems fair to me." He grinned. "Look at the two of you being reasonable adults. You may not like what the other faces, sometimes even daily, but you know it's an integral part of each other and something neither of you can just give up. That being said, it doesn't mean it doesn't cause some occasional stress. Like when Todd had the roof cave in on him a few months ago."

"Or when I got lost in the mountains after avoiding that arrow attack. Yeah, I got it. I did promise him I'd be extra careful. He knows we're supposed to stay out of sight and that Kate and Doug will be the face of the FBI. Which is a good thing, because if Giraldi is with Pierce, and he sees me, we're blown. Take my safety out of the equation; they won't move another gem if they think the feds are onto them somehow."

"We'll be careful. And there's no guarantee he'll even be involved today."

"No, there isn't. But I made sure to finish getting ready to leave the house in front of Todd." She pulled aside the light jacket she wore to reveal the Glock 43 in her shoulder holster strapped under her breasts and snugged up under her left arm. Then she pulled her spring-loaded tactical knife out of the right-side pocket of her yoga pants and touched the button. A wickedly sharp four-inch black blade with an angled Tanto point sprang free of the handle. "Knowing I'm not without resources made him feel better."

"I bet it did—" Brian's phone signaled an incoming text and he quickly opened the message. "Here we go. I have the coordinates." He copied the text and entered it into his map program as Meg folded the knife, tucked it away, and started the truck. "39.960465 north by -75.167340 west. Which takes us . . . It's just up the street on the right, about two blocks. This is good. The wait in the truck close by is going to really pay off. We're only going to be minutes behind them. Sending the directions to Kate."

Meg checked her side mirror and pulled out onto the road. Two cars back, Kate pulled out behind her. "Talk me through it."

"Go through this intersection . . . good. Now past this parking garage, still one more block to go." Brian was silent as they drove down the block between a four-story redbrick apartment building and a multilevel concrete parking garage, stopped quickly at the stop sign, and then proceeded. "It's here on the right." Brian's eyes rose from his phone. "Goddamn it. It's another parking structure."

"You think the coordinates are inside it?"

"Yes."

"The coordinates are only longitude and latitude. Not altitude. We're going to have to find the coordinates on every level and check to see if that's the starting point." Meg made the turn into the driveway, rolled down her window, and jabbed at the button, waiting impatiently as the ticket was printed and ejected into her hand.

Brian rummaged through his go bag and pulled out the bag of Pierce's laundry, and then sat back as they pulled through the gate. "You know what? We're pretty close to it here. But there're no cars, just a parking office."

"Up we go then."

Meg drove through the lot as fast as she dared. "There are still a surprising number of cars here at this time of the evening." They circled the lot to the ramp leading up to the second level. Up the ramp, and around, then she slowed their speed. "Tell me where."

"Just a bit farther . . . here!" He set his phone in an empty cup holder, unbuckled, and got out of the truck with the bag as soon as Meg braked to a stop. Leaving the door open, he opened the back door. "Hawk, stay. Lacey, come." Lacey jumped down and Brian offered her the bag. "Lacey, find Jameson."

They knew within the first twenty seconds there was nothing for her here, but Brian gave Lacey another ten seconds before ordering her into the truck. He jumped in, slammed the door closed, and pointed through the windshield. "Go."

They wound up again to the third level, now with Kate and Addison behind them at a conservative distance.

"This place only has four levels, so we've only got so many places to check. But why would they park so far up? There were empty spots down below."

Meg slowed to a stop and pointed to the southwest corner of the structure. "Because they're right next to both the stairs and the elevator. Multiple routes of entry and exit if they get jammed up."

"True. Lacey, let's do it again."

This time they hit pay dirt immediately when Lacey sat down next to a silver luxury sedan. Brian waved Meg into a parking spot on the far end of the level and then doubled back for his bag. They leashed the dogs, offered them both the scent again, and then followed them as they both headed for the open-air staircase running down the corner of the building. At ground level they stepped out onto Callowhill Street and the dogs turned west in unison. The handlers let the dogs have their heads and, with a brief word of encouragement, let them lead at a jog past a four-story glass-and-concrete building emblazoned with COMMUNITY COLLEGE OF PHILADELPHIA and CENTER FOR BUSINESS AND INDUSTRY.

Meg and Brian settled in at their usual easy pace, following the dogs as they tracked the trail around the corner and under the massive portico over the main entrance for the center. They drew up short when both dogs followed the trail directly to one of the two sets of double main doors and then sat down as the trail became obstructed.

"In we go then." Meg pulled on the curved door handle, but while it rattled, it didn't move. She yanked on the second handle, but it was also locked.

"Uh-oh." Brian tried the second set of doors, but also found their path barred. "This is a problem."

"It's after eight; the building could be locked down because it's after hours." Meg peered through the glass to the large open foyer. A long, unmanned security desk sat across from the main doors and in front of a bank of elevators. To the right, a glass-and-steel staircase wound up four floors. Potted tropical plants were scattered around areas of benching. But there wasn't a person in sight.

Meg turned as Kate and Addison jogged up behind them. "The doors are locked, and the place seems deserted."

"You're sure they went in there?" Kate asked.

"Both dogs are positive."

"Any other way to get in?"

"We can check."

"Can we call for security to let us in?" Brian asked.

"On what grounds? We don't have a warrant. It's a public place, but it's locked and after hours. We never saw them go in."

"Let's check it out," Brian said. "Doug, you backtrack the way we came, and Lacey and I will go in the other direction. That way we have one dog team and one agent left here in case they come out. Or in case someone else goes in and you can slip in behind them."

Brian, Lacey, and Addison all took off at a jog in their respective directions, leaving Meg, Hawk, and Kate behind.

Kate stepped up to the doors, examining the lobby beyond. "If it's locked, how did they get in? There's a security card scanner there"—she indicated the flat black box with a red light in the upper-right corner—"but they'd need a college security card to get through."

"Maybe someone gave them one," Meg said. "Though, more likely, someone met them here at the doors and escorted them in." She leaned into the glass, scanning the upper levels of the lobby. "I see security cameras. Maybe we can see who they met."

"Going to be tough. We can't actually support the fact a crime is likely taking place right now."

Within a few minutes Brian, Lacey, and Addison returned with the news that while there were emergency exits for the building, Lacey hadn't alerted on them, indicating someone had let them in that way. There were no other entrances, and the parking garage for the building below required a security pass to enter. Agreeing their only choice at this point was to pull back and wait for Pierce to leave, they crossed to the far side of Callowhill Street to Franklin Town Boulevard. A line of closed shops down a short handful of steps behind a row of support pillars gave them cover, and, as they waited, dusk did the rest. Meg and Brian pulled their binoculars out of their go bags and kept watch.

They finally spotted movement over thirty minutes later.

"I have them," Brian said.

"Me too." Meg handed her binoculars to Kate as two distant figures left the building, heading toward them, before turning onto Callowhill Street and walking out of sight.

Kate handed the binoculars back. "That was definitely Pierce." She shook her head in disgust. "Didn't even have a chance with this one. Let's take ten minutes to make sure they've cleared the parking garage before we go back. We're not parked near them, but we can't chance them not being in a rush. Then we'll head to DC. No point in waiting around. I suspect I'll hear from Pierce tonight. He has to know there was nothing we could do this time."

"Makes you wonder why he even suggested this as a possibility."

"I'm going to ask him about it."

Kate's call came a little over an hour later as they were on I-95, just crossing into Maryland. "I just talked to Pierce, who apologized for dragging us out for this one. He doesn't know the specifics on the drops until the last minute, and he had no idea the college would be locked down."

"How did they get in?" Meg asked.

"The guy they were meeting, Jon Blakeley, teaches jewelry design at the college. He let them know when the building was clear and they met him and he took them up to his classroom. He has a dedicated office, with a secure space for the jewelry he brings in and keeps on hand as part of his class."

"Why Blakeley?" asked Brian. "Is he another jeweler?"

"Yes. He teaches part-time, but his real gig is in custom-designed jewelry. He cuts his own stones and designs around them."

"The entire drop was behind closed doors then," Meg stated. "Any chance it went down on camera?"

"Sadly, no. The public areas of the building are monitored, but private teaching spaces are not. The teachers' union won that battle and that's why it all went down there. So tonight was a bust. The gems got through and we couldn't track any of it. But Pierce says the next drop will be in a few days. I'll let you know when I have more."

After Kate signed off the call, Meg stared thoughtfully out the window as she drove, her fingers absently tapping on the wheel.

"I can see the wheels turning," Brian stated. "What's going on up there?"

"I'm resetting. I went from weaponing up because of a potential risky situation, to reconsidering how we're doing this because tonight was a bust."

"I hear you, it's frustrating. Pierce is still new enough in the group that while they're trusting him to help complete the drops, they're not filling him in on all the details first. It's the reason why this whole plan works so beautifully. He doesn't know anything ahead of time, so they can't suspect him if we're successful."

"True." More finger tapping.

"And . . . ?"

"Want to do a little off-the-books investigating?"

"What have you got in mind?"

"Some of these jewelers are clearly part of the scheme, but we don't know which ones. What if you and I check some of them out?"

"What makes you think us walking in there and flashing our badges is going to do anything but clam them up?"

"That's not what I'm suggesting. What if you and I are looking at rings?" She reached over and tapped the plain gold band he wore on his left hand. "You'll have to leave Ryan at home for this, though."

"You want to go engagement ring shopping?"

"Sure. The worst we're going to do is waste some time. But if Jewelers' Row is the center of this, I think we need to pay it a visit. You in? Think you can fake being in love with me for a day?"

"Babe, you know I love you, just not that way. But yes, I can fake it 'til I make it. When were you thinking?"

"If Pierce doesn't think the next drop will be for a few days, tomorrow seems like a good idea."

"I can do tomorrow. Do we need to get permission to do this?"

"I'll keep Kate and Craig in the loop. But I can't see either of them objecting. It's just a simple fact-finding mission."

Brian glanced behind him, where the dogs were snoozing on the backseat, nose to nose. "Going to have to leave the dogs at home for this."

"It would definitely be weird for us to bring them."

Spirits lifted at the thought of proactive steps to take, Meg gave the truck a little more gas.

Time to take a different tack to see what they could shake loose.

CHAPTER 12

Blood Diamonds: Precious stones mined in African war zones, often by forced labor, and used to fund armed rebel movements.

Wednesday, August 7, 12:24 PM
Lippincott Jewelers
Philadelphia, Pennsylvania

The muted chime of the shop bell rang as Meg opened the door into the jewelry store and stepped through into quiet opulence. Thick silver carpeting cushioned her feet as she and Brian crossed toward brightly lit glass showcases atop black-veined, white marble pedestals.

This was their third jewelry store in a little over two hours.

"Good afternoon." A man in his midthirties wearing a navy suit, white shirt, maroon tie, and a shiny gold nameplate inscribed with NATHAN greeted them. "Welcome to Lippincott. How may I assist you?"

Brian put an arm around Meg's waist and pulled her closer. "We'd like to look at engagement rings."

Nathan lit up like a Christmas tree. "Lovely." He crossed over to a long showcase where rows of sparkling rings were displayed upright on cylindrical charcoal velvet stands. He indicated two tall steel stools topped with charcoal cushions. "Please come and make yourselves comfortable." He waited while Meg and Brian settled on the stools. "Now, before we really get started, so I can help you find the perfect ring, tell me something about yourselves. Starting with your names, please."

"I'm Cara, and this is Ryan. We've been together for three years. I run a dog training school and Ryan works as an archivist for the Smithsonian." They'd decided to avoid their true backgrounds in search and rescue because they didn't want any links back to their real profession. Instead, they'd selected familiar backgrounds they could carry off convincingly—Meg taking Cara's and Brian taking Ryan's. They'd co-opted their names as well, ensuring that if anyone actually looked into their histories, they would find a Cara and a Ryan in those actual occupations.

"Really? At the Smithsonian. You're a long way from home. Why did you come all this way?"

Meg braced her elbow on the top of the display case, propping her chin in her hand to gaze up at Nathan. "I heard there were two places to shop for the . . . type of stone I'm looking for. New York and Philly. So I talked Ryan into a little trip."

"I compliment your selection, Cara." Nathan glanced from one to the other. "Are you newly engaged?"

Brian grinned sheepishly. "I kind of went with a moment last night and popped the question. I wasn't prepared, but it just felt . . . right."

Meg beamed and laid her hand on Brian's. "It was right." She looked up at Nathan, hoping she appeared dreamily in love rather than dopey, which was how she felt. "But because it was spur of the moment, he didn't have a ring. And I told him it was okay because then we could pick it out together."

Nathan actually clapped his hands together in excitement. "I love it!" He spread his hands wide. "We have a range of options. Let's start with what style you like. Take a look at these rings for a minute while Ryan and I have a word." With a head cocked at Brian, he stepped several feet away.

Brian joined him and there was a moment of low conversation as Meg strained to hear while pretending to consider the rings in the case. Brian returned and, while Nathan was still behind him, mimed rubbing his index finger and thumb together with a closed fist. *Setting the price range.*

"So . . . what style speaks to you?"

"They're all so beautiful. But I guess what I'm really more interested in is the stones themselves."

Nathan reached into the case and withdrew a square diamond solitaire in a platinum setting. "Here's a lovely ring. A two-and-a-half-carat princess cut. This is a gorgeous diamond." He pulled the ring from the stand, and turned it this way and that for Meg. The diamond sparkled in the bright store lights. He held out his hand toward her. "May I?"

Meg extended her hand and he pulled it a little closer, eyeballing her ring finger. "Our rings are size seven, but I'd say you're about a six and a half. It will be a bit big, but it will give you the idea."

Meg slid the ring onto her finger and extended her hand to "ooh and ah," as she imagined she was supposed to.

"What do you think?" Brian asked. "It looks great on you."

"Hmmm . . ." Meg waggled the ring back and forth a bit more, as if undecided. "I think it's a little plain."

"Okay, now we're getting somewhere." Nathan slid the ring off her finger and pulled out three more. "Which of these do you like? This solitaire?" He slid forward a ring with a pear-shaped diamond surrounded by a simple bezel

rim. "Or perhaps this one?" The ring he set next to the first had a round center stone encircled with a halo of smaller diamonds. "Or this rectangular emerald-cut diamond flanked by thin baguette diamonds on the shoulders? It doesn't have to be any of these rings in particular; I'm just trying to get a feel for your taste."

Meg took a moment to consider the rings and then pointed to the halo setting. "I like that one."

"Inspired choice. Now, before we move on, let's talk about what you're looking for in your center stone. Have you heard about the four C's?"

Just at every store we've been to. "No. Are they important?"

"Are they *important*?" Nathan patted her hand. "They're the difference between a stone that looks no more convincing than a piece of glass and a stone that sparkles like this." He picked up the halo ring, turning it under the bright lights so it glinted and glittered. "First of all, we have the cut. We've touched on that—round, princess, pear, marquise, et cetera. Then we have the carats, which are the weight of the diamond. The larger the carat designation, the larger the stone. Both the cut and carat weight are determined by the cutter, but the last two C's, color and clarity, are inherent to the stone itself."

"I thought diamonds were colorless," Brian said.

"Goodness no. True diamonds come in a multitude of colors—pink, yellow, green, blue, even black. But unless it's a particularly large stone, like the twelve-carat pink ring Sotheby's sold last year for just under five million, colored diamonds are not valued as highly as clear diamonds. Since it's the impurities that give a stone its color, it has to be otherwise flawless to command that kind of price tag. The purest of diamonds are those that are both transparent and clear. There is a *D*-to-*Z* rating system for engagement ring diamonds. The closer you are to the be-

ginning of the alphabet, the more colorless the stone; the closer to the end of the alphabet, the more yellow over-tones in the stone." He extended the halo ring again. "Look at the pure color of the stone. It's an *F*. Then we come to the last of the four *C*'s—clarity. This is where we take the natural blemishes or inclusions into account. A flawless stone is extremely hard to come by, so most stones have some small number of inclusions."

"What's an inclusion?"

"If you examine the stone, especially with a loupe, you'll see some minor dark or cloudy shadings within the stone. That's an inclusion. The higher the inclusion count, the lower the clarity rating. This one, for instance, is a VVS2, or very, very slightly included." He slipped the halo back on its stand and set the other rings in the display case as he gazed down through the glass and selected a number of rings. "Considering a budget, we work with setting style and the four *C*'s to find you the perfect ring."

The bell rang again as the door opened and a man stepped in, a dark silhouette backlit by brilliant sunlight before the door swung shut. Meg looked back to the rings Nathan was setting out, and then instinct tugged her gaze up. She swallowed a gasp of surprise as the man stepped forward and she met McCord's gaze. His eyes flared briefly in recognition, but he quickly recovered, giving only the subtlest of head shakes as he angled away from her and toward the female salesclerk who came out of the back room at the sound of the bell.

Meg turned back to the rings Nathan had laid out. *Time to push.* "These are all beautiful, but the style and the four C's isn't all I'm looking for."

"Don't worry about that. Ryan and I have already covered that."

"No, that's not what I mean." Meg picked up a ring, a gorgeous halo with a round center stone in a bezel setting

of platinum surrounded by tiny diamonds that flowed down the shank of the ring in waves, giving the impression they wrapped around the band. "It's a gorgeous ring, but I want a little excitement."

Nathan squinted slightly at her, trying to translate her words. "Meaning . . . a ring with a story?"

"Exactly!" Meg let the excitement of the thrill of the chase fill her tone.

"We have some rings created with vintage stones. Most of those stones have been recut because older stones didn't have the same symmetry or as many facets as we expect today, making them seem dull. But with a little TLC and a good eye, we can turn the old into something glorious. If you give me a minute, I have a few of those in the back and—"

"No." Meg grasped Nathan's forearm, stopping him as he was about to step away. "That's not exactly what I mean by 'excitement.'" She dropped her voice so Nathan was forced to bend closer to hear her. "I'm looking for a stone with a more interesting backstory. You hear stories about diamonds that come from interesting areas of the world. Diamonds with stories behind them. Diamonds with a story to tell. *That's* what I'm looking for." She ran one fingertip down the diamond-encrusted edge of a band. "Engagement rings are exciting, but everyone I know has one. I want something different." She looked up to meet his calculating eyes. "Do you understand what I mean?"

"If you mean what I think you mean, those are illegal in this country."

Meg tried to channel her inner sixteen-year-old, disappointed when the boy she had a crush on asked her girlfriend out on a date. "Oh." She paused, worrying her lower lip. "I was really hoping for something special here, even if it cost a little more. Well, thank you for showing us all these gorgeous rings. We'll keep you in mind." She slid

off the stool and laid her hand on Brian's thigh in what she hoped looked like the familiar ease of intimacy. "Let's try the place next door?"

"Whatever you want, babe. It's your call."

"That's my call."

"Wait!" Nathan held out a hand to stay their exit. "Maybe I can do something for you. We have . . . contacts in this business. Let me look into it for you."

"Really?"

"No promises."

"Of course. Ryan, give him your number."

Brian rattled off his number and then held out his hand to shake Nathan's. "Thank you for your help. If you can help us find what we're looking for, then we're happy to build a ring around that, custom."

Nathan stared down at the number. "Let me see what I can do."

When they left, McCord was leaning negligently on a display case, flirting with the salesclerk as she showed him a tray of glittering diamond rings. But Meg never looked his way, and in her peripheral vision, he never took his eyes off the rings.

What on earth was McCord doing in a jewelry shop in Philadelphia when he had no idea of what she was working on?

CHAPTER 13

Cloud: An inclusion that can make a diamond appear hazy or even milky in appearance when viewed under magnification. Most clouds cannot be seen with the naked eye.

Wednesday, August 7, 7:41 PM
Jennings/McCord residence
Washington, DC

Meg rapped three times on Cara and McCord's front door and then opened it, leaning in. "We're here," she called. She stepped into the front foyer with Webb and Hawk, who shot through the door and straight down the hallway toward the kitchen, where a scrabble and the click of nails on tile told of an enthusiastic greeting by Saki, Blink, and Cody.

"Come on back." Cara's voice floated out from the family room at the rear of the house. "Just follow Hawk."

A series of texts with Cara a few minutes before had assured Meg that McCord was home, they'd eaten, and she and Webb were welcome to come over.

Because Meg had questions only McCord could answer.

Meg slipped off her shoes and walked down the hallway in her stocking feet, Webb following behind. She entered the large, open-concept kitchen and family room to find

McCord on the sofa, his laptop open on his thighs, busily typing while the Washington Nationals played on the big-screen TV over the mantel. Cara was curled up in a nearby chair, her feet tucked under her and a book open. The dogs were still happily greeting each other over by the large double dog bed beside the sliding patio door. The glass door was open, letting in a cooling evening breeze after a muggy day.

"Hey," Cara greeted.

"Hey." Meg walked over to McCord, who kept typing, with his eyes locked on his monitor. She waited a full fifteen seconds before finally poking him in the shoulder. "Hey!"

He looked up at her. "Hi." He saved his document and closed his laptop lid. "Have a nice day in Philadelphia?"

"It was useful. You?"

"It was good." He set his laptop down on the coffee table and picked up his mug, held it out. "Coffee?"

"I'd love some." Webb took the chair opposite Cara. "Meg?"

"Sure. Just as soon as McCord and I have a chance to catch up."

McCord threw a sidelong look and a confident smile at Cara. "I told you she wouldn't wait until tomorrow." He looked up at Meg and patted the sofa beside him. "Sit down and take a load off. Cara, do you mind grabbing two more cups?"

Cara tucked her bookmark into her book and set it down on top of McCord's laptop. "No problem. Give me a minute." Getting up, she headed into the kitchen.

Meg watched Cara go. "I should go help."

Before Meg could move away, McCord grabbed her wrist and pulled her down to sprawl next to him on the couch. "Cara's got it. You have questions. I have answers. More than that, *I* have questions. Why were you and

Brian pretending to be a couple looking at engagement rings?"

"We're working a case. Why were you in Jewelers' Row in Philadelphia chatting up the salesgirl?"

"Because I'm working on a story."

Meg sat back and crossed her arms over her chest. "What story?"

"What case?"

"Are we really doing this, McCord?"

"No, you're not." Cara set a tray with filled coffee mugs, cream, and sugar on the table. "Help yourself while you both explain yourselves. Todd, you too."

Webb pulled his gaze from the baseball game long enough to flash Cara a grin and rolled eyes. "Thanks."

Cara took her seat and picked up her own coffee.

Meg pulled the tray toward her and started fixing her coffee. "You know, you surprised the hell out of me today, walking in there like that."

"Mutual, let me assure you. What's the case?"

"I haven't said anything to you because there's no story yet." She frowned. "At the rate we're going, there may never be a story. You remember Special Agent Kate Moore?"

"From the Stevenson case last fall? How could I forget?"

"You also remember me getting a text from Craig on the night you moved in here? The one calling me into his office the next morning? The one where we figured I'd screwed up something and was being called on the carpet? Well, that meeting ended up being with Brian and Kate. Kate asked to use us for one of her cases and Craig green-lit the request."

"She certainly knows what the dogs can do."

"Exactly. And she used that knowledge as a springboard. She's working with the FBI Diamond Trafficking Program. Going after the illegal trade in conflict diamonds. The Philadelphia crime family is involved and

we're trying to intercept shipments as they go out to . . ."
Meg paused at the stunned look on his face. "What?"

"The story I'm working on . . . it's about conflict diamonds coming into Philadelphia through the Mob."

"Seriously? We're working on the *same case*?"

"Apparently so. This time without actually trying."

"That would explain the jewelry store visit. Let's com-
pare notes then." Meg quickly detailed the case and the information they'd gathered to date.

"Then the jewelry store excursion wasn't part of the
case proper?" McCord asked.

"No, but Craig and Kate knew about it and were on
board. From it, we've started a list of potential jewelers
who may be knowingly selling conflict diamonds. That
was part of the charade, posing as the antithesis of the
modern ethical consumer. We went in as a spur-of-the-
moment, newly engaged couple looking for a ring, and I
tried to sell the fact that I wanted the ring to have a backstory. Many of them at first thought I was looking for vintage jewelry. Some of them figured out immediately I was
looking for a conflict gem."

Cara's lip curled with distaste. "Did anyone not believe
you? Clay's told me a little about what he's working on—
the human rights abuses, the mistreatment of the workers,
and the terrible conditions. Why would anyone want
something that came out of that kind of sheer misery, even
if it is shiny?"

"You'd be amazed at what people will pay for." Disgust
coated McCord's tone. "Did they buy it?"

"Hook, line, and sinker, every one of them. I wasn't sure
if it would be convincing or if it would bellow 'law enforcement,' but apparently you see all kinds in retail."

"Any takers?"

"Not right off. Brian gave his number to about half of

the jewelers we talked to. Now, some we skipped right off the bat. There were a number that clearly posted information that they were ethical jewelers, so we didn't bother with those. If that's their selling point, we'd only have wasted their time and ours. We focused on the jewelers who said nothing about conflict diamonds outright."

"What was your gut impression?"

"Of the ones we talked to? Mostly that the clerks who quickly disavowed conflict gems seemed on the level. You could feel the distaste coming off them. It was the ones who tried to play a little coy, where Brian and I agreed they had an ulterior motive. Those were the ones who tried to sound out exactly what I meant by a ring with a 'story' attached to it. There were definitely a few where you could see the calculation. They know what they're selling."

"Or they're thinking they could sell you a perfectly legitimate stone and call it a conflict gem," Webb suggested.

"This is true." McCord toasted Webb with his coffee mug. "If you have someone wily, they might think they can put one over on you. It's illegal to buy or sell conflict diamonds, so if you ratted them out, they wouldn't actually be in trouble except for misrepresentation. And in the meantime they got your business out of the deal and made a pretty penny."

"Why would anyone openly sell a conflict gem?" Cara asked. "Isn't the point that they're illegal, so they're going to bury the real provenance?"

"By and large, that's exactly what they do," said McCord. "But in this case they're banking on the fact the buyer is in as much legal jeopardy as they are. They'll likely charge more to make it worth it to them to take that risk."

"I offered to pay a bit more for the product, just to

sweeten the deal," Meg said. Webb's expression, the way he sat back with his coffee, shaking his head, caught her attention. "What?"

"I understand the fact-finding mission, but isn't that entrapment?"

McCord jumped in before Meg could respond. "Actually no. Technically, entrapment is when a law enforcement officer coerces someone into doing something they wouldn't normally do. The thing is, for someone to be able to make an immediate sale, they'd have to already be dealing in these stones. Thus, no entrapment."

"Got you." When Meg just stared at him, one eyebrow raised, Webb simply shrugged. "Just making sure you're not getting into trouble. Wouldn't want to have to visit you in the Big House."

"What is this, 1953?" Amused, she shook her head at him. "But it's a fair question." Meg turned back to McCord. "What were you after?"

"The same thing as you, but you had a better angle on it. It's one thing to be the wearer of the ring, to want something with a complicated past. It's another thing to be the jackass buying the ring, looking for a way to save a few bucks by taking something that might be of questionable origin."

"If we'd known we were both working the same case, we could have gotten better organized on this. It's not going to look good if we both hit shops asking the same questions."

"I'll say. I was only getting started and I didn't assume those saying they only carried certified ethical stones were telling the truth. I suspect we overlapped less than you think."

"That's good." Meg pulled her phone out of her back pocket, opened up her notepad, and brought up the list of stores. She held it out for McCord. "Here's who we hit today."

McCord took the phone and skimmed down the list. "You did okay. Definitely more than me. But I hit one . . . two . . . three of them. But then I visited another four, you didn't."

"The ones who claimed to be ethical jewelers, did you get a feel for them?"

"I think they were all legit. It was clearly a major part of their business model. Still, I had to check. I can send you my specific notes on all the stores. Want to do the same?"

"I have no problem with it. But let's dot the *i*'s." She pulled out her phone and typed out and sent a text. "I'm making sure Kate is on board with our usual understanding that you'll sit on the story if we share our information with you." Her phone signaled an incoming text. "As I thought. She's in. Small world, she says. Also, she sends her greetings."

"Send mine back. Then give me the rundown of what you're doing and I'll fill you in on my research."

Meg brought McCord up to speed with Kate's plan for their searches and their success so far. "I haven't heard from Brian, so I assume he hasn't been contacted by any of the stores yet. But I wouldn't actually expect him to hear from anyone before tomorrow during business hours. So . . . what do you have that we don't?"

"You have one entry point into the family. I have another. But let's back up. What do you know about the Mafia?"

"Does watching *The Godfather*, *Goodfellas*, or *The Untouchables* count?"

"No."

"Educate me then. I know there's a history lesson in there somewhere you're dying to tell me."

McCord shrugged, but looked entirely unembarrassed. "You know me too well."

"You'd hope so, by this point."

"Let's get into it then. The Sicilian Mafia started it all off in Italy in the nineteenth century. But mass immigration to the US in the mid-to-late-nineteenth century and on into the early twentieth century splintered the Sicilian Mafia into a separate organization, the Italian-American Mafia. Also known as the Mob. They still interact with the Italian Mafia, but as equals, not as a part of the whole."

"Also known as the family."

"Yes. Though in this case, family does not actually describe blood relatives, but the numerous criminal organizations inside the larger Mob. Now, the idea of the Mob you likely hold in your head is their glory days in the early twentieth century, specifically during Prohibition. Al Capone and Eliot Ness and all that. When making and selling booze became illegal, they saw a giant business opportunity and stepped in to take advantage. This was when the Mob acquired its greatest power and had its hands in many cookie jars, including bootlegging, protection, prostitution, gambling, and extortion."

"Charming group," Webb said dryly.

"Don't you know it. In New York City alone, it's estimated the Mob was responsible for over one thousand deaths during Prohibition. But that's officially recognized deaths from clashes between the various families. That likely didn't include the quieter deaths and disappearances from within groups. Loyalty was unilaterally expected. Anyone who strayed, who talked to the cops, who didn't follow the rules, was taken out. They didn't kid around."

"I'm sure they still don't."

"Nope. Later in the twentieth century, the Mob got involved in union racketeering and gas tax fraud, and then got into the restaurant biz because they realized they could not only use restaurants as safe meeting spaces with no risk of being bugged, but also as bases for drug smuggling. Of course, in 1970 when the RICO Act became law, things turned around for them. It was right in the name—the Racketeer Influenced and Corrupt Organizations Act—a law specifically created with the Mob in its sights. Through the RICO Act, in ten years starting in the early 1980s, almost eighty bosses, underbosses, and captains were charged with various crimes."

Meg hesitated in the act of putting her empty coffee mug down on the table. "Captains?"

"Mob structure. Let me circle back to that. You need to understand that so you know who you're dealing with. Anyway, RICO was a disaster for the families, with each trying to sell the other out in exchange for immunity from prosecution for their own crimes. It was a bloodbath, and law enforcement through the eighties and nineties really whittled away at the Mob as a whole. Currently the Mob is only a fraction of its former size and power. And while there's some activity in the Midwest and on the West Coast, the most significant activity still takes place along the East Coast, especially in New York City and Philadelphia."

"What do they specialize in now?" Webb asked.

"They pretty much run the gamut. No need to be into bootlegging anymore, or prostitution, that's too small time for them, but they're still into protection, gambling, extortion, tax fraud, and labor racketeering. Add to that corruption of public officials, loan-sharking, and stock manipulation. And, of course, murder has always been part of their stock-in-trade."

"It's the most efficient way to stop a troublemaker, or to get rid of someone who knows the wrong thing," Webb said. "It's been a Mob standard from the beginning. Is part of the problem for them today the fact they're not the only game in town? You hear about the Mexican drug cartels and the Chinese Triad, so clearly their business is being chipped away by international actors."

"They're definitely feeling the squeeze because of all the competition. Go back to the days of bootlegging during Prohibition, and a big city like Boston only had the Irish and the Italians in competition for the illegal booze trade. The Italian Mafia won that one."

"In a hail of bullets from a tommy gun, I would assume."

"You would assume correctly. But yes, you're right that others, the ones you mentioned, as well as the Russian Mob, are horning in on their business. Even with all that, they tend to stay on top. Many think it's because of their strict hierarchical structure. Now, let's talk about that hierarchical structure; then I'll fill you in on the who's who in Philadelphia, because that matters to the case." He finished off his coffee. "Just let me get a refill first."

He started to push off the sofa, but Cara waved him down. "Sit. Keep working it through with Meg. Meg? Todd? More coffee?"

"I'll give you a hand." Webb stood and grabbed his empty mug and Meg's. "We can eavesdrop from the kitchen."

"I'll talk loud. Saves both of us explaining it again to you both later." McCord swiveled on the couch so he partially faced the kitchen. "The first thing to know about the structure of the Italian Mafia is, if you want to get past the ground floor of the organization, you have to be Italian. Preferably full Italian from both sides, but some groups will accept someone who's half Italian on his father's side."

Meg rolled her eyes. "Misogyny on full display there, I

see. All they care about is the Italian Y chromosome; who cares where the X came from."

"I wouldn't call them progressive," McCord agreed. "Now, as you've already mentioned it, you know about the godfather role. The don. The boss. He's the head of the family and he runs all operations and takes a cut of those same operations. Everyone reports to him. He's advised by the consigliere, a man who is often a close family friend or an actual blood relative. He counsels the boss, mediates disputes within the family, and represents the family in meetings with other crime organizations or businesses. But as important as the consigliere is, he's officially third in line to the boss behind the underboss, the second in command and often the heir apparent if the boss dies or is taken into custody. The underboss is the hands-on guy, sometimes with every operation, or sometimes only with the main moneymaking operations."

Cara returned, carrying two mugs, one of which she set in front of McCord. "There's only one of each? A boss and underboss and consigliere?"

"For those positions, yes. But from that point on, it branches out."

Webb handed Meg her coffee, flashed her a smile in response to her thanks, and took his seat with his own mug.

"Next one in the chain is the *caporegime*. Also called the capo, or captain. The capo leads his own crew of ten to twenty men in their dedicated task. This is where you get your distribution of business ventures. Different crews are responsible for a specific project, be it infiltrating labor groups, or drug running, or, in our case, smuggling of conflict diamonds. The capo organizes the soldiers in his crew."

" 'Soldiers'?" Webb asked. "Isn't that a little military-based for this kind of underworld group?"

"Not from their point of view. They expect their soldiers to behave like they're under orders, just like the military does. It works for them. It's the soldiers who are the real worker bees. Need to carry out a hit? Need to pressure someone to pay up or they'll lose their business? Need to move diamonds to a buyer? Those are all jobs for soldiers."

"So that's what Pierce is," Meg stated.

"Yes. Now, within the soldiers, there are different positions—recruiter, enforcer, courier, et cetera. And these are the guys who make the money. Do the drug deals, collect the protection or extortion money, ensure their portion of the gambling money comes to the family. They take a cut and then the rest of the money gets passed to the capo."

"And then does it continue like that? The capo takes a cut and passes it to the underboss? The underboss takes a cut and the rest goes to the boss?"

"Exactly like that." With an index finger McCord motioned to himself and Webb. "Now, if you and I got a sudden urge to join the underworld, the best we could do is join as an associate. Associates are the only non-Italian members of the organization."

"I'm intrigued. What exactly would we be doing in our careers with the Mob?" Webb asked. "You know, so I can plan my life of crime."

"Because your life of walking into burning buildings and bringing heart attack victims back from the dead isn't exciting enough?" McCord deadpanned.

"Sometimes you just need an adrenaline rush."

"Well, this could fill that need," McCord said. "Associates basically do everything a soldier does, but without the protection of the family. Which is considerable."

"How so?" Cara asked. "Just in looking out for each other?"

"This goes *way* beyond that. Once you're initiated into the family, you have the family's protection as a 'made man.' So, if you're a soldier, for instance, that means no one is allowed to kill you unless they have the permission of the soldier's boss. That also goes for other families as well—you can't kill another family's 'made man' either. Keep in mind the number of families in the US—twenty-four overall, with six active in New York State, three in Pennsylvania, not to mention all the factions operating in Jersey—and this is no small perk. Associates don't have that kind of protection. They can be killed by anyone in any family."

"Sounds like that may not be the best position in the family," Meg said. "You're safer as a made man, except that provision puts the ultimate power in the hands of the boss. He can have anyone killed inside his own family."

"They're very powerful men, no doubt about it. Okay, so now you have the breakdown, let's look at who's in Philadelphia, so you know the players. The boss is Joey Cianfrani, the underboss is Tony Peluso, and the consigliere is Mario Venuti."

"We haven't come across any of those names so far. But I'm sure they're known inside the Organized Crime Program. Do you have the name of the capo who's running Giraldi and Pierce? Or Giraldi and Marzano, as the family knows it."

"I don't know all the guys in the crew by name, but the capo running the diamonds is Vittore Falconi. He had a rep for being a brutal enforcer, but he worked his way up the ranks."

"You said each capo runs ten to twenty guys. Are they all working with conflict diamonds?"

"From what I've been able to tell so far, no. This group seems to manage the high-end smuggling. Rough stones, jewelry, stolen artwork, exotic animals—these guys seem

122   *Sara Driscoll*

to do it all. Anything highly taxed or illegal—and the more expensive, the better. I'm trying to dig deeper into this whole group. But I have to do it carefully. These guys wouldn't think twice about shutting up a reporter with a bullet."

Meg glanced at Cara. Her face was partially hidden behind the mug of coffee she cradled with both hands, but her set jaw, and the flat-eyed stare she pinned on McCord, told Meg exactly what her sister thought of McCord's penchant for risk taking. "Is this an adrenaline rush thing too? You like the thrill of the chase?"

"I like the thrill of the chase, but not at the expense of my life." McCord held out a hand to Cara and she reflexively laid hers in it. "I'll be careful. I know what I'm getting into. No story is worth dying for. I promise."

Cara nodded in understanding, but the compressed line of her lips gave away her discomfort.

Meg totally understood. She lived with a man who put his life on the line for the greater good every shift. But a firefighter had an entire crew who could come to his aid—and had—when his life was in danger. McCord worked solo.

She could only hope he wasn't getting in over his head.

he often had the advantage. It was all about contacts and connections, and most of those people would never talk to law enforcement for any reason. But they might talk to him.

He estimated he'd just hit the jackpot.

Nothing like a disgruntled employee wanting to spill the beans on a negligent employer.

It had taken hours of investigation to discover the shell companies, and then to uncover all the businesses they owned and do a deep dive into each one. But because of that research, he'd reached out to Curt Richardson, an ex-employee of Russo Logistics, and was now waiting to hear back. It might finally give him the forward momentum he'd been waiting for on this case.

Maybe this story would net him the Pulitzer he hungered for.

It had been too long since he'd sunk his teeth into a really meaty story. Yes, Meg's cases were definitely worth his time and effort, but lately he'd been feeling he needed to branch out, not leaning on her to set his feet on a certain path, but to find that path on his own. Perhaps if his second day on the job hadn't been September 11, 2001, he wouldn't be so focused on righting wrongs, both big and small. But 9/11 had shaped his psyche as a young newsman, molding his perspective on both America and its place in the world.

That perspective had led him to Iraq in 2006 and straight into the investigation of the Haditha massacre and the death of twenty-four Iraqi civilians, including women and children. It hadn't been his intention to get involved. He'd arrived in Baghdad in March, just as *Time* magazine published the first story suggesting the incident had not been a military action, but a methodical killing

CHAPTER 14

Blocking: A preliminary step in diamond cutting where the basic proportions and symmetry of the diamond are established and the first facets on both the crown and pavilion are placed.

Thursday, August 8, 10:09 AM
The Washington Post
Washington, DC

McCord tuned out the general clamor of the news-room bull pen—constant voices, the whir of printers, and phones ringing or alerting incoming messages—and sat back in his chair in his cubicle, studying the notes he'd just backed up on the *Washington Post* server.

He was closing in.

It had been a shock to walk into a Philadelphia jewelry store and right into Meg and Brian acting like a pair of lovebirds, which was just . . . weird. But to then find out they were working the same case—that gave him a boost because now he knew he was definitely onto something. Law enforcement often had the upper hand in investigations because they had legal access to information he didn't, but when it came to the grittier areas of society, spree. He'd thrown himself into the story, assisting with the more than four hundred interviews for the article the *Washington Post* published the following January. That story named the Marines involved and the exact circumstances of the incident that had killed so many, even a child only a year old.

He'd felt the burning desire to right that wrong, even if it made his own countrymen the guilty parties. Those grandparents, those children, weren't Iraqi insurgents and they didn't deserve to die. Instead, they'd been targeted by a war-weary Marine battalion berserking over the loss of one of their own from an improvised explosive device only minutes before.

Right from the beginning it had been a recipe for disaster. It was definitely a "wrong place, wrong time" moment, but the victims hadn't even lived long enough to know what had happened.

While the *Post*'s investigation had kick-started an NCIS investigation, and charges were laid, in the end all charges were dropped except for one charge for a single soldier. Accusations were laid against the *Post* that they were responsible for denying the soldiers a fair trial after they published NCIS photos of the massacre, and McCord had always felt the paper had contributed to the failure to bring justice to those who died that day.

McCord had no illusions that the Haditha incident— and his residual guilt that lingered even though he'd had no say in publishing those photos—had also shaped his career. It had definitely pointed him toward stories highlighting inequality in power balances. When whispers of illegal diamond shipments had surfaced, he'd nosed around, and had soon disappeared down the rabbit hole of African civil wars, mine management, and worker mistreatment.

He couldn't get Sykes, his editor, to agree to either the risk or the cost of sending him to the Central African Republic, so he'd concentrated his efforts on snuffing out the American end of the equation.

Because if there was no one to buy the gems, the diamonds wouldn't be worth mining.

Those investigations had led him to the Philadelphia crime family, and from there his story had spiraled outward to all their other business interests. So many business interests. Enough that he'd expanded his attention from mistreated African workers to everyone touched by the Mob. He knew his story would be unlikely to topple the Philly Mob, but it would erode their hold. But now with the FBI involved, they had a chance to bring them down.

If they were successful, it would take the boot off the necks of so many victims.

His gaze shifted guiltily to the pile of file folders to the left of his keyboard. Normally, he'd juggle several stories at the same time. Investigative reporting was a long game, and he'd typically have multiple investigations on the go, some in their infancy, some in the research trenches, some only needing polishing. In his head he ticked off the folders—the common factors in a rash of mass shootings, the sex trafficking trial of a notorious businessman, the social factors leading to a rise of measles in communities as it hadn't been seen in the past half century, and sexual harassment complaints levied against a popular senator. All important stories, all with victims deserving justice and to have their stories heard, but, somehow, the investigation into diamond trafficking had really sunk its teeth into him, and the resulting blinders had put every other story on the backburner.

He laid his hand on the pile. *I'll be back for you.*

His phone signaled an incoming text. He picked it up, scanned the screen, and every other story fell away.

Curt Richardson wanted to meet.

This could be the turning point in his investigation.

Here we go.

CHAPTER 15

Melee: A group of gemstones used to accent a larger, central stone.

Friday, August 9, 10:26 AM
S 16th Street
Philadelphia, Pennsylvania

With their dogs on short leashes, and once again dressed in athletic gear, Brian and Meg jogged toward the intersection of S 16th and Market Streets. As they hit the intersection, both dogs turned west, in the direction of the crosswalk as cars whipped by.

"Hawk, stop." Keeping up the pretense even in the downtown business and shopping core of Philadelphia, Meg jogged in place and made a show of checking her heart rate and steps on her fitness tracker. Beside her, Brian also stayed in motion, but scanned the people around them.

They were only a few minutes behind.

Another early-morning start, another local wait in the truck, but they'd been quick off the mark, had found the starting location beside a black SUV, and were hot on the trail.

The DON'T WALK hand flashed on, along S 16th Street,

with a countdown from fifteen, so Meg took a few seconds to look around and orient herself. To the east, Philadelphia's nineteenth-century French Second Empire–styled sprawling City Hall filled the entire end of the block, with its mansard roof, decorative columns and pediments, and tall, narrow clock tower topped by the figure of William Penn. Everything else surrounding them consisted of skyscrapers, mostly of steel and glass. The modern city meets the historical, all inside a single city block.

The DON'T WALK signal flashed 5 . . . 4 . . . 3 . . . as traffic sped by.

The light changed and they were off, slipping into the intersection before pedestrians crowded around them, and running across the street at an easy pace.

Kate and Addison were behind them, but would let them get at least twenty feet ahead before they followed.

Back on the sidewalk and weaving through pedestrians, they jogged past 1600 Market Street, a towering spear of black glass, reflecting the ominous black clouds scudding overhead. The dogs trotted easily, most often keeping their heads down, but occasionally one or the other would look up and scent the breeze as it tunneled between the tall buildings. They jogged past a silver tubular sign with arrows announcing the ONE LIBERTY OBSERVATION DECK beside the graphic image of a building with layered upper levels that clearly took its design inspiration from the Chrysler Building in Manhattan. Meg glanced up the tall expanse of the next building, but it was more of the same—the lower floors faced with marble, stretching into black glass as far as the eye could see.

Another thirty feet of sidewalk and the dogs abruptly swung left, directly toward the gold-and-glass revolving doors cradled between four-story black columns that marked the entryway to One Liberty Place.

"They're doing the drop in a major office building?" Brian questioned.

"Looks like it. Hang on, let's confirm. Hawk, come." Meg walked Hawk fifteen feet farther down the sidewalk. "Hawk, find Jameson." Without hesitation Hawk turned around, heading directly back to the doors. "There's no question, this is where they went."

"There's no way we're going to be undercover for this search."

"Why are we stopped?" Kate asked as she and Addison caught up.

"The dogs are saying they went inside. If so, we have a problem. That's a huge building," Brian said, "and while we're searching one section, they could be leaving through another."

"Then we're going to have to make sure that doesn't happen." Kate turned to Addison. "Do you see any other options?"

"I don't, even though this is a clear risk. If anyone from the family is monitoring, this will be the last op we run. Worse, if they catch us, it could be deadly."

"We're all armed and trained," Meg said. "You let us worry about that."

"Then let's get started." Pulling out her FBI flip case, Kate strode forward, pulled open the handicap entrance door, and led them inside.

The lobby of One Liberty Place was all white-veined black marble as far as the eye could see, from the white-and-black–checkered floor, over the long security desk, around the grand piano to their left, through the security turnstiles to the elevator banks, and all the way up to the ceiling soaring four stories overhead.

"Excuse me, you can't bring those dogs in here." A stocky older man in a navy shirt and pants, with a security badge on his shoulder, stood from behind his glossy marble desk. "You need to take them outside."

Kate already had her ID open and extended as she approached the desk with Addison. "Special Agent Kate Moore and Special Agent Doug Addison, FBI. Those dogs are FBI K-9s and we're working a case. You have an illegal smuggling transaction taking place right now in this building."

Meg left the negotiations to Kate and kept her attention locked on her dog. Hawk was head down and leading her directly toward the turnstiles guarding the entryway to the elevators. Low to the ground, he simply darted through the second turnstile from the right, but when Meg tried to follow, the bar locked in place.

"You can't go through there," the guard called.

"Hawk, come back, bud." Meg swiveled to face the desk. "Kate, they went through here. We need to follow."

"We're looking for two men. They would have entered within the last ten minutes. Did they check in with you?" Kate pulled out her phone and brought up a photo of Pierce. "This was one of the men."

"A bunch of people have come through here in the last ten minutes, but all of them had pass cards. I can look up IDs, but that's not going to tell you where they went."

Kate turned to Meg and Brian. "What do you need?"

"We need to track them up," Brian said, "but that's not going to tell us where they got off."

"We can figure that out," Meg said. "You need to shut down the elevators for approximately fifteen minutes while we do a fast scan."

"You're going to cover the building in fifteen minutes? That's impossible," Kate stated. "It has to be over fifty floors."

"Sixty-one," said the guard.

"If we cover the whole building, we'll lose the pass-off.

But we don't need to. The dogs have the scent. All we need to do is stop at every floor and check out the elevator lobby. The dogs will tell us if they've been there. If so, the search continues. If not, up to the next floor." Meg turned to Brian. "Let's make it easy. You take odd floors, I'll take even. Lock out all the elevators but two. Sixty-one floors, cut in half because there's two of us, a minute maximum per floor, likely only half that, and it will take about fifteen minutes. But we need to start *now*."

"Can you do this?" Kate asked the guard. "We need all but two elevators brought down to the ground floor and locked out, once we know no one is on them. We need the other two for our exclusive use. And I need a list of who has recently scanned through those turnstiles. That might tell us where they're going, if they're registered by company."

"They are. Hang on." The guard sat down at his computer and reached toward a panel of lights and buttons. "Go through that same turnstile now."

"Lacey, find Jameson." Brian followed his dog through the turnstile.

Meg passed through after them and both dogs tracked the trail to the left, to a bank of elevators, three on one side and two on the other. Both dogs sat down on the right side of the two elevators. "Good boy, Hawk. Good girl, Lacey." Meg unclipped Hawk, coiled the leash, and put it in her pocket as she walked back to the turn in the corridor. "Kate, we have it. They went up the right elevator of the double bank. We need those two elevators active and we need to shut down the other three."

"Give me a second," Kate called.

In another minute Kate and Addison came around the corner. "They're ours. Doug and I are going to split up and go with you, so if you have to move quickly, once you identify where they are, you're not alone. Officer Curry will stay at the security desk and is going to call me with the names and offices of anyone who swiped in and the companies that registered the cards. That might shorten this down. He's also sending all the elevators to the ground floor and will keep the other three there. He'll block anyone else from passing through the turnstiles until I let him know otherwise. I've called in agents from the field office to watch the emergency staircases and the outside exits. They're not getting out of this building unseen." She jabbed the elevator call button and the doors of the right-hand elevator slid open. "Doug, you and Meg go first; we'll be right behind you."

Meg led Hawk into the elevator. "Starting on two."

"We'll start on three," Brian said. "Safe hunting."

"You too."

The elevator doors closed and the vertical search began.

CHAPTER 16

Channel Set: A type of setting in which small diamonds, or other gemstones, are placed inside a specially cut channel. A small lip that extends very slightly over the edge of the gemstones keeps them secure.

Friday, August 9, 10:40 AM
One Liberty Place
Philadelphia, Pennsylvania

The doors opened on the second floor to pale wood-paneled walls and glossy smoked-charcoal tile floors.

Meg pulled the plastic bag from her jogging jacket pocket and offered it to Hawk. "Hawk, find Jameson." As she stepped into the narrow lobby behind her dog, she heard the low hum of the next elevator whooshing by on its way to the third floor—Lacey was also on the hunt.

Hawk put his head down, but Meg could immediately tell he was casting for scent, not following it as he circled the lobby.

Standing in the doorway to hold the elevator door open, Addison watched Hawk pass the entry to the corridor without a pause. "I don't know anything about this, but it looks to me like he's fishing."

"He is. Hawk, come." Meg led Hawk back into the elevator and punched the button for the fourth floor. "He knew the moment he stepped out, it wasn't the right floor."

"If every floor goes like that, it's not even going to take fifteen minutes."

Hawk quickly fell into a pattern. At each floor he'd leave the elevator, nose down, to circle the small lobby, paying special attention to the end leading to the connecting hallway, and then return to the elevator. Each floor took him at most twenty seconds.

Addison and Kate were texting, so Meg knew Brian also wasn't successful so far.

Kate called when they were finishing with the sixteenth floor, and Addison put the call on speaker. "I have the list of people who entered the building and the companies the cards are registered to. More importantly for us, what floor they're on. Sixth, ninth, twenty-fourth, thirty-second, forty-fifth, and fifty-ninth floors. Want to just hit those floors?"

"Are they only allowed access to the floor to which they are registered?" Meg asked as they rose to the eighteenth floor.

"No. They can get off anywhere."

"Then there's no guarantee they got off on the floor they're registered to. Perhaps the family rents office space for a legitimate business that fronts their illegal activities. Maybe they rent more than one location. Maybe the person they're meeting rents the space, so we can't track them except with the dogs." The doors opened on the eighteenth floor. "Hawk, find Jameson." She studied her dog as he circled the lobby. "I say we keep going. Brian?"

"Agreed. We need to be meticulous or we're going to miss something and they'll get by us."

Hawk finished his circle and returned to Meg at the elevator. "We'll stick to the plan then. Heading up to the twentieth floor."

"We're on the twenty-first," Kate said. "Call us if you catch something."

The twenty-fourth floor was on Kate's potentials list, but netted them nothing. The search continued.

But when they exited the thirty-second floor, everything changed. Hawk's relaxed posture instantly morphed into one of alertness and instead of circling to the right toward the lobby's dead end, he immediately veered left, entering the larger hallway and heading north toward a double set of heavy cherrywood doors at the end of the hallway.

"Hawk, stop. Come." She turned around. "Doug, come on out. Let Kate know we have them."

Addison already had his phone to his ear. Clearly, he'd already seen enough of the search to know when Hawk was onto a scent. "Kate, Hawk found the trail. Come to the thirty-second floor." He ended the call and slipped the phone into his pocket. "They're on their way. He's sure?"

"Yes. He wants to track the trail down the hallway, but I want to wait for Kate. If this moves fast, we need both of you with us."

The left elevator dinged and the doors opened. Lacey exited first and immediately caught the trail, following Hawk toward the lobby exit.

"Lacey, stop. Sit. That's definitely it. Are you going in?" Brian asked Kate.

"If they lead me to a location and I have no doubt they're sure, then, yes, I'm going in. At that point I'll have legitimate reasonable suspicion of a crime taking place to legally enter, based on Agent Pierce's intel and the dog's tracking abilities. Let the dogs continue tracking. Unless our guys used the emergency staircase, they're still on this floor."

"Hawk, Lacey, find Jameson."

The dogs trotted down the corridor in step, noses down in the still hallway, every skin cell lying where it had fallen only minutes before. For the dogs it was a flashing arrow pointing their way. When they came to the double doors, Kate pulled one open and the dogs led the way inside.

The young woman behind the oak desk looked startled and her likely standard greeting of "Green, Parker, and Williamson, may I . . ." trailed off into stunned surprise as two FBI badges were flipped open and presented to her.

"Special Agent Kate Moore and Special Agent Doug Addison. Two men came in here within the past fifteen minutes. One of them looks like this." She flashed Pierce's picture. "Where are they?"

"Mr. Williamson said it was fine for them to use the conference room to meet with Mr. Hatch."

"Where is it?"

The young woman raised a shaking hand to point down a corridor of doorways. "Down there. Around the corner and then first door on your le—"

Kate and Addison didn't even wait for her to finish, but sprinted down the hallway.

Meg stepped up to the desk. "Is there another way to get to that conference room?"

"The office plan is a big square. You'd have to go all the way around the other—"

Meg had already turned away from her. "I'll go the long way."

"I'll take this hallway," Brian said.

"Hawk, come."

They ran past rows of doors, potted plants, and clustered sitting areas. Around corners and startled employees, who exclaimed in surprise and backed into walls. Straight through a group of six men having what looked like an impromptu meeting in the hallway, and who scattered at her warning of "FBI, coming through!" Around, all the way to the conference room.

Meg knew she was in the right place at the sight of Brian and Lacey down the hallway, about fifteen feet from an open door. She stopped about the same distance away on the other side.

A crash and a shout came from inside the room.

Stay or go? Meg could see the same indecision on Brian's face, but she raised a hand, palm out telling Brian to hold. There were two trained, armed agents in the room, but if anyone got past them, she and Brian had them cornered. If one of them moved, it opened an escape route. Another crash, vicious swearing and then pounding feet. A tall, lean, blond man—definitely not Giraldi—ran out the door, heading to the right for the hallway and freedom. Only to be confronted by man and dog.

"Lacey, guard!"

Lacey went low on her splayed front paws, her lips drawn back to reveal her teeth, and let loose with a foreboding growl. The man jerked to a halt, nearly fell in his effort to abruptly turn, and took two steps in Meg's direction.

"Hawk, guard!"

More teeth, more growling, and the man hesitated long enough for Kate to appear with her Glock trained on him, ordering him to his knees. Only after the man was cuffed and pushed back into the conference room did Meg and Brian release the dogs.

They met at the conference room door to take in the carnage. Chairs lay overturned and books had tumbled from a bookcase to sprawl on the ground below. A heavily framed watercolor of a forest glade lay on the floor, tipped against the wall. Addison stood, panting, his T-shirt ripped at one shoulder, holding a handcuffed Pierce with one cheek pressed to the wall. Blood trickled from his nose to smear the wall. The blond man was seated in a chair, his cuffed wrists wedged between himself and the chair back. Two men stood at the far end of the room. One, standing with a tall, dignified bearing, glared at Kate with clenched fists. The other, a shorter, older man, well dressed in a neat suit and dark tie, cowered in the back corner. Rough diamonds tumbled out of a black velvet bag to scatter across the table, and a jeweler's loupe lay amidst the stones.

Clearly, it had been a struggle to contain Pierce and the other man. Pierce had put up a fight and Addison had to get a little rough with him to get him cuffed. But now when word got back to the family, he'd look like the loyal soldier they thought him to be. Meg only hoped Addison hadn't actually broken Pierce's nose.

"You're going to regret this when my lawyers finish taking you apart," the dignified man spat.

"Bless your heart." Kate loosened the reins on her Southern sarcasm before turning her back on him and raising her cell phone to her ear to instruct the agents downstairs to ask security to release the elevator lockdown and then to come up to thirty-two to help bring down the suspects. She ended the call and slipped her phone into her jacket pocket, turning to find Meg and Brian in the doorway. "Thanks for the assist out there." She looked down at the blond man in the chair. "This one moves like the wind."

Brian laid his hand on Lacey's head. She grinned up at him, tongue lolling, looking nothing like the fierce guard dog she'd been minutes before. "No one can get by these guys."

"I wouldn't want to face down those teeth. If y'all can just hang here until the other agents arrive, we'll meet you back at the field office after that."

"You got it."

Out in the hallway Meg and Brian shared a silent high five.

Finally a search that had gone right from start to finish.

CHAPTER 17

Plotting Diagram: A map of a diamond's inclusions.

Friday, August 9, 1:21 PM
Philadelphia FBI field office
Philadelphia, Pennsylvania

Pierce came in holding an ice pack against the side of his nose. Above it, his left eye was darkening to a muddy purple.

Addison looked up from his phone at Pierce's entrance and winced. "Ouch."

Pierce pulled out a chair and sat, removing the pack from his nose to lay it on the table. His face had been cleansed of blood, but his nose was puffy and bruised. "I appreciate the fact you didn't want to leave Bruno with any question about my allegiance to the family, but did you have to be so enthusiastic?"

Addison's cheeks flushed a ruddy hue. "Sorry, man. I didn't see that painting when I was turning to slam you into the wall."

"It would have been fine if I hadn't caught the corner of it with my face." With a frown Pierce glanced down at the trails of dried blood that trickled down his shirt. "But it certainly convinced Bruno. Before they split us up, it was clear he considered us on the same side. How long are you going to 'detain' us?" He made air quotes around the word "detain."

"Another hour or so, and then you'll all be transferred to federal holding until the lawyers arrive. We'll get you released on bail in the next day or two and you can be back in business. But in the meantime, we wanted to get your intel on the drop."

Rustling at the door attracted their attention and Brian sprung to his feet to relieve Kate of several of the brown paper bags she carried. He flashed her a smile. "See? I told you, you'd get lunch someday."

"Hopefully, I got everyone's order correct." Her gaze circled the table until it landed on Pierce and she grimaced. "Ow. You okay?"

"Yeah. Hurts some, but will look great to Bruno and the lawyers they send in. I'll tell them I want to argue police brutality."

"You were resisting arrest," Addison protested.

"Sure I was. It'll go nowhere, but they'd expect me to push for it, so I will."

"That'll look authentic. You don't think you'll have any trouble taking part in the next drop? This whole effort falls apart without you."

"I expect they'll look at me. They know that Bartholomew was arrested. Now this drop goes south. So they're going to search for a leak."

"That puts you in jeopardy."

"The only physical evidence is the burner phone, which you now have in custody and it can stay there. They have no way to track the custom app. And they can search me as much as they like for a wire, but they're never going to find one." He studied Hawk, who lay beside Meg's chair. "They'll never suspect we're doing this old school and in a completely untraceable fashion by technological means."

He looked up to meet Kate's gaze. "I didn't think this would work. Even after the test run, I doubted you'd make this work. I was wrong."

"Credit where credit is due—it's all about the dogs. None of this would work if they weren't pros. But now Bruno has not only seen us, but also the dogs. Isn't that going to be a problem?"

"Lacey can totally pass as an apprehension K-9. Hawk . . . maybe not so much, though he sounded pretty vicious. I'll cede that thought with them, that they're patrol-and-apprehension K-9s, not scent dogs, and you brought them, not they brought you. As far as seeing the four of you, as long as you continue to use the dogs and stay out of sight until the end, I don't think this is a problem next time. But you may only get one more crack at it if they pair me with either Giraldi or Bruno. Being seen once is one thing. Being seen twice will kick up their suspicions. We knew this angle on disrupting the chain might be short-lived depending on how the drops went down." He paused for a moment, his forehead creased as he was briefly lost in thought. "Actually, I can't see them using Bruno for diamond drops in the near future, not when law enforcement associates his face with diamond trafficking. So, really, it's still only Giraldi who might be a problem and he doesn't know you're law enforcement, just someone in his way at an art fair. Let's play it by ear." He eyed the bags. "One of those for me?"

"You bet." Kate slid a bag across the table to Pierce. "I went with the traditional loaded burger and fries, since I didn't know what you like. Please tell me you're not vegan."

"No, ma'am." He opened and pulled out a foil-wrapped burger and leaned down to sniff it. "That's a damned shame. I can't smell a thing because my nose is messed up, but I'm going to imagine this smells amazing."

Kate and Brian passed out the remaining bags and everyone settled in to eat for a few minutes.

Kate wiped her mouth with her napkin and lay it down next to her crumpled food wrapper. "Green, Parker, and Williamson, the office space where the drop took place. That's a law firm, mostly dealing with corporate law—mergers and acquisitions, setting up companies, corporate restructuring." She turned to Meg and Brian. "Henry Williamson was the fourth man we arrested." Back to Pierce. "How are Williamson and his law firm connected with diamond smuggling?"

"The law firm isn't." Pierce paused to take a drink of his soda to wash down his burger. "But Williamson is one of our associates. He's handy because he assisted in setting up several shell companies to shelter the activities of other businesses he helped the family acquire. And sometimes we use his space for private, off-the-grid meetings if we feel the heat is coming on strong. After Bartholomew got busted, they wanted this meet to be extremely private and somewhere totally unrelated to the gems or the buyer." He looked down to where Lacey sat by Brian's chair, her eyes following every bite Brian took. "You gonna share that with her? She did a good job. She deserves it."

"I agree, and she had an excellent meal about a half hour ago with extra treats added in for a job well done. She'd like my burger, but she doesn't get it." Brian stroked Lacey's head. "Down, girl." She sighed and settled with her head on her paws.

"Anyway," Pierce continued, "this seemed to be the perfect place to meet. It was set up as a meeting with Williamson over some of their legit businesses. Williamson was supposed to meet us at the beginning and then bugger off, but you never gave him the chance and burst in before he could extricate himself. That's actually going to have ramifications."

"Because we arrested him too?"

"Yes, and because he'll likely lose his partnership and may end up being disbarred. He'll be useless to the family at that point. They're going to be *pissed*." A sharkish smile punctuated his words. "And this will be a local news story and they won't like that either."

"As part of Philadelphia's law community, I assume Williamson will have the best of the best in terms of representation?"

"I'm sure he will. And he may skate out from under it yet. The weak link in the chain is going to be Norman Hatch."

"That's the fourth man?" Meg asked.

"Yes. He's a diamond broker who does big business in both New York and Philadelphia's Jewelers' Rows," Kate said. "We're keeping him totally separated because he's already asking for his lawyer, and he's nervous enough I think we'll be able to pitch a deal to him for reduced charges. He may sell Williamson down the river." She sat back in her chair with a satisfied sigh. "But that's not our problem. That's up to Assistant US Attorney Jacobs, and she'll keep us in the loop as to how it's all going. What's next for us, then?"

Pierce rubbed his jaw, his gaze fixed on the table. "I'm not absolutely sure."

"You think this bust will stop the sales of the stones?" Brian asked.

"I wouldn't think so. But it may put a damper on moving them in the short term. There are going to be discussions about sitting on them until things cool down. But Falconi, my capo, is going to push for keeping them moving."

"This is how he makes his money, right? If he sits on them, he makes nothing."

"Right. And, as soldiers, that goes for us too. There's incentive in keeping the stones moving. I'll push for that and stress we don't want to risk being caught with them if someone, somewhere, is turning up the heat. But it's going to be days before we reorganize because they'll want to track down where any potential leaks might be."

"You better be careful," Addison warned. "We don't want you in concrete shoes at the bottom of the Delaware River."

"You and me both. If they thought I was nobody, a bloody execution and a body toss might be all I'd get. But if they ever find out I'm law enforcement, they'll 'Jimmy Hoffa' me right away. Trust me, I'm keeping that in mind."

"I'm also keeping in mind that I'd like to see your capo and some of the upper reaches of your Philadelphia crime family put away for this."

"I think we'll be able to manage that, but we need to wait until we've connected more dots on the commercial end of the smuggling. Then we can sting them. And I'm in sync; I don't want this all to be small potatoes, but larger portions of the organization as well. Let's think about it."

Putting their heads together, they started to form a larger plan.

CHAPTER 18

Chip: A jagged, shallow defect in the surface of a diamond that reduces its value and poses a potential problem with durability.

Friday, August 16, 8:06 PM
N Judson Street, Lower North Philadelphia
Philadelphia, Pennsylvania

Brian reached out and laid a hand over Meg's bouncing knee. "You're shaking the whole truck. For the love of God, *stop*."

"Sorry." Her cheeks warming in embarrassment, Meg instantly stilled. "The waiting is getting to me."

"I'm there with you. This whole case feels like a giant case of hurry-up-and-wait and we're spending more time in Todd's truck than I ever would've thought possible. But think about last week's success. This strategy has paid off. And, on the bright side, no one is shooting arrows at us this time."

"You got me there."

"We can just sit back and relax. And be ready to jump at a moment's notice and then run around like maniacs."

Meg laughed. "That does seem to be how this goes."

They'd been called into a mixed residential-and-commercial neighborhood just north of the City Center. Meg and Brian both recognized this was different from the previous areas they'd visited when they came in via Fairmount Avenue to drive past what looked like a castle, complete with massive stone crenelated turrets marking the corners of a stone wall rising nearly to the top of the tower. Ivy climbed the stone facing, and while the walls held medieval-styled indented arrow slits, they were filled with thick iron bars.

Meg could only spare the massive edifice a quick glance as they drove past. "Why is there a fortress in the middle of Philadelphia?"

"And here I thought you were the expert and knew *everything* about old buildings." He grinned when she shot him a squinty glare. "According to Google Maps, it's the only reason in modern day you'd have a fortress like this in the middle of a metropolitan center. That's the old Eastern State Penitentiary." They whipped past a sign saying the site was open for daily tours. "Hey, look, next time we're here during the day, we can go in and take a look at the old derelict jail. You know, just in case you didn't get enough of abandoned prisons at the Old Montgomery Jail."

An image of the century-old jail, with its rusted bars, caved-in roof, and actively collapsing concrete walkways, came back to Meg. She shuddered. "God, no. Hard pass."

As they waited in the truck for the text with Pierce's location to arrive, Meg turned away to look out the window at the row of redbrick town houses across the road. They'd found street parking on a block north of the intersection Pierce had suggested. A narrow, one-way street, they'd been lucky enough to find a spot large enough for the truck under the spreading limbs of a gingko tree. Dusk was leaching into night and while N Judson sank into shadows, the streetlights ahead on Aspen had already winked on.

"Any more leads on the jewelry stores?" she asked.

"Since you asked me yesterday? No. If there was, I'd have said something. Kate has the list of the three stores that got back to me. She's going to check them out."

"She should send us back in. They're expecting us."

"I told her that. I think we put her in a bad position. She didn't expect us to actually unearth anything useful. And we're not agents." Brian gave her a sidelong look. "Let's be honest. It's not you she's worried about. You're an ex-cop. It's me. The dog guy."

"I'm a dog guy . . . theoretically."

"You're a great dog guy. But you also have all that extra cop training."

"And she doesn't think I could protect you? I wouldn't let anything happen to you."

"I know that, but look at it from her perspective. She's responsible for us. But speaking of the jewelry stores . . . how'd you like ring shopping?"

Meg fixed him with a side-eye stare. "Fine." She didn't like where this was going. "Why?"

"I just thought some of those rings looked good on you." He held up his left hand, wiggled his ring finger, the gold band a subtle shine in the last of the evening light. "You and Todd ever talk about taking the plunge?"

"Into marriage?"

"Sure."

"Sort of."

Brian let a full five seconds pass before prodding her. "Meaning?"

"Are you bored? Is this why you're quizzing me?"

"Sure, I'm bored. And you just finished telling me you are too."

"Suddenly I don't mind being bored. What are you, the marriage police?"

Brian's bark of laughter had both dogs looking up at him in confusion. "Yeah, that's me. I was just wondering after our trip to Jewelers' Row if that made you think about it, that's all."

"You're worse than my mother."

"Any comparison to your mother is a high compliment, so thank you. And you're skating around my question."

"This makes me really sorry I didn't know you when you and Ryan were dating. I could have given you the third degree." She paused, staring out the front windshield. "We've talked about it, okay? Well, not marriage so much, more about kids."

Brian's eyebrows nearly got lost in his hairline. "Babe, that was *not* where I thought this was going, but do tell."

"We agreed that moving in together was all we needed to work on for now, but we both want kids. Maybe in a few years, when Hawk starts to slow down as he ages. No hard-and-fast plans, you know? We'll take it as it comes. And maybe marriage will come before that."

"Seems sensible." He gave her a little nudge with his elbow. "You know I'm only poking at you because you guys are amazing together. And I want to see you as happy as Ryan and I are."

"You love being married?"

"*Yes*. It's the best. Knowing you're coming home every night to someone who truly gets you and is committed for the long haul? That's what we have and what I'd like to see for you. And I think you're almost there. That's why I asked."

"You're a nosy pain in the ass." She tried to look stern, but she couldn't stop the smile that tugged at the corner of her lips.

"But you love me anyway."

"Of course I do. And—" Meg cut off as her cell phone rang and she pulled it out of one of the console cup holders. "Why is Kate calling instead of texting?" She answered the call, putting it on speaker. "Hi, Kate. Everything okay?"

"Call off the search." Kate's tone oozed disappointment. "We lost our trail."

"They canceled the drop?"

"No, they're not sending Pierce."

Meg and Brian exchanged uneasy looks. "Does he think they're onto him after the last drop went south?"

"No. Falconi has him making contact with someone out of town about some kind of black-market animal trophy they're smuggling in."

"Disgusting."

"Agreed. Pierce didn't sound happy about it either, and not just because of the change of plans. But that blows tonight's operation."

"Can he tell us anything about the drop? We came all this way. We could at least scope out the area."

"And you're just going to follow any pair of guys you see walking down the sidewalk? That's a waste of your time and the dogs' skills. Without Pierce, or without a more specific location clue, there's nothing for them to do. Pierce doesn't know the exact location of the drop and he doesn't know who they're sending. It's a crew of about twenty guys, remember. They could be sending any of them."

"Yeah, I guess you're right. Are you heading to DC or the field office?"

"DC. I'm in court tomorrow, so if it doesn't need to be a late night, it would be better for my testimony."

"Okay. Us too, then. Talk to you tomorrow?"

"You bet." Kate ended the call, and a moment later, the green hatchback sped by with Addison at the wheel.

"Well, hell. We did so well last time. I was hoping that was the beginning of a trend."

"Maybe next time." Brian pointed ahead out the front window. "Home, James."

Meg checked her side mirror and pulled into the narrow lane. "I assume we're retracing our way back?"

"Basically." Brian checked the map on his phone as they turned onto Aspen Street. "The next cross street, North 24th Street, is one way south. Take it. That will lead to Pennsylvania Avenue and, from there, back to I-676."

Meg stopped at the stop sign, signaled, and made the turn onto N 24th Street. Another residential road, but one wide enough to allow parking on both sides of the street. Another block south and the side-by-side town houses opened out to mixed-use buildings—a barbershop, closed for the night; a pizzeria next to it; a pub across the street, the sidewalk running alongside packed with occupied tables and chairs—the people of Philadelphia enjoying a meal or drinks after dinner on a warm summer evening.

Meg registered the men walking beside the patio, heading north as they continued along the sidewalk. For a moment her mind went absolutely blank . . . and then her brain kicked in and she had to force herself to gently brake and not react by screeching to a halt. She looked in the rearview mirror, squinting at the two figures moving away from her.

Brian twisted around in his seat to look out the rear window of the truck. "What's wrong?" He jerked as Meg hit the gas, and quickly turned around to face forward again.

"I need to circle back down this street, but there are too many one-ways. Check your map. How do I do it?"

Brian didn't even question, he just turned his attention to his phone. "Take a right here on Fairmount, then your first right is North 25th Street. Take it. We can't go as far up as Aspen, because that goes the wrong way, but we can take one of these side streets."

"I need the one closest to Aspen that goes back toward North 24th Street."

"That's the third street on the right. Meredith." He grabbed the door handle and held on as she made the turn onto N 25th Street too fast. "Meg, what's going on?"

"We just drove past Giraldi."

"Seriously? Are you sure?"

She threw him a slit-eyed glare. "He tried to kick my dog. He practically splintered my shin. I'm not going to forget his face."

"I guess not. We passed a couple of restaurants back there. Didn't you say that McCord outlined how they owned restaurants and used them as safe meeting places?"

"Yeah. Maybe they just had their meet."

"Or maybe they're on their way to it." Brian pointed to the street coming up on their right. "This is Meredith."

Meredith was another narrow one-way street with parking on the south side. But up ahead, an SUV was parked, blocking traffic as two people tried to maneuver a large crate into it. Meg slowed, her fingers tapping with irritation on the wheel; then she abruptly pulled into an open spot and killed the engine. "Screw it. We go on foot from here."

"What am I looking for?"

"I don't know what the other guy is wearing, but Giraldi's wearing a dark jacket and pants."

"Not a surprise, considering who we're dealing with, but he's likely wearing a jacket in this heat for the same reason we are—to hide a weapon."

"That's my take on it." She reached for her cell phone. "I'm getting Kate back. We can track Giraldi for now and

54   *Sara Driscoll*

they can join up with us when they circle back." She speed-dialed Kate, hardly letting her get a greeting out when she answered. "It's Meg. We just spotted Giraldi."

"*What?* Where?"

"Walking up North 24th Street. Brian and I circled around and are going to try to find them again to track them. Can you come back?"

"Yes. Hang on, putting you on speaker." There was a pause and then her voice returned, sounding slightly tinny. "We just got onto I-676 and we're going over the Schuylkill River. Doug, can we push it a bit faster?"

"Not without killing us or someone else." Addison's voice came from a distance. "Get me directions and I'll get us back as fast as possible."

"Working on it. Meg, we're on our way. We'll follow your trackers, but I want you to stay in touch."

"Will do. Meg out." She disconnected and slid her cell phone into the side pocket of her yoga pants. "Let's go."

They climbed out of the truck, leashed the dogs, and jogged down the narrow sidewalk; Meg in front, with Brian behind her.

In the distance the scream of sirens rose, getting louder and louder. Just before Meg and Brian reached the corner to turn onto N 24th Street, two cop cars sped south, lights and sirens running.

"Damn it!" Brian ran faster, but Meg stayed with him. "Even if those aren't meant for them, if that's really Giraldi, it might be enough to spook him."

They rounded the corner, heading south again, the sidewalk opening up enough so they could run side by side. With the dogs not leading this search, they fell into their normal jogging position, running beside their owners, easily keeping pace even at this faster speed.

Meg peered down the street, but the double row of cars and the trees lining both sides, some of them clearly decades old, partially impeded her view. "I can't see them. Do you think they might have ducked into one of these businesses to avoid the police?"

"If we have to go door-to-door, we'll never find them. Maybe they took a side street to stay out of sight?"

"Maybe. We're coming up on one. We'll check it out."

"Did you recognize the other guy?"

"Honestly, I didn't see him. I was so surprised to see Giraldi, I didn't look past him."

At Perot Street they stopped on the corner, each looking down the road on their own side.

"There's a guy walking away from us on this side," Brian said. "Assuming it's the right guy, I'd say they split up."

"I only see one guy too. But I don't see them together on North 24th, so I think them going separate ways is a good guess. We can split up and follow them, but I have to take the unknown guy. It's way too dangerous for me to take Giraldi. It won't matter if the new guy catches a glimpse of Hawk and I because he won't connect me with a previous drop."

"Agreed. And Giraldi and I never came face-to-face, the same way you did, so it's doubtful he's going to recognize me."

Meg peered down the street on Brian's side, then back to her own. "I'm not sure which is which. Both have dark hair, both are wearing dark shirts or jackets. We need to make this call fast, before we lose line of sight. Then I'll text Kate to let her know we've split up, and they'll have to do the same once they arrive. You stay in touch with Doug; I'll stay in touch with Kate."

"That works." Brian took a quick moment to study one man, then the other. "I think the one on my side is Giraldi. I got to see him standing next to you at the art festival, so I got a size comparison. He's big, really big. This guy is the bigger of the two. I think that's Giraldi. Lacey and I will take him."

"Be careful. Giraldi isn't someone to play around with."

"None of them are safe to play around with. Stay in touch when you can. Be safe."

"Back at you."

They peeled off from each other, Brian crossing the street to jog back toward the penitentiary, and Meg taking the corner onto Perot, jogging almost halfway up the street before dropping into a walk so she didn't get too close.

Perot was another narrow, one-way street, but now that lack of space was a detriment. A row of trees lined the same side as a run of parked cars, but they were old enough that all their foliage was far overhead, and the trunks gave her nearly zero cover. The line of cars did better, and the man was on the far sidewalk with zero cover from cars or trees, but Meg knew she and Hawk were still in plain view. She estimated approximately a zero percent chance that he wasn't armed in some way, be it gun or knife. He was likely also an enforcer, and from the size of him, he'd be a dangerous man in hand-to-hand combat. But she was only trailing him; she'd never get close enough to him to need to show him her own skills in that arena, skills she'd picked up in her training to join the Richmond PD.

The man was walking fast, but Meg and Hawk easily kept up with him. He glanced over his shoulder only once, just a quick flash of the side of his face, too brief for her to build an ID, but she was sure he'd seen her.

A normal person would think she'd made a turn while walking her dog. A suspicious person would think he was being followed. But his pace never altered.

At the end of the street, he took a left, disappearing from view.

That was a problem. They had no known scent to track, so Meg needed to keep him in sight or they risked losing him altogether. "Hawk, come!" They burst into a run, crossing the empty street and sprinting for the corner, dropping into a walk a few feet short of the edge of the last building. "Hawk, stop."

Her back against the wall, Meg leaned out ever so slightly to peer around the edge. She caught a flash of black as it disappeared at a run behind a redbrick building across the street and down a half block.

Moving fast. Definitely made us.

And whether he thought she was law enforcement or from a rival Mob clearly didn't matter. He knew someone was after him. And if they didn't move fast, they were going to lose him and Kate would be coming back for nothing.

"Hawk, come!"

They ran across the street and down the block. The Fairmount Art Center sat on the corner, the front door at an angle to the intersection. "Hawk, sit. Stay." Hawk waited at the bottom of the steps while Meg ran up them, then slipped behind a tall white pillar to catch a glimpse around the corner.

And froze in shock.

It wasn't just any man standing on a short support fence to hoist himself over a tall black iron gate. It was Giraldi.

Brian had made the wrong call.

CHAPTER 19

Fire: Spectral colors reflected from a diamond's interior when it is moved while being exposed to light.

Friday, August 16, 8:23 PM
N 25th Street, Lower North Philadelphia
Philadelphia, Pennsylvania

Fear shot through her veins like a dousing of ice water and she pulled back, momentarily uncertain.

She had about three seconds to make the decision.

Call off the chase, let Brian know he doesn't have Giraldi, and let this one go.

Or man up and get the job done. If you stay on Giraldi and Kate takes him into custody as the man Bartholomew identified as the Mob smuggler in Franklin Park, he won't be a threat to you any longer. You know how cruel he is. Who will he hurt next if you don't try?

She peered around the pillar again to find Giraldi just clearing the top of the gate, and remembered fury washed the fear clean away. With a command to Hawk, they ran flat out toward the gate as Meg pulled out her cell phone and used voice commands to send a text to Kate.

In pursuit of Giraldi who knows we're following. North 25th and Fairmount and on the move.

Giraldi was already over the top of the gate and dropping onto the far side. One glance showed Meg they were in trouble. The tall locked gate separated a short driveway from a well-lit parking lot beyond, and, on the far side of the parking lot, a second gate stood open to allow cars to pass through. But while she could climb over the fence in front of her as Giraldi had, her dog couldn't. She'd taught him to vault a four- or five-foot fence by using her own back as a springboard, but this fence was easily over six feet. If Hawk even cleared it in the first place, there was no way he'd land well on the other side.

No choice but to circle around.

She was pulling away from the gate when Giraldi slowed and turned midflight, his right hand swinging toward them. Her vision narrowed on the dark shape in his hand.

A gun.

"Talon, down!" Hawk flattened to the ground, and Meg dove to half cover him as the shot rang out, whining over her head.

People screamed and the sound of running feet echoed through the parking lot. Meg risked raising her head just enough to see Giraldi running for the far gate as people took cover behind cars or ran for their lives.

That stunt had bought him several precious seconds. Whether he'd really aimed for her, she wasn't sure. Especially when she suspected he didn't know who she was. While women didn't take a full role in the family's criminal activities, there was no doubt they played a supporting role and there would be ramifications for taking one out without a boss's permission. And Giraldi would know full well the hell that would rain down on him if he killed anyone associated with law enforcement. It was why he ran instead of standing his ground.

She'd just have to catch him, even if it meant holding him until Kate could arrive to do the official arrest. He was now a clear and present danger to everyone around him because she knew he wouldn't hesitate to kill anyone who got in the way of his escape. Even if she stopped her pursuit now, he wouldn't know she'd given up, so he'd still be a risk until he felt he was absolutely safe. She had no choice but to stay on him.

Meg jumped to her feet. "Hawk, up!" This way was blocked, so they'd have to go the long way around. And she needed her dog to be unrestrained for a chase like this, so she unleashed him. "Come!" She coiled his leash and jammed it in her jacket pocket and then ran flat out. Back down the short driveway, they slowed only long enough in taking the corner to the right to ensure they didn't run full speed into anyone. They wove down the busy sidewalk—it was a warm summer evening and the citizens of Philadelphia were out in force—making Meg glad Hawk was running free or they'd be so hampered they'd never have a chance to catch Giraldi.

They rounded the corner of a large gray-stone building with tall, ornate windows and a central arching tower of stone and black marble with gold figures depicting the creation of the arts over the row of entryway doors. The spotlit sign beside the entrance read PHILADELPHIA MUSEUM OF ART PERELMAN BUILDING, and people streamed out through the doors onto the sidewalk. Meg abruptly changed her trajectory and darted around a couple who stepped onto the sidewalk and then paused to look back toward the museum. The man's yell—"Hey! Slow down!"—followed her to the corner, where she stood panting, her dog at her side, staring out over a busy street.

The blast of a car horn drew her attention to the right to where a car was stopped in the middle of the lane. A dark figure streaked across the road, momentarily breaking the glare of headlights, to disappear into the encroaching gloom on the far side. In the dim light the figure—too big to be anything but a man—ran between the angled cars parked at the side of the road and into the grass and trees beyond.

A park. Which meant people out enjoying a lovely summer evening, every one of whom would be considered a threat by Giraldi.

"Hawk, ready." Meg gauged the traffic streaking by, balanced on the balls of her feet. *Wait . . . wait . . .* "Come!" She sprang off the curb as a sedan roared by and pounded across the road, her eyes on oncoming traffic on the other side of the road. But she'd timed it perfectly and they had a full two seconds after they stepped onto the sidewalk before the next car swept by.

After him.

In front of them lay a huge park complex. Well-lit by Victorian gaslight-styled streetlights, she could see a long, rambling building to her left and an extensive greenspace to her right. They tore off into the greenspace, zigzagging between trees, looking for any sign of quick movement. Pedestrians were out strolling in the park, so Meg watched intently for anyone moving too quickly. She swung to the right, but then corrected, realizing the movement she tracked was someone jogging with their dog.

Then she saw him, cutting across a road that wound through the park, heading to transect her own path. She didn't take the time to question his intent, but ran faster with an encouraging word to her dog. Giraldi disappeared for a moment in the trees and then reappeared, curving around a raised overlook and sprinting onto a long expanse of grass that gently rose toward the building.

They were only about eighty feet behind Giraldi, the time they'd lost having to circle the Perelman Building being made up in his lack of speed and change of direction. It looked to Meg like he was starting to tire and knew it, which probably explained his change in direction. Either he didn't know she was still behind him, or he had a specific plan in mind.

It felt good to take all that jittery energy and pour it into forward momentum. To be proactive. To *do* something. Her breathing was deep, her heart pounding, her fingertips tingling, but this was what they trained for. All those early morning jogs, *this* was why they did it. So when they had to act, they had the speed and stamina they needed.

They ran onto grass. Flanked by sidewalks, statuary, and tall light standards, the space was dotted with pedestrians, dog walkers, and a couple lounging in the grass. At the far end of the grass, a beige stone building reminiscent of a Greek temple, with tall Corinthian columns, glowed with inset lights.

Icy fingers of dread trailed up the back of Meg's overheated neck as she realized Giraldi's plan.

The main building of the Philadelphia Museum of Art. A huge tourist draw on its own, it boasted the long sweep of steps made famous in the movie *Rocky* when underdog Rocky Balboa used the steps as part of his training regimen, pausing at the top to look down over the expanse of the Philadelphia skyline, his fists raised in victory. Many came to tour the museum, but even more came simply to climb the steps like Rocky or to have their picture taken with the statue of the fictional boxer at the bottom of the staircase.

He's going to lose himself in a crowd. On a summer evening, the front of the building is likely teeming with tourists. And since Hawk doesn't have a recognizable scent to follow, he'll never be able to pick him out of the crowd.

She sent another voice text to Kate, updating her position as they pursued Giraldi.

Eighty feet now felt like eighty miles. Giraldi pounded up a flight of stone steps, sprinted across a road and then up another set of steps. Then he banked left, following the footpath that circled the building.

Meg weighed her options. She was gaining on him, but probably not fast enough to catch him in time. She glanced down at Hawk, running smoothly beside her, panting hard but not even close to blown. He could run faster than she could, even this far into the chase. She could order him to go after Giraldi when they got close enough. But as fast as that thought bloomed in her mind, the image of her Richmond PD German shepherd, Deuce, dying in her arms after being shot by a fleeing suspect, wiped it clean away. Deuce was a patrol dog, trained to apprehend and take down suspects; Hawk was search-and-rescue, a SAR K-9, and though he'd saved her life before when she was held at gunpoint, that kind of viciousness only rose to the surface when she was in danger. But it didn't matter, even if she could order him to do it, she wouldn't. Giraldi might hesitate to shoot her from a distance; he wouldn't hesitate to take out a snarling dog only feet away.

It was up to her. She was armed and a good shot, but she only wanted to stop him, not kill him, and no one could shoot accurately while sprinting full speed and breathing hard. Not to mention all the innocent people around to risk taking a shot.

But she needed to stop him. At this point he had to suspect she was law enforcement. If he went back to his capo and told him he was under surveillance, they'd go underground and Kate and the FBI would lose their entire case.

Around the side of the building, they followed a curving road lined with parked cars, and then sprinted over the top of an overlook into the gardens below, the gap closed now to sixty feet. Giraldi disappeared around the front of the building, Meg and Hawk following only a few seconds behind. But even those few seconds gave him an outsized advantage when he headed down the front steps just as she and Hawk cleared the corner of the building. Meg had a brief view of a laser-sharp gaze and a mask of fury as he looked back toward them before being swallowed by the crowd.

The wings of the museum shaped the forecourt as a giant letter *U*, the wide stone-tiled terrace alive with people coming from the museum or climbing the steps to the top. Kids ran around the fountain, or hopped over a series of short concrete domes, set in a line to keep vehicular traffic out of the forecourt. Couples strolled, hand in hand, and clumped family gatherings dotted the space.

Trying to keep her eye on the place where Giraldi disappeared, Meg ran full tilt toward the top of the stairs. As she reached the top, two teenage boys beside her threw their clenched fists into the air and jogged in a circle, pumping their fists while they hooted with victory. Meg had an impression of the skyline of Philadelphia spread out before her, its tall glass skyscrapers alight in the darkness, before she plunged into the crowd, scanning for a dark head or a flash of a dark jacket pushing through the crowd in front of her.

"Hawk, with me."

They wound through jostling bodies moving both up and down the stairs, and over short landings crowded

with picture takers or people who found the climb too tax-
ing and needed a breather. But no Giraldi.

Dread scraped at the edges of Meg's determination.
"Hawk, stop." She stood beside him on the edge of one of
the landings, staring down, and then turning to scan upward. *Did I miss him in the throng?* But there was no sign
of him. "Hawk, come." They ran down the remaining
steps, but the clenching in Meg's gut said they'd missed him.

Standing on ground level, Meg spun in a circle, looking
for any sign of frantic escape, but nothing stood out, just
the general frenetic movement of crowds melting into the
shadows of a warm summer evening.

He was gone.

Hawk whined softly.

Meg knelt down beside him, running her hands over
him and praising him for a job well done, before pulling a
jerky treat out of her pocket. Dogs took a loss at the end
of a search hard, so Meg was careful to keep her voice
light and positive even though inside she was kicking herself for having gotten *that* close, only to lose him in a
crowd of tourists.

She pulled out her phone to realize she'd missed three
texts from Brian and four from Kate. She scanned Kate's
texts—a running update of their location and finally a
message that Kate was on foot and incoming—and sent a
return message.

**Lost Giraldi on the steps in front of the Philadelphia
Museum of Art. I'll wait for you here.**

She scanned Brian's texts and then speed-dialed him.
"It's me. Did you lose yours?"

"Yeah."

"Did you get a look at him?"

"No. Bastard ducked into a restaurant and disappeared

into the back. I got jammed up by two waiters who wouldn't let Lacey into the place because the health department would shut them down. They didn't care that we're FBI. And then by the time we untangled ourselves from that mess and ran around the building, he was nowhere in sight. It was a brilliant way to lose both of us because I had Lacey with me."

"Did Doug get to you?"

"Not yet. Are you with Kate?"

"No, but I think she's close."

"From your tone of voice, I assume you lost yours?"

"Yes. But I got a look at mine at the same time he got a look at me. It was Giraldi."

Brian's low curse expressed exactly how Meg felt as well. "He didn't hurt you? Or Hawk?"

"No, he never got close enough. He stayed on the move and he clearly knows his city. Ever seen *Rocky*?"

"The movie?"

"Yes."

"Of course."

"Know the scene where he jogs up all those steps and dances around with his fists in the air in front of what looks like a Greek temple?"

"Sure."

"That's the Philadelphia Museum of Art. That's where I am right now, at the bottom of those steps. With the roughly two hundred tourists he disappeared into. Between the tourists and the lack of light, I lost sight of him and never found him again. And Hawk didn't have a known scent to follow through a crowd of that size, so Giraldi was impossible to track that way. He could have gone in just about any direction at the bottom of the steps, including back up them if he could do it with a group, so I have no idea where he is. And with no scent to trail, neither does Hawk. We're zero for two."

"Kate's not going to be happy about this."

Meg walked over to a dry fountain off to one side of the bottom of the steps and sagged down onto the short wall that circled it, her breath still sawing. "Yeah, I know." She stared glumly off at the brightly lit statue of a man on horseback on the other side of the street. "I kept in touch with her via text during the chase, and I know she and Doug were doing everything they could to get back in time, but we likely put them in an impossible position. It was a stupid and impulsive move on my part, thinking we could hold them until Kate and Doug got to us. I'm sorry for dragging you into this."

"Hey, none of that. I've got a brain and can think for myself. And I could have talked you out of it. But I thought we could do it too. If you're going down for this, I'm going down with you."

"Thanks." Feeling as lousy as she did over losing Giraldi, Brian's stubborn loyalty boosted her spirits.

"And, honestly, if the positions had been reversed, and it'd been Kate and Doug on their own spotting Giraldi, I bet they would have made the same attempt we just did. They're as involved in this case as we are, and it was a split-second decision."

"The worst part is that now the family knows someone is looking at them, they're only going to be more careful. And our cover is now well and truly blown. If they want K-9, it's going to have to be Lauren, Rocco, Scott, and Theo from now on."

"They're pros. They'll be able to step into this case. And we can advise from the sidelines. Bright side—Pierce wasn't anywhere near this drop, so if they think he's any kind of weak link, that may take the pressure off him. They might even start to think that Giraldi is the weak link."

"There is that. Where are you?"

"About a block from the truck. I'm going to meet Doug there."

"Kate's coming here." Meg stood. "I'll wait for her, then we'll walk back to you."

"See you in about fifteen."

She ended the call, and then waited with Hawk for Kate to arrive as the trail grew ever colder.

CHAPTER 20

Brillianteering: The process of cutting the final facets on the diamond including the upper, lower girdle, and star facets.

Monday, August 19, 2:11 AM
Jennings/Webb residence
Washington, DC

Meg woke to the sound of a low growl.
She sat bolt upright in bed. Enough moonlight shimmered between the parted bedroom curtains for her to find Hawk, lying in his dog bed, head up and alert.

Listening.

Out of habit she reached over to rouse Webb, but her hand fell on cold sheets. Her brain flashed a little more awake. *On shift at the firehouse.*

Hawk growled again and rose from his bed. Even in the dim light, Meg could see the fur running down his neck to his back was standing on end.

Then she heard it, a quiet scrape that could have been the sliding door that led out to the patio closing.

Someone's in the house.

"Hawk, stay. Quiet." She whispered the command as she reached for her phone. She was law enforcement, but she wasn't stupid. If a home invasion was taking place, she'd investigate, but there was a good chance she'd need backup. She didn't dare place a voice call; instead, she put her phone on silent and whipped off a quick text to 911.

HOME INVASION. FEDERAL OFFICER NEEDS ASSISTANCE.

She followed with her address. It was pushing the line a little by labeling herself as a federal officer when K-9 handlers weren't officially sworn officers, but she knew it would speed up the emergency response.

An image of Giraldi's furious expression filled her mind.

He'd not only escaped, but he'd gotten a look at her for a second time. While there might be a small chance it was a random home invasion two days after a Mob courier/enforcer slipped from her grasp, she highly doubted it.

She set her phone on the bedside table since her sleep shorts and tank didn't have pockets, and she wasn't about to take the time to change. She then slid out of bed because she and Hawk certainly weren't going to lie around like sitting ducks. It could be nothing, in which case she'd happily make embarrassed apologies to the Metropolitan Police officers when they arrived. If not, they needed to move. *Now.*

Her gaze shot to her dresser, where her SAR knife lay in its sheath next to her folded tactical knife, and then to the antique wardrobe beside it that held her gun safe. Either the Glock 19 or Glock 43 inside the safe would be the superior distant defensive weapon, but she'd need to turn on a light or use her phone flashlight to type in the code on her weapon safe. Then there was the bigger problem that after she properly entered her code, the locking unit would beep twice if it was correct. In the deadly stillness of the house, that would be an unacceptable giveaway of her awareness, position, and weapons capabilities.

Knives it was then.

The creak of a kitchen floorboard confirmed Meg's suspicion—someone was in the house. Webb wouldn't come home in the middle of a shift, but if he did, he'd use his key, not come in through the back. Cara and McCord had a spare key, so they'd let themselves in through the front door as well . . . not that anything short of a life-or-death emergency would bring them in the middle of the night. The backyard shared by the two sides of the duplex was completely enclosed with no gate, so the only way to gain access to the back of the house from outside was to scale the fence.

Anyone who would do that was clearly up to no good.

Meg crossed to her dresser and quickly strapped her SAR knife in its sheath onto the outside of her left forearm. She calculated the advantage of a silent approach with bare feet stacked against the disadvantage if anything broke during a fight that might cut her exposed feet or if she had to run any distance, and stepped into the running shoes neatly lined up beside the wardrobe and laced them on. Her fingertips quickly found a hair elastic on the dresser top and tied her hair back into a high ponytail to keep her vision clear at all times. Just before leaving her bedroom, she grabbed her tactical knife, her thumb settling over the release button, but keeping it closed for now.

"Hawk, come." Her words were just a whisper of sound, but it was more than loud enough for her dog's keen hearing.

They crept silently across the bedroom, Meg giving quiet thanks she'd recently trimmed Hawk's nails so instead of clicking over the hardwood—which would have sounded like gunshots in the silence—he quietly padded at her side. Meg paused in the doorway, trying to discern anything in the darkness, and straining to hear any sound from downstairs.

Sometimes owning a century-old house had its disadvantages—the way aged floorboards creaked in odd spots, for instance. But after a month living here, she and Webb knew every creaking floorboard in the house and unconsciously walked around them. Now that irritation was Meg's advantage. She could move silently through the house, whereas an intruder could not. *That squeaky third step on the way up, for instance.*

A sudden thought struck her, sending a chill down her spine.

What if he's wearing night vision goggles?

Of course he would be. She would. Entering a strange house in the dark? It would be likely any intruder would walk into a wall or a piece of furniture. She hadn't heard him bump into an end table, or her ugly-as-sin recliner, or a kitchen chair. Which gave him a significant advantage. She knew her own house, she was out of bed and stalking him, after all; but if he caught a glimpse of her, two knives were only going to go so far, especially if he was carrying a firearm. Of course the way to combat night vision was with bright lights—a flashlight or a lamp would blind him. She laid a hand on Hawk's back to attract his attention and gave him the hand signal to stay, and then doubled back to her bedside table. Reaching into the narrow gap between it and the wall, she pulled out the emergency, heavy-duty flashlight she kept there for power outages. Constructed of metal, it had a wide head with a long, narrow body, giving it the advantage of being not only a light source, but a makeshift club. And that dual usage was what she'd need to blind him and then attack while he was disoriented. It might only give her seconds, but that might be all the time she'd need to gain the upper hand.

Considering he'd likely have at least one firearm, her choices were to get close enough, the gun couldn't be used, or stay out of his line of sight. How she'd deal with him would very much depend on a combination of the intruder and the speed of arriving law enforcement, so she was going to have to do this on the fly.

Back in her bedroom doorway with Hawk, she paused.

Silence.

Time to move.

She gave Hawk the hand signal to come and crept down the hallway as quickly as she dared. She stayed close to the wall, where the floors were most secure and quiet. Past the guest bedroom on the right, and the bathroom beside it. Meg gauged its suitability, but quickly changed her mind when she evaluated the long, narrow room—too easy to be spotted and blocked from the single entryway, which would make them obvious targets. It would be a death sentence.

Her gaze shifted down the hallway to the room closest to the staircase, the narrow third bedroom that stretched across the rear of the house they'd furnished as shared office space. There was room for both Hawk and her to hide behind the door and it had the added aspect that if the intruder thought she'd still be in bed, one quick look would tell him that room had an entirely different purpose.

They tiptoed across the hall and slid behind the open door, squeezing in between the wall and a filing cabinet. Meg tucked Hawk into the corner so she'd be able to step into the doorway unimpeded, if needed. Beside her, Hawk pressed against her leg, his body tense. She laid a hand on his back and slid it up to identify his body positioning and bent down to his ear. "Talon, stay." She could barely hear her own words, but she knew her dog would pick them up. She needed him to stay out of sight to begin with, so he didn't get caught in the initial altercation, but, more importantly, so he could be a surprise weapon.

She switched hands, settling the heavy flashlight in her right hand as the initial weapon, and the tactical blade in her left. She pressed the button, the blade springing free with a nearly inaudible *click*. She waited, closing her eyes in the almost total blackness to concentrate everything on her hearing.

Seconds ticked by, each feeling like a minute. Meg was impressed by the intruder—except for the odd whisper of noise that could be attributed to the house settling, he was nearly silent.

What else would you expect from a Mob enforcer? This is what he does.

A loud creak followed by absolute silence heralded his arrival on the third step. She'd previously found that part of the staircase nothing but irritating, but Meg had a new appreciation for it in particular, and the house's quirks in general, now they allowed her to track the intruder in real time.

Then she heard it—a quiet footstep at the top of the stairs.

He was on the second floor.

It was easier to track him now as he circled the top of the stairway and continued down the hallway, only feet away, by the slight brush of carpet under his feet. She held her breath as she judged him to be standing in the office doorway, scanning the room. She searched for any sign of a light source, but found nothing besides inky blackness. *Definitely using night vision.* She grasped the flashlight more firmly, her thumb settling over the power switch. Her advantage was going to be in those few seconds of blinding light, and in all the training she'd done during her days in the Richmond PD.

He moved on from the office doorway just as she'd hoped as he searched for her bedroom. She let him get what she estimated to be another three or four feet down the hallway, and then slipped silently around the door, leaving Hawk behind. When she stepped out in the hall-way, she purposely scuffed her shoe along the carpet and then turned on the flashlight, aiming for where she anticipated his head would be.

As she expected, his head whipped around at the whisper of sound, and she caught him square in the eyes with the flashlight beam.

CHAPTER 21

Hearts and Arrows: Patterning achieved in a round diamond through a high degree of facet precision.

Monday, August 19, 2:15 AM
Jennings/Webb residence
Washington, DC

She had a split second to evaluate the situation: It was, indeed, Giraldi. He was all in black and wore double-lensed night vision goggles on a multistrap head mount. And he held a matte black handgun with a suppressor in his black-gloved right hand.

Giraldi roared with pain at the searing, blinding light, and ripped his night vision goggles off with his left hand, dropping them to the carpet as he pivoted toward the attack. A gunshot rang out, not the usual *boom* of a handgun in a confined space, but the *pop* of a silenced shot. The bullet punched a hole in the wall a foot from where Meg stood, but she didn't have time to give any thought to how lucky she'd been that a blinded Giraldi couldn't see well enough to aim to kill.

As Giraldi continued to swing toward her, the gun coming around to bring her into range, she pulled back and slammed the flashlight down with everything she had on the upper edge of his right wrist, just behind his thumb, targeting the radial nerve, knowing a direct hit would spasm his hand open. Giraldi grunted and the handgun spun out of his grasp, hitting the hardwood at the edge of the hallway runner and sliding fifteen feet away. The force of the strike reverberated up Meg's own arm, all the way to her shoulder, causing her to drop the flashlight. It hit the floor, rolling until it hit the baseboard, where it lay still, shining a beam of light along the floor and washing the hallway in a dim glow.

Giraldi easily had about seventy-five pounds on her, most of it muscle, so surprise was her only advantage now. Meg switched hands, seating the hilt of the tactical blade in her right hand and leaped. He threw up his left arm and her blade streaked down the outside edge, slicing through cloth and flesh. He blocked her with his right forearm, sending her stumbling backward.

Giraldi pulled his left sleeve away from his open wound and fixed his cold gaze on her. "Now you've made this difficult for yourself. If you'd just stayed put, this could have been quick and painless." His smile was ferocious. "Now I'll be happy to make it hurt."

"There was never going to be any other way. Quick and painless isn't in your repertoire." Meg kept her body loose and her weight on the balls of her feet, ready to react. There was no question he was going to come for her, and speed and agility might be her only options. She also knew there'd be no way the dropped gun was his only weapon. Another gun in an ankle holster, perhaps. Or a knife or two in his pockets.

"You'll never know now." He sprang for her with surprising speed, his eyes locked on her knife.

She tried to buy herself some time with a knee to his groin and had a brief flash of satisfaction at his furious curse. But as he tipped forward, he used his bulk to take her down with him to the floor, wrapping one meaty fist around her right wrist, cruelly grinding the bones together. Meg hit the hallway runner with enough force from his weight to knock the air from her lungs even as he drove her right hand into hardwood, knocking the knife from her grasp. It clattered across the floor, skittering over hardwood to shoot between the balusters and fall onto the staircase in a series of muffled thuds, ending in a faint drop to the floor below.

Gone, but at least she still had her SAR knife, though it was now trapped under his bulk, Giraldi's substantial weight pinning her down in a full-mount position. She struggled, trying to buck him off, and then attempted to knee him in the back, but he leaned too far toward her as he kept her right wrist pinned to the floor with his left hand.

Kneeling above her, his body centered over her hips, with her left arm pinned to her side, he grinned in enjoyment at her attempt to free herself and let her tire herself out. "Maybe I'm being too hasty. Maybe I should have some fun with you before I put you out of your misery."

She didn't give his threat of rape even a moment's thought, but estimated their relative positions and jerked her head up, squeezing her eyes shut and ramming the apex of her forehead as hard as she could into his nose. She heard the crunch of bone, felt the wet splatter of blood, and knew she'd hit home.

Giraldi roared with pain and reared away to avoid a subsequent blow, yanking his right arm back. She saw the blow coming, but with her arms pinned, there was no way to block it. He caught her just below her left eye in a battering blow with his elbow that slammed her head back against the floor. Her skull exploded in a flash of lights and agony. He drilled her a second time and she felt her cheek split open as she fought to not lose consciousness. It was when he pulled back for a third strike that Meg saw her moment.

"Talon, *fass!*"

Hawk wasn't an attack dog, but she'd trained Deuce as part of her position on the Richmond PD. Police dogs weren't trained to attack with English commands in case someone accidentally said a key word, so, often in America, they were trained in German. Most of the time Hawk was a good-natured, docile Labrador, but after their run-in with Daniel Mannew on the top of the Great North Mountain in West Virginia, when she'd seen Hawk in action untrained, she'd realized he could be used as a weapon in extreme situations. She'd trained him only in the basics, but she knew it would be enough.

Hawk burst from the office doorway, leaping on Giraldi's back, his teeth sinking into the back of Giraldi's upper-right arm, almost at the shoulder. Giraldi screamed in pain and thrashed, Meg completely forgotten as he tried to rid himself of seventy pounds of ferocious dog. He rose up on his knees, jerking his body from side to side, trying to dislodge Hawk.

It was enough room for Meg to scramble out from under him and to her knees. Her left arm now free, she grasped the hilt and smoothly pulled her SAR knife from its sheath. The blade was short; it was never meant as a weapon, merely as a tool. But Meg kept it razor sharp because a dull knife on a search was as good as no knife at all, so she knew it would suit her purposes now.

Giraldi slammed himself against the hallway wall and Hawk's continuing growl wavered with pain as he crashed into lath and plaster that cracked under pressure. But he didn't let go.

"You son of a bitch!" More furious about the treatment of her dog than about herself, Meg gripped the knife harder and struck out, aiming for Giraldi's midsection. "Talon, release! Come!" But as the knife made contact, she knew she'd misjudged in the dim light and her blade only skittered over his ribs instead of sliding deep. Damage for sure, but simply not enough.

Hawk let go of Giraldi, who, without his weight to counterbalance as they struggled, fell sideways while Hawk bolted past him to stand with Meg.

Time to get out of the limited space of the hallway and downstairs, where escape and, hopefully, arriving law enforcement awaited them. She pointed down the stairs. "Talon, go!"

Hawk took off at a run, Meg right on his heels. She grabbed the curving top of the banister, using it to slingshot herself around the corner and give herself extra speed as she took the first two steps against the wall, keeping out of Giraldi's reach from over the banister. She knocked a picture off its hook and it bounced down the steps, the glass shattering when it hit hardwood on the ground floor.

Faster!

Giraldi was right behind her on the stairs, his long arms working to his advantage as he caught her ponytail, jerking her back and nearly off her feet as searing pain burned through her scalp. She staggered up a step, bracing her back leg as he tried to haul her up toward him.

From below, all she could hear was Hawk's frantic barking.

She dropped the SAR knife she still clutched in her right hand and reached back with both hands, locking them around his wrist where he clutched her ponytail. Then she threw all her weight down on the step and yanked with all her might. His weight shifted as he overbalanced, tipping forward down the stairs, and she dragged at him one more time with all the strength she had left, the effort pulling a combination of a groan and a scream from deep inside. Then she let go and locked each hand around one of the molded hardwood balusters that marched up the outer edge of the staircase. She ducked low and, squeezing her eyes shut, held on.

Giraldi's bulk crushed her momentarily, and she had a brief impression of his hands scrabbling for purchase, but then he rolled off and crashed down the stairs in a repetitive *thump, thump, thump*.

Then . . . silence, broken only by the distant wail of sirens.

Meg opened her eyes and peered down the stairs, the streetlight coming through the front windows giving scant illumination. Giraldi lay at the bottom of the staircase, facedown and limbs sprawled awkwardly, surrounded by glass shards. Blood pooled around his left arm and darkened the left side of his body. His shirt was torn at the back of his right shoulder, and bloody pale skin peeked through the gap. Hawk had definitely done some damage when he latched on and held on for dear life. For her life.

Hawk stood about four feet away, his lips peeled back in a snarl, but Giraldi didn't cower or try to move away.

Meg grabbed her SAR knife off the step and used the banister to drag herself to her feet. She swayed for a moment, then stumbled down the stairs, one hand clutching the railing. She carefully approached Giraldi, her blade held at the ready in case he attacked. She nudged him with the toe of her running shoe, but he remained motionless.

Harder. Still, no response.

She was sure he wasn't faking it. Giraldi didn't seem like the type to play dead; if he'd been conscious, he'd still be trying to take her down. But had she killed him? She bent over and pressed two fingers against his throat and was rewarded with the answering thump of his heartbeat. Relief streaked through her. She didn't want her home to be the site of violent death, even if she was justified in defending herself and her dog.

"Hawk, guard."

Her shoes crunching over broken glass, she hurried into the living room, tapping one fist against the hall light switch on the way to fully illuminate both rooms. She ripped the plug for one of the matching pairs of table lamps from the wall, then used her bloody SAR knife to slice the cord from the lamp. Running back to Giraldi, who remained motionless, she knotted a length of cord around his right wrist, then dragged both arms behind his back and lashed them together. She pulled the knot tight enough that if he came to, he wouldn't be able to simply wriggle free.

Her knees suddenly weak, she knelt down in the living room doorway, well clear of the glass shards, but close enough to react if Giraldi moved. "Hawk, come here, boy." Still breathing hard, she had to pause to pull in air. "Let me check you out." He walked over and stood quietly under her hands as she examined him, probing for any points of pain, relieved when she found none. But she noticed he never took his eyes from the stranger on the floor. "Good boy. We're lucky he didn't hurt you. He would have if given the chance." She dropped her head against Hawk's, looped her arm around him, and just held on for a minute as her body finally reacted to the attack. She released a shaky breath. "Wasn't sure we were going to make it for a minute there. But you really came through for me when it made all the difference in the world. Love you, partner."

Hawk's response came through loud and clear as his tail wagged hard enough to shimmy his entire body. For good measure he followed up with a slurp up her right cheek that coaxed a smiling laugh from her that turned into a small groan. Her smile melting away, she lifted a hand to her left cheekbone and even that soft touch made the battered tissues sing with pain. When she pulled her fingers away, they were wet with blood.

"That bastard really clocked me. I'm going to look like I went a few rounds with Rocky in a few hours. Todd is *not* going to be impressed." Exhausted, she dropped her head back to rest against Hawk's.

The sirens grew louder and in less than a minute were accompanied by the squeal of brakes and car doors slamming. Meg looked up to find the living room awash with red and blue strobe lights.

The cavalry had arrived.

CHAPTER 22

Simulant: A material that has a similar appearance to a gemstone, but does not have the same mineral makeup or the physical and optical properties of the stone it imitates.

Monday, August 19, 2:29 AM
Jennings/Webb residence
Washington, DC

Cara, in a light robe over her pajamas, and McCord, in shorts and a faded *Washington Post* T-shirt, with his cell phone gripped in a white-knuckled fist, ran through the open front door, only to be stopped by two cops.

But Cara wouldn't be held back. "Meg? Meg!" She whipped back to the cop. "She's my sister. Where's my sister?"

Sitting on her living room couch with Hawk, Meg dropped a bag of frozen peas from her cheek and stood. She stepped farther into the living room so she could be seen. "Cara, in here."

"Oh my God!" The cop stepped back and Cara ran to Meg and wrapped her arms around her. "We woke to the lights and sirens. What happened?" She pulled far enough away to really look at Meg. "And what happened to your cheek?" She raised a hand to touch her sister's face, then dropped it. "You need to have that looked at."

"I will." Meg looked over Cara's shoulder to meet McCord's worried gaze. "It was a home invasion. This case just got a little too close to home. Literally."

McCord's gaze went sharp. "Who?"

"Giraldi."

McCord's gaze darted around the living room and then into the hallway. "Did he get away?"

"No, they just took him to the hospital."

He studied the eye that was starting to swell shut. "He did that?"

"He objected to my not just lying there and taking it when he tried to kill me." She pulled away from her sister to look down at the dog who stood at her side, leaning in so he didn't lose contact with her. Meg sank down on the sofa and wrapped an arm around Hawk. "I got in a few hits. So did Hawk."

Cara settled next to Meg on the sofa, stroking a hand down Hawk's back. "Of course he did."

Hawk's tail thumped in pleasure at both touch and praise.

McCord sat down on the ottoman facing Meg. "How did he find you? One thing's for sure, if he came after you, he had to connect you after that last chase."

Meg nodded grimly. "I don't know how he found me, but let me assure you, I'm going to find out." Raised voices drew her attention to the front door.

"I live here." There was no mistaking Webb's voice or the whiplike urgency in it. "Get out of my way."

"Hang on." Meg stood, sidled past Cara, and stepped toward the front foyer to find Webb framed in the door-way, dressed in his navy DCFEMS uniform, his body tense like a cat's, coiled, and ready to spring. "Todd, I'm here. Officers, please let him through."

Webb pushed past the officers to cross the foyer in long strides. Reaching Meg, he wrapped both arms around her, pulling her in so tight she nearly couldn't breathe as he bent his head down to hers. "My God, Cara called and told me the house was surrounded by police cars and I panicked." He released her to slide his hands over her shoulders to clasp her upper arms, shifting her back just far enough to look into her eyes before his gaze dropped to her left cheek. He skimmed his fingertips gently over blood-smeared, swollen flesh. "Someone hit you." There was no mistaking the barely leashed fury in his tone.

"Yeah, but I broke his nose and stabbed him in the ribs with my SAR knife. And then knocked him down the stairs, leaving him unconscious. All in all, I win. And Hawk tore up his arm and shoulder, so we both won." She gave him a lopsided smile that morphed into a wince as pain shot through her left cheek. She rested both palms on his chest, as much to comfort herself as him. "I'm okay, really. Though I admit to being a little shaken up." It suddenly occurred to her that he must have come in at top speed from Engine Company 2. "Wait. What are you doing here? You're not allowed to leave the house while you're on shift."

"They couldn't have stopped me from leaving, not that they tried. Smaill tried to come with me, but I made him stay at the house."

"Are you going to be disciplined for this?"

"No, Chief Koenig will understand a family emergency. But I would have come even if it meant disciplinary action. We were back from a two-alarm blaze, had cleaned up, and I was settling in to catch a few hours horizontal when Cara called. I just grabbed my keys and ran. What happened?"

"Home invasion."

"*What?*" His hands went tight on her arms and Meg winced. "Sorry. Sit down. I want to look at that cheek. It's starting to swell."

"Yeah, I have a feeling I'm going to be pretty colorful before the day is out."

McCord and Cara flanked her on the sofa and Webb took the ottoman while he examined her, gently palpating her cheekbone and around her eye socket.

Meg flinched and sucked air through gritted teeth. "Careful."

"Sorry. I want to make sure there's no orbital floor fracture, which is common from this kind of injury. Close your eye. You know concussion symptoms probably better than I do at this point. Do I need to worry about that too?"

"No. He hit like a freight train, but I didn't lose consciousness and I'm not having any vision problems. I have a headache, but that's not surprising because . . . freight train. But I promise to let you know if anything develops."

"It doesn't feel like you broke anything, but we'll keep an eye on it. If I have any suspicions, you're going to the ER for X-rays. Now, let me get my supplies. We need to close that wound." He started to rise from the ottoman.

Meg caught his hand, pulling him back down. "We will, but the cops are collecting evidence upstairs, so it will have to wait a little bit. Then we'll get that amazing glue you have to use on me on a regular basis."

"It does seem to be my calling lately."

She touched her fingers to the cut and pulled them away to check for blood. "At least the bleeding has stopped. I haven't looked in a mirror, though. Probably better that way."

"Probably." Webb picked up the bag of frozen peas and

laid it carefully against her cheek and over her left eye. "Icing it is a good idea while we wait. Do some more."

"I will." She took the bag from him. "Now stop fussing so I can tell you what happened." She took his hand in her free one, partly for comfort and connection, and partly to keep him from poking at her. She then took the whole group through the events of the night, from waking to Hawk sounding the alarm, to her attempt to stay one step ahead of Giraldi, to the struggle between her and Giraldi and Hawk, ending with Giraldi pitching down the stairs.

"Experienced fighter," McCord said. "Notice he didn't pound on you with his fists, which would have done as much damage to him as to you. Used his elbow. A little less force, but he would just expect to do more of it to the same end result."

"Less force means less chance of concussion." Webb kept his worried gaze locked on Meg. "You can't afford another one."

"Thank God for Hawk joining the fray when he had you trapped and was pounding on you." Cara stroked a hand over Hawk's head. "I hate to think what might have happened without him."

"I can tell you exactly what would have happened. Todd would have come home in a few hours to my dead body because Giraldi significantly outweighed me, and that straight up gave him the advantage." She looked sideways at McCord. "You need to be careful. They tracked me. If they can find an FBI handler, they can find a reporter."

"I'm okay. They don't know I'm involved."

Meg met Webb's eyes and her shoulders slumped. "I'm sorry. There's some damage upstairs. A bullet hole in the wall that may have gone right through to the office. And Giraldi cracked the wall lower down when he crashed into it, trying to dislodge Hawk after he clamped onto him."

Webb squeezed her fingers. "That's the least of our concerns. Remember Kirk, the firefighter we bought the house from? He reno'd this place to begin with. Guaranteed I can hire him to do some repairs to put it back to mint condition. Don't give it a second thought. The house can be fixed. You nearly couldn't be."

"I can't believe we didn't hear the fight going on," said McCord. "We share a common wall, and even if we were on the far side of the duplex, you'd think the odd thump would have come through to wake us up."

Cara threw him a dark look before giving Meg an apologetic shrug. "I wish we had. But between Clay's white noise machine and Cody's snoring, nothing was loud enough to wake either of us up. Even the dogs slept through it. It took lights and sirens to penetrate."

At that moment a Metropolitan PD officer stepped into the living room. "Ms. Jennings, your cell phone keeps ringing upstairs. A 'Craig Beaumont' keeps trying to reach you."

"Word has filtered through, I see." Meg tapped McCord's phone. "They're not going to let me touch mine for now while the crime techs look the house over. Do you have Craig's cell number?"

"Yeah." McCord brought up his contact list, scrolled down to Craig's name, selected it, and extended his phone to Meg.

"Thanks." She put the call through to Craig. It was immediately picked up. "It's Meg. McCord lent me his phone so I could call you. I can't get to mine currently."

"Are you okay?" Craig's words were staccato sharp.

"Yes. I'm sorry they got you out of bed."

"What the hell else would you expect them to do? One of my people was attacked. Do you need me to come over?"

"To my house full of Metro PD officers? No, thanks, we have enough cops already. I need to know how he found me, Craig. I need to know who else knows my address now." She met Webb's worried eyes. "It's not just me. Todd wasn't here tonight because he was on shift, but Giraldi would have cheerfully murdered us both. And Hawk. I need to know they'll be safe." When Webb shook his head and started to say something, she simply squeezed his hand. "It's not a matter of wanting, Craig. I need it."

"I do too."

"And Brian. We need to check on him too. If they found me, they could find him."

"I'm on it. Do I need to arrange for Giraldi to be brought here?"

"I told officers he was involved in our federal case, which is how it got back to you. But you may need to send Kate or Addison in to take him into custody."

"They're both already up and ready to move out."

"They took Giraldi to George Washington University Hospital with a knife wound, a hell of a bite wound from Hawk, and whatever other injuries occurred when he went down my stairs. They can pick him up there and bring him in. Craig?"

"Yeah?"

"I want to watch the interrogation. They're not going to let me in there, but he tried to kill me and my family. I want to hear what he says. It may not be much, because I know he's going to lawyer up, but I want in anyway."

"I have no problem with that. If he's at George Washington, he could be a few hours getting here. And I'd like to see him nice and tired when we talk to him. We might have a better chance of getting through his defenses that way. Can you come in at eight?"

"Yes. Will you be there?"

"Wouldn't miss it. See you then." Craig hung up.

Meg handed the phone to McCord. "Kate and Doug are going to go pick up Giraldi when they spring him from the ER. Then we'll convene at eight to interrogate him."

"You'll just observe?" McCord asked.

"Yes. I assume both Kate and Doug will do the questioning, but Craig's coming in too. Brian's about to get a wake-up call from Craig, so I think I'll call him and see if he wants to come in." She met Webb's eyes. "Giraldi's not getting out again. There are too many charges and he went after FBI personnel with an intent to kill."

"But who's coming for you after him?" Webb's eyes were hard and the furrow between his brows was deeper than ever. "Because in a group like that, there's always someone else."

"And if there is, I'll be ready." She held his gaze to make sure he understood her certainty. "They're not going to win. Giraldi coming after me was a mistake. It's the beginning of the end for them. They just don't know it yet."

CHAPTER 23

The Newspaper Test: Cubic zirconia is, essentially, a type of glass that doesn't have the refractive properties of a diamond. The same is true for all other imitation diamonds. If one can read the print—even if blurry—through a diamond lying flat on a newspaper in adequate light, then that diamond is a fake. A natural diamond has such high refractive properties that light is unable to travel through it on a sufficiently straight path to avoid extreme distortion.

Monday, August 19, 8:46 AM
J. Edgar Hoover Building
Washington, DC

Kate and Addison were late bringing Giraldi into the interview room. Brian and Meg waited patiently in the adjacent observation room, standing by the two-way mirror, looking into a starkly simple room centered around four chairs and a table with an embedded restraint bar. High up on the wall at two different angles, cameras were mounted to record the interview.

When the interview room door finally opened, Meg looked over her shoulder to the clock on the wall to mark the time. "That took longer than expected."

Brian pointed through the glass into the room. "That might be why."

Kate entered first and stood out of the way, holding the door open. Then Giraldi shuffled in, his hands cuffed behind his back. He moved stiffly, his upper body held motionless, his right shoulder and his left forearm distinctly bulky under a washed-out gray sweatshirt.

"I'd say his treatment at the hospital took a little longer than expected." Brian held up a hand and Meg automatically high-fived him. "Nice job. You really did a number on him."

"It was one hundred percent self-defense. And some of that probably happened when he went headfirst down the staircase," she said.

"Well, you helped him there too. And he deserves every single injury."

The door behind them opened and Craig entered the observation room. To Meg and Brian's surprise, he was followed by EAD Peters, who closed the door behind him, his gaze skimming over Hawk and Lacey napping against the far wall before moving on to the handlers.

"Sir, I didn't expect you here." Meg glanced from Peters to Craig. "Is there a problem?"

"No problem," Craig said.

"As long as you don't call one of my people being attacked a problem," Peters said. "In her own home. Personally, I'd call that a problem. But not with you." His eyes searched Meg's face, pausing for a long time on her cheek, his eyebrows snapped together in displeasure.

She hadn't looked good after the fight. And Webb's treatment, while necessary, certainly didn't improve her appearance in the short term.

Standing still under Peters's scrutiny, her mind flashed back to the early hours of the morning . . .

* * *

Once the police had cleared out earlier that morning, they went upstairs with Cara and McCord. They surveyed the damage in the hallway from both the fight and the subsequent investigation. Blood splattered the carpet around large missing chunks, removed by the crime techs—areas of greater staining taken as evidence. A section of wall approximately two feet off the floor, and easily as wide again, was crushed, the original plaster crumbling to the floor below, revealing broken strips of lath beneath. A single bullet hole pierced the wall at about the level of Meg's throat, and only a foot from where she'd been standing at the time of the shot.

McCord came to stand next to her as she studied the hole. "Nine millimeter?"

"That, or a .40 caliber would be my guess. Either way, if he'd come around just a little more before firing, either of those bullets going through my neck would have ended things quickly."

McCord squeezed her shoulder and moved away, heading to where Cara was studying the shattered wall.

Standing near the office door, staring at the floor by the damaged wall, Meg shivered, realizing how close she'd come to a brutal sexual assault followed by what would likely have been a slow, painful death. At the time, in the middle of the crisis, she hadn't had the time to feel fear. Now it closed in on her, clogging her lungs and jacking her heart rate.

Then Webb stepped in from behind, wrapping his arms around her, snugging her in against him, and her pulse rate slowed as the air in her lungs thinned.

"You beat him." Webb's voice was low in her ear, his words steady and sure, the logical first responder calm in the face of a crisis. "He may have gotten a few points in, but you won. Remember that. Don't let him ruin our home for you. He doesn't have that kind of power. We'll clean this up, repair the wall, replace the carpet, and it will be like he was never here."

She'd taken a deep breath, and nodded. And, squaring her shoulders, stood a little taller.

While Cara sat beside her on their bed, the covers still thrown back from when she'd left it following Hawk's alarm, Webb sat facing her in the office chair McCord had rolled in as he cleaned and sealed her wound, and then carefully covered it with a row of short Steri-Strips. Only then, after promising to come back tomorrow to help clean up the plaster and to take up the carpet, had Cara and McCord gone home to their dogs and their bed, allowing Meg and Webb to do the same.

When she tried to get Webb to go back to the firehouse to finish his shift, he flat out refused and wouldn't even hear any argument to the contrary. He wasn't leaving her, not with the attack so fresh in her mind. And in his own. He was covering well, but Giraldi's attack had affected him as deeply as it had her. He took crises in stride like the first responder he was, but she knew him well enough to sense his fear for her and the anger he tamped down, could feel it in the tenseness of his muscles and in all the things he didn't say. She knew he'd resolved at the beginning of their relationship that it wasn't his place to put restrictions on her career, but that in itself created its own stress for him. Exhausted, they went to bed without talking anything out, but, comforting them both, he'd spooned around her, holding her until she'd finally drifted off.

By seven o'clock, when she pulled her exhausted body from bed, Meg was stiff and her face was even more swollen and colorful, leaving her feeling a bit like Frankenstein's monster. What she lacked in ugly stitches, she made up for with a black-purple eye, now entirely swollen shut. Not sure how well she could drive, she called Brian to request he and Lacey pick up her and Hawk on his way to the Hoover Building.

"You had that properly treated?"

Peters's question brought Meg back to the present. "Yes, sir. My partner, Todd . . . you met him during the Garber case. If you remember, he's a firefighter/paramedic."

"Handy man to have around," Brian quipped. "He's always patching you up."

Meg tossed as much of a slit-eyed glare at Brian as she could with one eye swollen shut, and turned back to Peters. "He made sure there were no broken bones, then closed and bandaged the wound." She couldn't help raising a hand to her cheek, feeling under her fingertips the row of neat parallel strips Webb had carefully secured.

Brian caught her hand, pulling it from her face with a slight shake of his head. He gave her fingers a reassuring squeeze before he released them.

"Anyway," she continued, "he's satisfied I'm okay to work. No concussion, no broken bones, just a small gash, and a hell of a shiner. And given a week or two, even that will be gone." She turned to the glass to find Giraldi seated at the table with his left hand now free and one end of his handcuff attached to the table's restraint bar, while another man took the place beside him. The newcomer was short and round in stature, with only a thin halo of hair remaining on his otherwise-bald head. The fancy Italian suit and the custom leather briefcase pinpointed his vocation. "I assume that's Giraldi's lawyer?"

"That would be my guess," said Craig as Kate and Addison took the chairs on the opposite side of the table. "Looks like they're finally getting started."

Kate laid down a folder and clasped her hands over the top of it, looking entirely at ease. "Please note, gentlemen, that this interview is being recorded. Present are Special Agents Kate Moore and Doug Addison. Please state your names for the record."

"Giovi Vitale, counselor for Mr. Giraldi."

"Luigi Giraldi."

"Thank you, gentlemen. Mr. Giraldi, I'd like to read you your rights again, since that was previously done by the Metropolitan PD, but you are now officially in federal jurisdiction. You have the right to remain silent." Kate recited the rest of the Miranda warning. "Do you understand each of these rights, as I have explained them to you?"

"He understands," said Vitale.

"I'd like to hear that from Mr. Giraldi."

"I understand." Giraldi's words were clipped and angry.

"Excellent. Mr. Giraldi, can you explain why you entered the house owned by Megan Jennings earlier this morning?"

Giraldi just looked at her.

"Mr. Giraldi?"

"My client didn't realize whose house it was," said Vitale.

"That doesn't explain why he entered the house."

"He thought it was the house of a colleague."

Addison fixed him with a flat stare that clearly communicated they weren't the idiots Vitale seemed to be taking them for. "He hopped the fence and jimmied the lock on the back door of this 'colleague's' house?" He put air quotes around the word.

"Absolutely not. He went in the front door. It was un-locked."

"With night vision goggles and a Heckler and Koch P30L? His colleague must love him. And we have a wit-ness who says he came in the back."

"This witness was sitting up at two AM to see it hap-pen?" The derision in Vitale's tone was crystal clear.

"No, she was upstairs in bed, but she heard it."

"You have fingerprints to prove he came in that way?"

"Unless your client is stupid"—Addison shot a quick look at Giraldi, who sat at ease in his chair, keeping his mouth shut and letting his lawyer talk for him—"he's al-ready told you he was wearing black nitrile gloves, so you know there aren't fingerprints. But we have a reliable wit-ness. We also have DoorCam footage from the house across the street that shows no one going into the house via the front door after Ms. Jennings and her dog came home after their evening walk."

It was subtle, but Giraldi reacted to the word "dog," his eyes narrowing and his hands clenching into fists.

Meg was about to call it out, but Kate beat her to it, leaning forward to study Giraldi more closely. "What's wrong, Mr. Giraldi? Don't like dogs?"

"Dog attacked me. Vicious. I want it put down."

"You can want that all you like. That's a trained law en-forcement K-9 who was protecting his owner."

"That dog is a fucking weapon."

Kate simply raised her eyebrows politely at his bad lan-guage. "We seem to have struck a nerve. Mr. Giraldi, if you hadn't been in Ms. Jennings's house with your night vision goggles and your P30L, there would have been no need for the dog to protect his owner."

Vitale held up a hand, like he was calming rough waters. "Agent Moore, I think you'll see my client is justifiably angry. He was in the wrong place at the wrong time and was attacked. In fact, by the law of the District of Columbia, Ms. Jennings can be brought up on assault charges for attacking my client."

"Bullshit!" Inside the observation room the word shot out of Meg's mouth before she could stop it. She glanced over at Peters, frowning at the anger carving grooves around his eyes and mouth. "Sorry, sir."

"I've heard the term before, Jennings. I've even used it a time or two myself. And this is a good time because it is bullshit."

Peters returned his attention to the interview and some of the tension between Meg's shoulder blades relaxed fractionally.

Kate sat back in her chair, looking utterly relaxed and unimpressed. "Now you're just playing with us, Counselor. You know very well that while DC doesn't have a 'stand your ground' law or a Castle Doctrine, all Ms. Jennings needs to prove is she had reasonable grounds to believe she was in imminent danger of bodily harm. Mr. Giraldi snuck into her house in the middle of the night with a firearm and night vision goggles and shot a hole in her wall at the first sight of her down the hallway. So let's dispense with all this 'wrong place, wrong time' garbage. Mr. Giraldi, you illegally entered Ms. Jennings's house with the intent to kill, or, at the very least, harm her. And most likely her dog. Which is why you've been charged with first-degree burglary and two charges of second-level assault of a police officer—"

"Wait." Vitale's clenched fist hit the table. "Two charges?"

"He assaulted two officers, one human, one canine. The assistant US attorney in charge of Mr. Giraldi's case was definitive on that point. And on the charge itself. Second-level assault of a police officer, a felony crime."

Meg hadn't been sure if they'd press a charge of aggravated assault or assaulting a police officer, which could include civilian consultants associated with law enforcement. Satisfaction warmed her as the charges piled up, especially that he would be found accountable for attacking her dog.

"That woman had a knife," Vitale countered. "It's not assault when you're defending yourself. And my client didn't know she was law enforcement, so assaulting a police officer won't stick."

"It will. But we'll come back to that. Next we have the weapons charges," Kate continued. "Possession of an unregistered firearm, unlawful possession of ammunition, and assault with a deadly weapon, all felony charges." Kate gave Vitale a sweet smile. "Your client is going to go away for a long time. And that's just to start. You know, it's interesting."

Vitale leaned on one chair arm, his face an expression of utter boredom, as if he had no concerns that any of the charges would actually stick. "What's interesting?"

"We know your client is a soldier in the Philadelphia crime family. He has a couple of roles, but one of them is as an enforcer." She turned to look at Addison. "Now, why would an enforcer make a hit on a woman all alone in her house except for her dog? That's not the Mob way."

"Sure isn't," Addison agreed. "Easier to do something remote like a car bomb. Or, since she was at home on her own, why not just toss a Molotov cocktail through the window and let her and her dog burn to death, trapped inside? Why risk failure by going into her house? Why such a personal hit?"

"Ah, I think you have it there." Kate met Giraldi's eyes. "It's personal. You could have taken her out in any number of ways, but you didn't want to attract that much attention. She was on your tail, not once, but twice, and you knew it. And because of those two occurrences, you knew she was law enforcement in some way. You also knew you'd be pulled out of your current role if you made a fuss about her because the powers that be would consider you a liability in that role. Instead, you took it into your own hands and opted to just make her disappear." Kate waved her spread hands wide, like a magician. "The plan wasn't to kill her in her bed. The plan was to knock her out and carry her out of the house. The dog can't talk, so you were happy to leave him behind. But Ms. Jennings needed to disappear."

"It's really too bad for you Ms. Jennings had the guts to go toe-to-toe with you," Addison said. "That really ruined your plans."

Behind the glass Brian shoulder-bumped Meg and tossed her a grin.

"Though, truthfully, you didn't think the whole thing through well enough," Addison continued. "You know what really scaled the deal? The dog."

"Yes." Kate's tone was pure satisfaction. "That was a mistake. Not only did Hawk hear you come in, but he woke Meg. And then, I hear, he was paramount to bringing you down. How's the shoulder?"

Giraldi's face looked like it could have been etched in stone. "Fine."

"I'm so glad to hear that." Kate's tone was flat, conveying a true lack of interest in his injuries. "Now, I can see how you might have written the dog off. He's just a goofy Labrador. He'd just cower in a corner when faced with you." The corner of her lips tipped up. "Surprise. Not so much. You know, in my experience dogs will move heaven and earth to protect their owners."

"From what I understand," countered Vitale, "she used the dog as a weapon."

"As I understand it, your client was assaulting her at the time. She didn't call her dog until she was pinned and beaten by someone at least fifty or seventy pounds heavier, and specifically after he threatened rape." She turned to Addison. "Guess we need to add a misdemeanor charge of threats to do bodily injury." She swung back to Vitale. "As I was saying, she acted entirely in self-defense."

Giraldi's hold on his tongue snapped. "You have no proof."

"I have the word of an FBI K-9 handler. That's good enough for me." She opened her file folder and pulled out a color photo of Meg, taken a half hour previously and held it so both men could see. "This is what you were doing to her, a woman who was only two-thirds your body weight."

From where she stood, Meg could see the picture, which showed her injury in living color. Giraldi didn't even blink, but Vitale winced.

"Personally, as a woman, if I had a dog and was in danger of being overpowered, raped, and murdered, I'd call him to help too. It went wrong for you in every way possible. You expected Ms. Jennings to be docile, and she not only wasn't, she met you head-on, and that's when it all went to hell. Now let's talk other charges."

"You've covered everything having to do with my client entering Ms. Jennings's home," Vitale protested. "What else could you possibly have?"

"Oh, you'd be surprised. Agent Addison?"

Addison studied the two men for a moment and, even

through the glass, Meg could sense the building tension. *They have to know he can connect them to Mob activity, they probably just don't know what Mob activity.*

"We have the reason Ms. Jennings has been following your client," stated Addison. "That's the reason you're not sitting down at Metro PD, talking to a couple guys there. You're here at the FBI because we were already watching you, Mr. Giraldi. We know you're involved in the transfer and sale of illegal luxury goods—most recently in rough diamonds. We know you were involved specifically in the delivery of illegally smuggled conflict diamonds on the third of August in Franklin Square. A witness to the event has positively identified you by your mug shot, Mr. Giraldi. He confirmed you were one of two men making the delivery that day. He couldn't help us with the other gentleman, but he was quite definite you had delivered the illegal stones to him. Therefore, you're also being charged with smuggling goods into the United States, the prohibited importation of rough diamonds outside of the Kimberley Process Certification Scheme, and the misrepresentation of the certification of those diamonds."

For the first time Giraldi started to show signs of alarm, but Vitale calmly laid his hand on his arm. "I believe I'd like to have a word with my client, Agents."

"Of course." Kate picked up her folder and pushed away from the table. "The agent outside will take you to a room where you can have some privacy."

"Both hands on the table." Addison circled the table and unlocked the cuff from the restraint bar and then cuffed Giraldi's two wrists together.

Kate opened the door and called in the young agent standing outside, who took charge of Giraldi and led him outside into the hallway, trailed by Vitale.

Kate and Addison left the interview room, and, seconds

later, the door to observation opened. Kate entered first and then stopped short at the sight of Peters. "Sir. I didn't realize you were coming down for this interview."

"He tried to take apart one of my people." Peters glanced back into the now-empty room. "Of course I'd want to see it."

"I think you backed Giraldi nicely into a corner," Craig said. "He may want to make a deal, but I'm sure that's a family lawyer. He's not going to want to damage the family's . . . business ventures."

"No, probably not," said Addison, walking over to the laptop in the corner and ending the recording. "The family will pay for his lawyer, but they'll expect him to go down quietly. And to not take the whole group down with him."

"That will partly depend on Giraldi," said Peters. "But if he's interested in saving his own skin, especially because he knows the kinds of jobs they've sent him out to do, he'll go down with his life."

"As opposed to fighting and getting a lighter sentence and then someone taking him out in jail," suggested Craig.

"Exactly. He'll have seen family members who didn't toe the line serve as a warning to others. He may even have been the enforcer who carried out one of those warnings."

"He'll also know the lawyer is really there for the family's benefit rather than his own," said Meg. "The family pays Vitale's way, and is his *real* client. He'll smooth the way for Giraldi as much as he can, but, in the end, from what I understand about how this all works, he's as much there to ensure his client's silence as to actually represent him and make sure we give him a fair shake."

"That's my read on it." Peters turned to Kate and Addison, pinned them both with a level stare. "You're going to have another go at Giraldi after he and Vitale have their little talk, but I'd like you to press him on how he tracked down one of my people in their own home. Is it because Jennings has been in the papers occasionally because of her cases? Or is it because we have a larger problem here at the FBI? You know how the Mob likes to get cozy with law enforcement."

It was the possibility Meg hadn't actually spoken out loud, but it had been a festering suspicion for hours.

"I'll do my best to nail that down, but that thought also crossed my mind." Kate absently slapped the folder against her open palm. "They're breaking all sorts of local, state, and federal laws. It would be to their advantage to have someone inside the Philadelphia field office to muddy the waters for them occasionally."

"How much contact have you had with the field office agents?" Craig asked.

"Some," Addison admitted. "As you might imagine, we have a couple of guys who've worked with the Organized Crime Program overall, and the Diamond Trafficking Program, specifically. You're thinking it's someone there."

Peters paced away a few steps, turned, and paced back. "I'm mostly thinking out loud. We have information that shouldn't be out there. Was Ms. Jennings followed home one night and then Giraldi waited until the right moment to attack when she was alone? Did they track her by identifying and trailing her live-in partner? Did they track her through the Bureau? If there's a hole, we need to find it and plug it. Though if someone from the Philadelphia field office is involved, Pierce would have been taken out already, so that doesn't feel right either." He turned to Meg. "Any chance one of your ex-colleagues at Richmond PD could be involved?"

Meg shook her head. "No. I don't stay in touch there as much as I should, and as far as I know, no one there knows we've just moved." She paused for a moment, looking back into the interview room, back to Giraldi's now-empty chair. "Honestly, I don't think he knew he was dealing with an ex-cop. An ex-cop who'd trained a patrol dog. I think he believed he was going after an average animal handler"—she threw an apologetic look at Brian, who just shrugged in agreement—"and her search-and-rescue dog. SAR dogs are known to have a significant drive to find their target, but they're not known for bringing that target to the ground. They find, they comfort, they assist. But I'd trained Hawk in the basics of protection. He's not, by nature, an aggressive dog—"

"Unless you're in jeopardy," Brian interrupted.

"Unless I'm in jeopardy," Meg echoed. "Then look out, as Giraldi discovered. But his unpreparedness—entering a house with a dog and not considering it to be any kind of early-warning system or threat to his own safety—tells me he doesn't know I'm ex-PD. So then we're back to the question of how did he find out where I live?"

"Giraldi might be willing to trade that information," Addison said.

"He might. Again, that would be to the detriment of the family. Assuming they have someone inside law enforcement—and if they do, federal law enforcement would give them the best protection considering the crimes in question— they're going to want to keep that person unknown."

"We'd have to interview Giraldi without his lawyer present. With his consent," Kate clarified.

"That would be the only way."

"Giraldi's going to know that, though, won't he?" Brian asked. "He's been around the block a few times and knows with the lineup of charges you're levying against him, he's going to potentially go away for a decade or two. If he knows the family isn't going to help him, will he try to help himself?"

"He'll be weighing his options," Peters stated. "A long life behind bars, or a shorter sentence he never lives out because of a shiv to the gut. He's going to be practical. This is the life he chose, and was paid handsomely for it. This is the result. He's made his bed; now he'll have to decide if he's going to lie in it. Push for his cooperation." His gaze traveled the room, catching the eye of each one of them. "We may have stumbled onto something bigger than just this one investigation. If so, we need to put a stop to it. Now."

CHAPTER 24

Provenance: A record of ownership used as a guide to authenticity or quality.

Her hammering heart in her throat, Meg stepped out onto the wooden plank stretching between the twin ropes of the suspension bridge. Earsplitting cracks like gunfire reverberated into open space as the wood splintered under her weight. She clutched at the frayed guide ropes as if her life depended on it.

Because it did.

Fog blanketed her surroundings, giving her only about six feet ahead to see, but the echo bouncing back to her sketched the contours of the space below.

Wide. Deep. Empty.

Deadly.

But fear drove her forward. *Where's Hawk?*

Another step on widely spaced boards, with nothing but snaking fingers of fog filling the spaces between as the bridge oscillated up and down and the wind whistled around her. Meg couldn't be sure if whoever built the bridge ran out of materials and chose to place the boards a foot apart, or if the intervening boards had crumbled and disappeared into the void below.

As she would if one of the boards didn't hold.

"Hawk! Hawk, where are you?"

Is that his answering bark in the distance?

The wisps shifted around her, swirls of dark and light, and then some of the fog below dissipated just long enough for her to glimpse what lay beneath her feet: a winding silver thread of water hundreds of feet below. Jagged rocks. Seabirds in flight. Then the fog closed over again, blanketing her in a misty embrace.

All she could do was close her eyes and hang on as her heart hammered, her breath stuttered and jerked, and a high-pitched whine filled her ears.

Hang on. You can do this. You have to find Hawk. If he's ahead of you on the bridge, he could die without you to guide him.

Her eyes snapped open and she set her jaw, grasped the guide ropes more firmly and took another step forward. But the wood crumbled beneath her hiking boot and she pitched forward with a scream. As she went down, she scraped her left cheek on the ragged guide rope, shaving off layers of skin as her head jerked sideways. That slowed her descent minimally; then she landed hard across several planks, her head and left shoulder dangling over the side of the bridge, her arm swinging wide to grab at nothing more than clouds. Simultaneously she locked her right hand in a white-knuckled grip on a plank and lunged back with her left, missing the first time and then latching onto the support rope. But that tipped her weight onto her hips, and with a shriek of tearing wood, the board supporting them cracked in half, the wood falling away to spin into the fog below. Only her right boot hooked onto the plank that had previously supported her, and another under her chest kept her from a deadly drop in the abyss.

She lay still for a moment, panting and shaking, as the wind blew her loose hair into a cloud around her face. She dragged her upper body onto the bridge and took a moment to try to catch her breath, her lungs pumping like bellows as she pressed one cheek against rough wood.

Get up unless you want to die here.

But getting up was easier said than done with no support for her knees. She raised her head, evaluating the planks marching away from her and, stretching forward, grabbed a plank with both hands, tested its stability, and then slowly pulled herself forward. When that plank got too close for good leverage, she reached for the next.

At that moment the fog thinned enough for her to see about twenty feet down the bridge and her heart nearly stopped. The air she dragged in on a gasp of shock was icy cold and thin enough to prickle like needles.

Hawk stood on the bridge, his feet braced over two planks, swaying as the bridge bobbed in the wind. He turned back to look at her, his brown eyes, always so steady and loving, now wide with fear. He whined, and tried to turn farther.

"No! Talon, stay!"

She had to get to her dog. Then go forward, or back? In the fog she didn't know which path to the end of the bridge was shorter. Or safer.

One step at a time. She had to get to him first. Now that she had a solid surface under her knees, she could get back on her feet. Grabbing the support ropes on either side of her, Meg shifted back slowly, testing the plank's ability to take her full weight. So far, so good. Up on her knees, change her grip on the guide ropes, one foot on the plank. And up to her feet.

One plank forward. Another. *Getting there*—
The bridge abruptly shifted beneath her, either from Hawk changing his balance or Meg changing hers, rolling to the right, tipping her even farther in that direction. She lurched to the left, trying to balance the load. For a heart-stopping few seconds, the bridge teetered back and forth as Hawk desperately tried to keep his balance.

"Talon, stay! Hold on!"

The undulations slowly stopped until they were left where they'd started in the soft oscillations from the wind. Meg slowly straightened, and, eyes firmly fixed on the next board, stretched out a booted foot to test even a little of her weight on it.

"Meg?"

Meg's body froze at the sound of her sister's voice, only her head whipping from side to side to look all around her, but the only thing visible in the pocket of fog was Hawk.

Is Cara out on this bridge too?

"Meg?" Louder this time.

Who to save first? The dog she could see, or the beloved sister who was lost in the fog?

"Meg, you need to wake up." Webb's voice this time.

Reality finally penetrated her sleep-fogged brain.

Meg lurched upright on full alert as the light on Todd's side of the bed snapped on and she found herself no longer suspended over a deadly drop, but at home, in her own bed, her left cheek aching with pain.

Another attack?

Her heart rate kicked into overdrive, but then she realized Hawk still lay in his dog bed beside her, not on alert from an unknown intruder, but with his head up and eyes attentively fixed on the bedroom doorway. Because someone he knew stood there.

Cara?

Cara stood in the gap in sleep shorts and a T-shirt. Her

arms were wrapped around herself as if she was freezing on this warm August night.

Meg's gaze flicked to her bedside clock: 3:38 AM.

Her gut clenched. The only reason for Cara to be standing in her bedroom in the middle of the night was an emergency. Something so bad, she hadn't picked up the phone, but come herself.

Had the Mob gone after Cara and McCord when they didn't succeed with her?

She flung back the thin sheet and rolled out of bed. On the other side of the bed, Webb got up, clad only in a pair of boxers, and stepped into the walk-in closet on his side of the bed, partially closing the door.

"What happened?" Meg scanned her sister from head to toe, but she appeared unharmed. Meg circled the bed to take her sister's hands and drew her down to sit on the padded cedar chest at the end of their bed. "Where's McCord?"

Cara's face was bleached even in the low light of the single bedside lamp. "That's the problem."

"What do you mean?"

"Clay's missing."

Webb reappeared in dark-wash blue jeans, a black T-shirt, and bare feet. "What do you mean 'missing'? He didn't come home last night?"

"No. Sometimes he doesn't if he's following a story out of town. I get that, even if it's last minute. But that's not what this is."

"How do you know?"

"Clay and I have a system. Some of the stuff he does when he's involved in an investigation is dangerous. So we have a deal—when he's out in the field, he texts me every twelve hours, if not before. A response to a previous text, a smiley face, a 'knock-knock' joke. *Something.*"

"He's dropped out of contact?" Meg prompted.

"Yes. And that's not like him."

Meg glanced up at Webb to find his gaze already locked on her. She knew he was thinking the same thing she was—during the course of his investigation, McCord had run into someone from the family and something had gone badly wrong. It would be bad if they figured out he was a reporter. It would be worse if they'd in any way connected McCord to Meg or to the FBI.

"When should you have heard something from him?"

"By no later than one thirty. But I didn't want to over-react, so I waited. And paced. And freaked out the dogs. And, finally, I couldn't wait anymore."

Meg squeezed her hands. "You did the right thing coming here. The first thing we need to do is make sure it isn't something innocuous, like he's stranded somewhere without a cell signal. It happens."

Cara shook her head, her lips pressed into a tight white line.

"It could," Meg insisted. "Or he could have gotten in an accident and hasn't been able to reach out yet."

"No." Cara's voice was firm. "I know Clay. He's dependable and he'd never purposely worry me, especially on this story and after your attack. He knows the deal. So he either isn't allowed to contact me or . . ." She hesitated, then gathered herself and forced the words from her mouth. "Or he can't."

There it was, the thing they were all skating around. Considering the case he was investigating, a car accident wasn't the most obvious possibility. McCord unconscious, or hurt, or even dead, was.

I'll be careful. I know what I'm getting into. No story is worth dying for. I promise.

McCord's words to Cara echoed in Meg's head. He knew what he'd promised. If he was out of touch, it was only because something had gone very wrong.

Meg surged to her feet. "I'm calling Craig."

"What's he going to do?"

"Mobilize the team. McCord is essentially working on our case. More than that, he's one of us now. And he's missing. You mess with one of us, you get all of us." She turned to Webb. "Take Cara downstairs and put on a pot of coffee. I'll be down in a minute."

She saw understanding in his brown eyes—she needed space, to be brutally honest with Craig, and didn't want Cara to be within earshot.

"Can do." Webb held out a hand for Cara, and when she reflexively put hers in his, he drew her to her feet. Still holding her hand, he led her out into the hallway and down the stairs.

Meg lunged for her cell phone, speed-dialing Craig.

It rang a full four times before the line was picked up. There was an elongated pause before Craig's sleepy voice came down the line. "Beaumont."

"Craig, it's Meg. I'm so sorry to call in the middle of the night."

"What's wrong?" His voice was already sharper, years of experience having taught him how to react to a crisis with split-second reflexes. "Are you okay? Is it another attack?"

"No, I'm fine. But I don't think McCord is. He's missing. He and Cara have a system of contact, so no matter what he's doing, without fail, he won't go more than twelve hours without touching base in some way so she knows he's okay."

"It's been more than twelve?"

"Fourteen. Craig, he's working this case. If he's stumbled onto something the family is doing and they've figured it out . . . Or if they've connected him to me through Cara or simply by his home address . . ."

"Then it's all gone to hell. Who do you need?"

"Everyone. We need to determine where he was, and then we need to follow his trail. If we can give them a starting point, the dogs can find him. And we take down whoever has him."

"Meg, you know there's a chance—"

"Don't go there. I can't go there without it messing with my head. This is a rescue, not a recovery."

"A rescue it is then. You call Brian and Kate. I'll take Addison, Lauren, and Scott. And I'll keep Peters in the loop. Get everyone to the Hoover Building. We'll figure out what's going on and be on the road to Philly by daybreak."

"Thanks, Craig."

"No thanks required. It's McCord. Now go." He hung up.

Meg took a breath and tried to gather her ragged sense of hope and hold it close.

Then she dialed Brian.

CHAPTER 25

X-Ray Fluorescence: A diamond's ability to emit secondary X-rays when it is exposed to an X-ray. This characteristic is used to identify a diamond or other stone by indicating its chemical elements.

Friday, August 23, 4:50 AM
Fourth-floor conference room, J. Edgar Hoover Building
Washington, DC

Brian came in with Lacey on his heels and scanned the table. "Sorry, am I late?"

Meg looked up from the coffee she clasped in both hands. "Not at all. Kate's not here yet and Craig's still downstairs waiting for Martin Sykes."

Brian pulled out the chair next to Meg and sat down. "Sykes? Isn't that McCord's editor? You called McCord's boss in the middle of the night?"

"Who else would know better what McCord's been up to than his boss? It occurred to me after I talked to you that we should bring him in. Craig agreed, so I got his number from Cara and got him out of bed. He was grumpy I got him up, but once he found out what was going on, he didn't quibble about coming down to help."

"Why would he? It's McCord."

It's McCord. That had been the thread running through every conversation since she started making phone calls. Sleepy pickups, followed by an unquestioning willingness to assist. The entire team had turned out, and not a single one of them had considered any other option. What a change from their first case with McCord, when he was simply a generic investigative reporter regarded with suspicion by all of them. He'd won them over, one by one, time after time, his research and investigative abilities advancing cases, saving lives, and helping apprehend guilty suspects. He was a crucial part of their team, even though he didn't work for the FBI.

He was one of them. And when one of them went missing, it was all hands on deck.

Meg looked around the table. Lauren Wycliffe, in yoga pants and a light hoodie, with her normally perfectly styled blond hair simply pulled back into a no-nonsense ponytail, sat at the head of the table. Rocco, Lauren's border collie, sat patiently beside her, with just the black-and-white crown of his head visible. Next to her, Scott Park, tall, blond, and rangy, slouched in his chair, his eyes at half-mast as his chin seemed to sink into the collar of his Henley. Theo, Scott's bloodhound, was out of sight, but Meg knew Theo—why sit when you could lie down? Hands down, Theo was the best tracking dog they had, but he was cursed with the typical bloodhound stubbornness and low energy. Still, no one could move that dog like Scott, and if they were needed, they'd be there and on the trail.

Kate came through the door clutching a cup of take-out coffee and looking uncharacteristically dressed down in jeans and a cap-sleeved T-shirt. "Sorry, I had to find coffee or I'd be useless. Where are we?" She pulled out a chair and sat.

"Waiting for Craig and McCord's boss." At Kate's

raised eyebrows, Meg continued, "I decided it would be a good idea to call him in and Craig cleared it. My sister, McCord's partner, doesn't know the details of McCord's work like Sykes does. Sykes also has access to the *Washington Post*'s computer systems and can dig out any notes McCord has uploaded for safekeeping. Craig's waiting for him downstairs and will bring him up as soon as he gets here."

Kate took a long sip of coffee, and sagged back in her chair. "Giving me a few extra minutes for the caffeine to kick in, which is probably not a bad thing." Her Tennessee accent seemed stronger this morning, as if exhaustion knocked down her normal effort to smooth it out to better fit in with the East Coasters who filled the Hoover Building. "When I went to bed close to one, I didn't think I'd be up in less than three hours. I'm worn slap out. Just let me mainline caffeine for a bit and I'll be back up to my usual speed and mental acuity."

Craig pushed through the conference room door, followed by a tall man, with gray hair, a square jaw, and broad shoulders, carrying a laptop bag. Craig's gaze circled the table. "Morning. Thank you all for coming out. This is Martin Sykes, McCord's editor at the *Washington Post*. Mr. Sykes, please take any chair."

Sykes moved over to pull out the empty chair between Lauren and Meg. "Just Martin is fine." As he sat, he gave Meg, whom he'd met several times before, a brief nod. "I don't know how to thank you all for this. If McCord's in trouble, I'm not sure how I'd get him out."

"We'll make sure that happens," Kate said. "Give us anything you can to help us accomplish that goal."

Sykes pulled a laptop out of his bag and then booted up. "I can get into the *Post*'s system remotely. That's where McCord keeps copies of all of his notes. Whatever he knew at the time of his last upload will be there."

"Let me log you into the Wi-Fi," Meg offered. She waited while he logged on and then typed her own credentials into the network.

"Thanks." Head down and eyes locked on his screen, he opened up his browser, typed in an address, and started navigating through the *Post*'s system. "Give me a minute to look through this."

Kate's phone, facedown on the table, vibrated, and she picked it up and scanned the incoming message. Her gaze shot to a low black tripod unit with a keypad and central speaker sitting in the middle of the table. "That's our Philadelphia contact. He just got my message about McCord and wants to call into our meeting." She turned to Sykes, studied him for a moment. "It would be more useful, Martin, if we could bring you more fully into this case, but you understand my reluctance."

"I get it. Been in this business for forty years. You clearly trust McCord as a confidential partner in your cases, so it's not like you consider all journalists untrustworthy."

"Mr. McCord has proven himself multiple times."

"You had to start with him somewhere. I'm an old newspaper guy. I know how to keep my mouth shut. And in this case some things are more important than a story." He looked up from his monitor to lock gazes with Kate. "McCord is more important. Whatever you tell me, I'll keep it under wraps."

Kate gave him a nod of approval. "We have Special Agent Finn Pierce inside the Philadelphia crime family working as a courier and enforcer. He's been helping us monitor illegal conflict diamond drops so we can apprehend not only the family members involved, but the brokers and jewelers as well. Agent Pierce's life will be in danger, if not forfeited, if it gets out he's law enforcement, which is why we needed your assurance."

"It's not getting out through me." His tone was emphatic. "You have my word."

"Let's loop Agent Pierce in then."

Scott, nearest the teleconference unit, pulled it closer. "We can call him directly through this. Text him to be ready for us to call, then tell me his number. I'll put the call through."

Kate read out the number to Scott, who keyed it in, then pushed the teleconference unit into the middle of the table as the sound of a ringing phone burst from the speaker.

"Hello?" The voice was a little tinny, but clear.

"Finn, it's Kate. Thanks for joining us."

"No problem. A journalist disappearing was news to me. There's no talk about it."

"It happened possibly as recently as last night, so there may not have been time yet."

"You're sure he's been taken and it's not just something like his phone died?"

"No. He'd have found another way to get through by this time. He has a system of staying in touch when on an investigation. He makes contact at least once every twelve hours, and we hit that point at one thirty this morning. He's been out of touch since before then; we just don't know when."

"So anytime since yesterday afternoon." Pierce's tone was flat, like he was purposely trying to keep the expression from his voice. "That's a big window."

Meg exchanged worried glances with Brian. Pierce was saying what they were all thinking, but it was worse to hear it out loud.

"We know. It's why we're concerned. We have the entire Human Scent Evidence Team here, as well as Doug Addison and Martin Sykes, McCord's editor at the *Washington Post*. He's searching through all the notes McCord uploaded to the *Post*'s servers right now. Martin, anything?"

Sykes was head down as he clicked and scanned through documents. "I'm into his files. He keeps detailed notes. Which is great, but means there's a lot of information when you need specifics quickly at your fingertips." He paused, his eyes zipping back and forth as he followed the text on-screen. "I have a hierarchy list of the family. Boss, underboss, list of capos and soldiers. The name Falconi comes up a lot."

"That's Vittore Falconi," Pierce said. "He's my capo and runs my crew of soldiers."

"Lovely group," Sykes muttered, returning his attention to his monitor. "McCord has this broken down into areas of business. Extortion, gambling, loan-sharking. Drug, gun, and diamond trafficking. He's also done the footwork and found a bunch of shell companies owned by the family used in their various dealings. He lists Robertson Brothers, United Partners, Americoil, InterAct Inc., Onyx Corp., and the Sortino Group as shell corporations. The name Henry Williamson, or Green, Parker, and Williamson, is listed with almost all of them."

"That's the lawyer and the law firm that would have set up all these companies."

"I get the connection with the Sortino Group," said Pierce. "That's Cianfrani's mother's maiden name."

"That's the boss, right?" Kate clarified.

"Yes."

"He has lists of properties owned by those companies. It's no short list." Sykes looked up. "If McCord's disappeared, do you think they might have taken him to one of those locations?"

"That depends," said Pierce.

Sykes stared at the speaker in the middle of the table, as if trying to make eye contact with Pierce. "On what?"

"I'm not gonna sugarcoat this for you. I know these guys and what they're capable of. It will depend on whether they need to keep him alive long enough to get something from him. If not, your journalist is already dead. Then they'll dump his body in a location totally unconnected from any of their properties."

Seated beside Sykes, Pierce's words hit Meg like a physical impact. Pierce was doing nothing more than saying the quiet part out loud, but it was the thought Meg was trying to avoid at all costs.

McCord dead.

Don't go there. I can't go there without it messing with my head.

She closed her eyes, trying to steel herself against the blow of losing McCord. He was relatively new in her life, but had become such an integral part of it. From his encyclopedic knowledge, to his network of contacts that helped them dive into society's underbelly in a way the FBI simply couldn't, to his dogged efforts to save her sister's life when she was drowning, to his willingness to risk himself climbing through disintegrating buildings—he'd become an invaluable partner, even if he did sometimes drive her crazy, like the brother she'd never been given by blood.

She opened her eyes at the touch of a hand wrapping around her fist to find Brian leaning in toward her, his eyes locked on hers. He gave her hand a squeeze, holding on for a few seconds—*Don't make assumptions. Don't give up hope*—before letting go. Looking up and across the table, she met Craig's steady gaze, seeing an identical message.

She took a deep breath and let it out slowly. She wouldn't lose hope until there was no cause to hold on to it any longer.

Craig leaned forward, as though using his intensity would press the point. "That's not a premise we're going to contemplate right now. We're going to treat this like a rescue operation."

"I agree," said Kate. "And from what I know about McCord after working with him on two cases, he knows enough that it would be worth their while to keep him alive."

"McCord survived three years as a reporter in Iraq while being shot at and bombed," said Meg. "He's also crafty as hell. On top of that, he'll know my sister has raised the alarm and we're coming for him. He'll hang on as long as humanly possible."

"Then it's going to be a matter of finding him before he can't hang on anymore," said Addison. "Finn, do you have any ideas on that?"

"A couple. And I can check them out while you're on the road here. But do McCord's notes point in any particular direction? If they do, that will save us time."

Sykes's eyes stayed locked on his monitor. "He's listed a few white-collar businesses located inside office buildings."

"That seems unlikely to me," Addison said. "Finn? Opinion?"

"Agreed. It's going to have to be somewhere they won't be seen taking in a struggling or unconscious man. He's not going to be going with them willingly, if he's smart. It's also going to be somewhere that's either soundproofed or where noise won't be noticed."

Meg winced, clearly understanding the noise would be produced torturing information out of McCord.

"Unless McCord's actual investigation is what got him into trouble," Brian stated. "Like if he was discovered somewhere he shouldn't be."

Meg took another sip of her coffee and then sat, worrying the cup with one thumb. "Let's think this through. More likely than McCord getting nabbed on the street is him being somewhere they'd object to finding a stranger."

A thought occurred and the flame of hope burned a little brighter. "Maybe they don't even know he's a journalist."

"That would be a fast track to getting himself killed," said Pierce, dousing the tiny flame with a bucket of cold water. "The only reason they'd have for keeping him alive is if they think he knows something. Like who he's told about their activities, that kind of thing. Do you think he'd figure that out?"

"Yes. He's smart and he's savvy." Meg turned to Sykes, who'd been scanning documents the whole time they'd been discussing possibilities. "Working with the theory he was somewhere he shouldn't have been and got caught, where could that be? Last contact with him was at one thirty PM, but that doesn't mean he went missing immediately afterward. In fact, knowing McCord the way I do, he'd have waited for darkness to hide his tracks. Keeping an after-hours entry in mind, do we want to rethink the office building angle?"

"Possibly." Pierce spoke the word slowly, seemingly buying time to think. "But a lot of those buildings have security, either in person or via camera. McCord sneaking in, to begin with, might be problematic, right there."

"Actually," Craig said, "if that was the plan, he'd be better going in to see another business in the building and then redirecting when security wasn't watching him. But we're likely looking at after hours, which decreases the chances of that strategy. What else do you have?"

"There are a couple of industrial sites that might work. The first one is a construction company. Donato Construction."

"Construction, of course," Brian responded. "Why wouldn't they have their fingers in that pie?"

"According to McCord's notes, their modus operandi is the usual Mob template: underbid on construction jobs, and then underpay their employees to make a profit.

There's a list that includes the company head office, as well as active construction sites," Sykes explained.

"Might be some possibilities there," Scott said. "If they're closed and gated off, like most construction sites, they could be holding McCord there, since it's after hours."

"Noted," said Kate. "Though considering what time most of those sites open up, we're only hours away from them becoming active again, which might make it less likely. What else?"

Sykes opened another folder and scanned the contents. "A waste management company. He doesn't have much on it, though. Either he wasn't far into it, or he didn't consider it a solid lead." He opened another folder and whistled. "By that standard *this* is the solid lead. This is the biggest file yet." He scrolled to the end of the text. "It also has the most recent information."

"So it's what he was looking at last," Meg stated.

"That's how I read it."

"What is it?" Pierce asked.

"Logistics and transportation. Russo Logistics Group, owned by InterAct."

Brian's laugh had a cynical edge to it. "That's certainly no surprise. You did say drug and gun trafficking."

Sykes scrolled and kept scanning. "Also cigarettes."

"Really? When you can buy them legally?"

"Legally, sure. But at what cost? It's all about the taxes. Buy cheap in Missouri for a tax of seventeen cents on a twenty-pack, sell it in DC, when it's normally nearly five dollars in taxes for that same twenty-pack. Smuggle it across several state lines and sell to vendors for cheap."

"Owning a logistics company would be a great way to hide the transportation of illegal goods," said Meg. "Where is this place?"

"Yardley, northeast of Philadelphia. More importantly, according to these notes, it's located near I-295, I-195,

I-95, and US-1, and it's about twenty minutes away from the Northeast Philadelphia Airport."

"That's a small regional airport," Pierce said. "That location also puts it about ten minutes from the state line and Trenton, New Jersey, so they have any number of ways to move contraband around and between states by road or air."

"You're also looking at a central depot that would reasonably be expected to have security to protect all the materials moving through it." Addison sat back in his chair, looking thoughtful. "How big is this place?"

"Big. He included an aerial view of the facility." With his index finger Sykes traced the lines of buildings. "A main front-facing building that's open to the public. The rest of the complex is behind security fencing. It's rows of warehouses ringed with loading docks surrounded by trucks. You wouldn't see a lot standing outside the fence looking in."

"You're suggesting McCord snuck into this place and got caught?" Addison's tone was dubious. "Would he really trespass onto a property for a story?"

"You don't know McCord." Meg braced her forearms on the table and leaned forward to look around Brian at Addison. "That's exactly what he'd do."

CHAPTER 26

Kimberley Process Certification Scheme: A process established by the United Nations General Assembly in 2003 "to ensure that diamond purchases were not financing violence by rebel movements and their allies seeking to undermine legitimate governments."

Friday, August 23, 5:12 AM
Fourth-floor conference room, J. Edgar Hoover Building
Washington, DC

"Leave it to me to find out if he's there," Pierce said through the speaker. "If they've gone off the deep end and are holding a well-known investigative reporter, I should be able to at least confirm it. Then the best way to figure out how to get him back is to know what he knew. What's in his files?"

"More detail than we likely need," said Sykes, scanning through lines of text. "But that's the way McCord researches a story."

A smile tugged at the corner of Meg's lips, even through the gut-churning worry. "He once told me a story's like an iceberg. Readers see what's on top, but it's the massive amount of research hidden from view that builds the story. So, what's underneath?"

"Details of the facility itself. Ambient storage and transportation. Refrigerated storage and transportation. The number of vehicles that go through in a year and the number of tons of goods. Their delivery radius." He held up an index finger to forestall questions as he skimmed down the page. "This is all groundwork, all public information, so he could figure out if something was hinky through his investigation. Let me give you the basics. Russo Logistics Group deals with three things—warehousing, packaging, and transportation. You need a warehouse and staff to manage the product? They can provide that. Need food grade storage facilities or trucking to move your product over state lines? They can do that too. They're bonded and can take care of taxes and customs." He was silent for a moment as he scrolled farther. "There are a lot of details here you shouldn't need—things like cross-docking, lot traceability, turnkey solutions, and cold chains—but I can get this transcribed into a single document so you have it on hand just in case."

"That would be helpful," said Kate. "Now, something supposedly drove McCord there. Does anything stand out to you?"

Sykes paused for so long, Meg's left eye twitched out of pent-up frustration.

Then Sykes broke the silence. "It looks like he took a two-pronged approach. He tracked down any Philadelphia contacts, or used his local contacts to connect him to new ones. Because by that time he knew Russo was owned by a Mob shell company, and was trying to connect them with what they were moving, but he was using his underground contacts and trying to avoid any soldiers so the Mob didn't get wind of his investigation. That was of limited use. And then he found a disgruntled ex-employee on the Internet."

"That's business today," said Craig. "Piss off an employee and then watch them take it out on you on every online review site available."

"That's exactly what happened," Sykes continued. "This guy, Richardson, he was one of their long-haul drivers. They let him go when he became too expensive to insure after a number of accidents. He told McCord they didn't maintain their fleet and that's why the accidents were happening. When he stirred up trouble, complaining on every review site he could find, accusing them of unsafe practices, they sent someone after him to rough him up a bit."

"That sounds exactly like something we'd do," Pierce said.

"Wasn't you, was it?" Kate asked.

"Not in this particular case. They only use me as an enforcer occasionally. If it makes you feel better, I make it look worse than it is, lots of bruising, but I try to stay away from the serious injuries."

"Glad to hear it." Kate turned back to Sykes. "Did roughing him up shut him up?"

"It did. But McCord promised him anonymity and a chance to get some of his own back. And he jumped at that. And that's where McCord hit pay dirt."

"I bet he did. What's the scoop?"

"Richardson outlined a bunch of stuff. Poor vehicular maintenance. Hiring undocumented workers as long-haul drivers, paying them only a few dollars per day and working them so hard they hardly ever saw their families. Having their drivers not record their travel time by disabling the mechanisms designed for that purpose, which is a violation of federal safety regulations, all so they could put in illegally long hours. Or not maintaining product temperature in both the trailers and warehouses. But that's all

run-of-the-mill logistics company stuff. Where it got interesting were the issues specific to this site. For instance,
two warehouses are restricted to almost all personnel."

"Really?" Kate drew out the word thoughtfully. "Wonder what they were keeping in there?"

"Richardson didn't know. Now, only one of the two appeared to be an active warehouse. Trucks loaded up there,
but they weren't always fully branded Russo trucks. Most
of them were plain white trucks or panel vans. McCord
assumed they were moving illegal goods and wanted to
make sure nothing connected a truck back to the depot if
they got caught."

Addison, who'd been making notes, stopped and looked
up. "That sounds like illegal contraband technique. Moving drugs or guns, or even the cigarettes you mentioned,
trying to keep it all on the down low. At worst they'd lose
a shipment, but the rest of the business would remain in-
tact. They'd take an inconsequential loss while making
huge gains elsewhere. Did McCord think they were keeping the rough stones there?"

Sykes took a moment to skim the information. "Not
that I can see here. My guess is he had no proof."

"Which would be why he'd want to go and take a closer
look," Brian said.

"There's something else here, though. Richardson was
suspicious about the other warehouse."

"Was something different going on there?" Craig asked.

"He thought so. Full truck bays there, but it almost
never had trucks at it. Very little activity around it. Locked
up tight, with no way in, but once Richardson got curious
and wandered over to take a look. And got a whiff of
something."

"What?"

"Weed."

Meg jerked to look at Brian, to find him staring past her to Sykes, his eyebrows arched high. She swung back to face Sykes. "As in they're storing it there, or they're growing it there?"

"This guy thought growing it."

Addison was shaking his head in disbelief as he put down his pen. "You're telling me this Richardson thought they had a grow op going at a logistics warehouse and no one noticed? Do you know what a grow op smells like? It's nearly impossible to hide that stench. It's a distinctive and recognizable smell. It's going to attract attention in a state where marijuana is a Schedule one controlled substance. Possession is a misdemeanor with fines and jail time. But selling more than thirty grams is a felony with a protracted jail sentence. Growing it, even if it's just for your own use, is a felony. So running a big, smelly grow op is a nonstarter."

"That's where the location of this place comes into play. It's just outside of town where it could house numerous large buildings and have the space to move that many trucks in and out. Also it borders farm country. And the property directly behind it is a chicken farm."

"*A chicken farm?*" Scott looked around the table, searching for someone else who also wasn't making the connection. "Why would that matter?"

"We sometimes have chickens at my parents' animal rescue," Meg said. "The plain fact of the matter is chickens stink. Even if you have just a few of them. Now imagine hundreds or even a few thousand of them. That would be quite the stench. Definitely enough to cover up one little grow op. Even a grow op that wasn't that little."

"That's why Richardson says no one ever seemed to notice, or at least commented on the smell. It wasn't detectable over the smell of the farm, which permeated every corner of every warehouse. It's so bad that they've lost employees over it, but there isn't anything they can do."

"Those grow ops use a lot of power," Lauren said. "You think that would go unnoticed?"

"It's a logistics site." The speaker crackled slightly as Pierce spoke. "With specialized storage and twenty-four/seven operations. They could hide that kind of power usage simply by reporting the addition of a new refrigerated warehouse that required compressors to cool the air. It's not like it's a house and they're trying to disguise a power spike. They already use an immense amount of electricity."

Kate drained her cup and set it down on the table. "I think we have our direction, then. Meg, you know McCord best and now know what he knows. What would be his next step?"

"To find a way to get in there to confirm his suspicions. Then, afterward, he'd turn everything over to us. He'd also likely want to be in on the raid so he could write a kick-ass story, but he would let law enforcement make the catch. This place never shuts down, so I can see him sneaking in under cover of darkness to confirm Richardson's information." She turned to Brian, saw the same worry as hers brewing in his eyes. "In which case they've had him for at least eight hours. And God only knows what they've done to him in that time if they felt he was a threat."

"Agreed. There's no time to waste."

Craig pointed at Sykes's laptop. "Martin, how about you and I go through everything in McCord's notes while the teams deploy to Philadelphia. Due to the time constraint, we've had you review this quickly, but now you'll have time for a deeper dive." He scanned the room, meeting each handler's eyes before moving on to the next.

"That will also give me time to get detailed satellite photos of the facility that will give us better information than McCord's Google Maps shot. I want you all going in. We don't know the lay of the land. We don't know which warehouse is which, so we're going to have to depend on the dogs to track McCord's movements. Meg, do we have scent to work from?"

"Yes. Before I left home, I had Cara bag some of McCord's dirty laundry. I have an item for each team." She looked down at Hawk, snoozing beside her chair. "Not that Hawk will need it."

Craig swung around to Kate and Addison. "We're going to need a warrant."

Addison pushed away from the table and stood. "You leave that to me. I know exactly which judge to get out of bed. She's not going to be thrilled with the hour, but I think I can get her behind a warrant with what we have. I'll send an electronic version to you before you'll need it. Going in now to investigate the entire complex is going to be the only way to confirm these claims without giving them a chance to clear out."

"Or have a mysterious warehouse fire that torches the place to the ground, but has an odd smell," Kate agreed. "It needs to be a 'one and done' operation. I'm sorry we'll lose you for the raid, though."

"Getting the warrant is more important. I don't need the glory; I just want it done. You'll need backup, so bring in some of the Philadelphia boys."

"That's exactly what I thought. Pierce?"

"I'm here."

"Can you try to confirm any of this before we go in?"

"That's next on my list. I'll put my ear to the ground and see what's shaking. I'll pass on anything I get, but I have to stay out of your raid."

"I know. We need to keep your position safe, at least until we see who we bag out of this."

"Right. Let me work on it from this end to see if I can unearth anything. But if I was you, I'd hurry. It's going to take some time to get here. And time is the one thing your journalist doesn't have."

CHAPTER 27

Global Witness: A London-headquartered, international, non-governmental organization, established in 1993, that was one of the founding members of the Kimberley Process Certification Scheme (KPCS). Global Witness withdrew from the KPCS in 2011 after it said the process was not working.

Friday, August 23, 7:37 AM
Russo Logistics Group
Yardley, Pennsylvania

McCord slowly woke to pain.
His head felt like it was about to explode, and, as he regained consciousness, he became aware of other small agonies—his ribs were on fire, his nose throbbed, his jaw ached, and his shoulders burned.

Opening his eyes, he found himself staring at his own lap, his dirty navy pants spattered with blood.

Mine?

McCord slowly tipped his head up. Pain radiated through his neck and burst through his skull at even that minor movement. He inhaled on a gasp, but air only moved reluctantly through his mouth; his nose seemed to be cut off from his lungs. Squeezing his eyes shut, he held the position, waiting for the pain to fade as his stomach rolled greasily. He fought to stay conscious, somehow knowing that to let go, to go back into the darkness, was dangerous.

A low moan escaped him in response to the pain. The sound filling the room was muffled, stirring confusion until enough neurons fired to deduce that his jaw ached because he was gagged. A jerk to free his hands told him they were bound behind him.

The sharp pain in his head dissipated, finally settling instead into a low ache. Cautiously McCord opened his eyes, squinting, struggling to focus his blurry vision on anything beyond a few feet away. He was in a storage room of some sort, surrounded by shelves full of light bulbs, ballasts, bottles and vats of chemicals, stacks of empty plastic buckets, and stakes. Several huge spools of tubing of different sizes and stacked bags of clay pellets were lined up against the far wall.

Memory crashed over McCord, dragging him back to the previous day before everything went wrong.

For McCord, his entire investigation was now centered on one location: Russo Logistics—the company he'd traced back to InterAct, a shell company he'd linked to the Philadelphia crime family.

His story had begun with diamonds, but had expanded to include so many other facets of the Mob underbelly. As a newsman he'd amassed a stable of contacts over his career, but for this story, he needed a specific subset. His contacts in the criminal world had served him well in the past, and had contributed to his efforts to assist the FBI in bringing down a child sex trafficking ring the previous summer. However, a lot of those contacts didn't give a rat's ass about diamonds. It was simply too far out of their world.

But drugs and guns ... that was another angle alto-gether.

When he'd asked his Philadelphia contacts, a lot of them focused only on drug and gun trafficking, but quiet murmurs had whispered of a local network of distribution spreading out to neighboring states.

McCord had come to recognize the power of the Mob from the silence coming from many of his informants. Nothing he'd offered had convinced them to talk; fear was a suffocating influence. But a few had given him threads to tug. And many of those threads had come together in Yardley, Pennsylvania.

Logistics made sense in so many ways—a closed com-pound with layers of security, acres of storage facilities, a pool of vehicles to transport your product wherever you needed it to go, and all the permits required to cross state lines if needed. The ability to hide illegal activities behind their legal business not only gave them cover, but also gave them a way to launder funds gained through those enter-prises.

It was brilliantly simple and clearly effective.

He needed to confirm his theory in person before bring-ing the whole thing to Meg and Kate to avoid sending them off on a wild-goose chase. His biggest concern was security, but if he went in at night, he thought he'd be able to take a look around and perhaps even take some photos.

Remote research came first. Satellite photos showed a rural area with mixed zoning. It was close to numerous interstates and not far from the Pennsylvania/New Jersey state line, was backed by a poultry farm surrounded by cornfields, and was just down the street from a small in-dustrial park housing multiple businesses. But nothing replaced in-person scouting, so McCord had driven in from DC to see the complex with his own eyes earlier that day . . .

He parked over a mile away at the side of the road with the intent of walking the rest of the way. From the moment he opened his door, he was assaulted with the foulest odor he'd ever experienced—a mix of ammonia, animal feces, and rotting meat. Two hundred yards down the road, as his eyes started to burn, he acknowledged the clever advantage of putting a grow op near a chicken farm—no one would ever be able to discover it by scent alone, since nothing was detectable over the smell of factory chicken farming.

McCord spent hours that afternoon hunkered down in a cornfield with a pair of binoculars watching the facility to see how it ticked—rows of separated warehouses, multiple trucks driving in and out, and drivers and employees, all dressed in Russo navy blue, streaming over the complex. The odd glimpse inside a warehouse after a truck left a loading dock, and before the garage door was rolled back into place, showed each warehouse swarming with workers.

Busy place.

But workers moving from building to building showed him how to blend in. All he needed was a pair of navy pants and a navy short-sleeved shirt, both of which he happened to already have in the car, thanks to a little Internet research and a quick shopping trip the day before. He also brought along an empty cardboard box as part of his disguise, because no one would question a worker in a logistics facility running a package from warehouse to warehouse.

He retreated to the car and waited until darkness fell, then changed clothes and retraced his route back into the cornfield, where he waited for the perfect opportunity. He'd already picked out the location where he'd go over

the ten-foot chain-link fence surrounding the complex—
right behind the middle warehouse that backed onto the
poultry farm's cornfield and in a blind spot from the complex's security cameras. He'd get back out at the same
spot. Scaling the fence in both directions should be a snap
with the hiking boots he wore that were similar to the
steel-toed boots worn by employees.

It was after nine thirty when the complex quieted down
somewhat, the constant truck traffic slowed, and McCord
judged there were few enough people roaming outside to
make his unseen incursion possible. He broke from the
cornfield at a run, tossed the box over, scaled the fence,
and dropped onto the asphalt on the far side in under sixty
seconds. He picked up the box, seating it in his arms as if
it had heft, and headed across the asphalt and around the
first warehouse, strolling as if he didn't have a care in the
world.

Sometimes the best way to hide was in plain sight with
confidence that screamed *I belong here.* As long as no one
noticed the lack of the Russo Logistics patch high on his
left sleeve, he'd be fine.

He reviewed the aerial map of the facility in his head as
he walked the property. Most of the warehouses were well
lit and bustling, even at this time of night, as employees
concentrated on inventory organization and packing new
shipments for the next day. However, two smaller warehouses at the back of the property were mostly dark and
had no foot traffic. Scanning the space between buildings
and deciding the coast was clear, McCord strolled up to
the first building—better to look lost and ask for forgive-
ness, rather than permission—and brazenly tried the employee door.

Locked.

He circled the building to the only other door on the far
side, to find it also locked.

Without pausing he headed for the next warehouse, but had to duck into the shadows under the eaves when the adjacent door burst open, nearly hitting him. As he pressed against the wall, McCord had a brief impression of height and muscular bulk as a man strode away, the door swinging shut behind him. Before he even had time to consider the risk, McCord sprang forward, catching the handle just before the lock engaged. For a moment he stood there, his back against the door, watching the man rapidly cross the driveway between warehouses, knowing if he turned around and saw the crack of light shining through the unlatched door, he was done. If the guy could have heard the pounding of his heart as it hammered, he'd have been found in an instant.

But the man never even slowed, and disappeared around the corner of one of the warehouses.

McCord blew out a pent-up breath and pulled the door open a fraction of an inch more.

Silence.

Fish or cut bait. You want this or not?

Without giving himself time to do a risk assessment of the perils of walking into what might be a Mob hideaway with nothing more than an empty box, McCord opened the door and slipped through, easing it closed behind him. The *click* of the latch sounded like a thunderbolt in the quiet and he froze, but no one came running.

There, standing in the entryway, the smell hit him.

Dank. Skunky.

Cannabis.

Victory gave him a kick of adrenaline. Richardson was correct. They *were* running a grow op right next to the transportation system that would deliver it to their network of dealers. A few photos and he'd get out and let the authorities do the rest.

But, for now, he was entirely exposed and needed to

move. He was standing at the end of a long hallway running from one exit door to the other on the far side, slightly off-set from the center of the building. Unlike the other larger warehouses he'd seen through open loading docks, this warehouse wasn't a single open, soaring space jammed to the roof with racks and boxes. This building appeared to have a single room running down the left side of the corridor with exits at either end, facing a number of smaller rooms on the right-hand side, based on the number of doors.

Grow ops needed space, so the obvious first choice was the room on the left. None of the doors had windows, so he'd have to be careful. No one could see him out in the hallway, but at the same time, he couldn't see anyone in the room. He crossed the hallway, grasped the knob, and slowly eased the door open. Bright light spilled out and he nearly coughed from the dank plume of scent that billowed out, but he held his breath and bore down as he listened for movement. More silence. He opened the door farther and stepped through.

And stopped dead.

The entire room was filled with plants under blindingly bright grow lights.

He'd hit the mother lode.

Years ago, when Colorado first legalized marijuana, McCord had written an article on residents trying legal home grows for the first time—the tricks and the challenges of producing your own weed. He remembered a lot of that research, so he recognized what he was looking at: Rows of tall, bloom-covered marijuana plants grew out of clay pellets in large white buckets. Drip hoses ran from the top of each bucket to the next. Drain lines in the bottom of each bucket allowed for the circulation of nutrients. Heavy stakes supported bright green, healthy plants, heavy with buds. Panels of brilliant grow lights suspended overhead. The hum of the HVAC system as it circulated air using carbon filters in an attempt to pull out as much of the overpowering stench as possible in real time, while the plants pumped out unending streams in a constant battle.

Thousands and thousands of plants.

This was a major operation. When law enforcement came in, it would be to hand out reams of felony charges.

Get your proof and get out of here. This is enough to bring in the FBI with a warrant; if the diamonds are here as well, they'll find them.

He dropped the box to the floor, pulled out his phone, and started taking pictures, being careful to note all aspects of the operation.

He was snapping a picture of one of the ceiling-mounted HVAC units when the attack came out of nowhere.

Something slammed into him with breathtaking force, knocking him clean off his feet as his phone sailed away to clatter against the concrete floor. McCord didn't even have time to get his arms up before a fist smashed into his face, and pain exploded as bone cracked. He had a brief view of a head and shoulders above him, backlit by the brilliant grow lights, and balled his fist and struck out with all his strength at the man's jaw, pain shooting up his arm as he made contact. But the force was sufficient to whip the man's head to the side, driving his body far enough backward for McCord to buck him off and scramble away in an awkward crab walk.

Get to your feet. Make it a fair fight.

He crashed into the legs of another man, unseen, standing behind him. He looked up to see the bulky man he'd seen exiting the building.

Shit.

That brief pause was all the man needed to pull back

and bury his steel-toed boot in McCord's ribs. With a grunt McCord reflexively curled into a ball, trying to protect his torso, but the strikes came again and again, pummeling him, knocking all the air from his lungs.

Then his attacker grabbed his head in both hands and cracked it against the concrete floor.

Agony exploded and McCord sank into unconsciousness.

CHAPTER 28

A Rough Trade: A report produced by Global Witness, said to be the inspiration for the movie *Blood Diamonds.*

Friday, August 23, 7:42 AM
Russo Logistics Group
Yardley, Pennsylvania

McCord had no idea what time it was. Here, in the closed room, there was no hint of natural light to indicate daylight. It could be midnight or noon, but McCord suspected he must have been unconscious for hours.

Definitely concussed.

Time to pull it together and take stock. He had no idea if they'd checked on him since the fight or if they'd yet to return. But at some point, they'd come back and it wouldn't go well for him.

Better to not be here.

He had to trust he'd passed the twelve-hour window Cara depended on to know he was all right; had to trust she'd already raised the alarm, and Meg had raised the alarm in turn.

Meg. Her attack only days before came back to him. Giraldi might be in custody, but the family's modus operandi would be more universal than a single soldier. The easiest way to solve the problem of Meg had been to eliminate her. They wouldn't hesitate to do the same to him, unless he could convince them he knew something they needed. Something that would take time to extract.

McCord had to believe Meg was calling in reinforcements and he just needed to buy enough time for them to get here. He could pretend to still be unconscious, but they would likely only buy that for so long. After that, he needed to find a way to stall.

He hoped he wasn't simply giving them time to torture him before killing him, rather than just giving in to a swift death. He needed to believe deep down someone was coming for him. That he mattered, and help was on the way. Because to not believe that would lead to despair and hopelessness.

But to stall, he needed to figure out who he was dealing with. He closed his eyes, picturing the faces of the two men he'd seen. The one who'd taken him down before taking McCord's right hook was a stranger. Likely a soldier. But the other man . . . he seemed familiar somehow. Then it came to him. Falconi. Pierce's capo, the one running the soldiers responsible for the diamond deliveries.

If Falconi was here, there was a good chance the diamonds and possibly other luxury goods were here as well. And once they figured out who McCord was—and there was no reason to think they wouldn't when he always carried his *Washington Post* business cards in his wallet— they'd want to know what he knew and with whom he'd shared that information. And it was only a matter of time before Falconi and his goons returned.

His heart pounded as he broke out in a cold sweat. He shifted on the chair, ignoring the tearing pain in his shoulders and wrists as he tried to twist and yank his hands free. But sixty seconds of struggling simply left him winded and swearing.

He had to hang on. He had to have faith.

They'd be out looking for him, but would they find him? Had he left enough of a trail to follow? The dogs were good, but even they needed a starting point.

Was he truly on his own? The thought terrified him.

Come on, Meg, put the team together and figure it out. I'm not going to be able to help you this time.

McCord forced himself to steady his breathing. If he was going to pretend he was still unconscious, hyperventilating would fool no one. He needed to drag every ounce of courage from the depth of his soul. If this was where he was going to make his stand, he was not going to make it on his knees with his head bowed.

He'd been in danger before. Years before, in Iraq, he knew how to find the courage to hang on, to run faster . . .

Tuesday, March 25, 2008
Sadr City, Iraq

He was with the US Army's 2nd Stryker Cavalry, covering the group and helping them get medical supplies and humanitarian aid to the residents, when the cease-fire with the Mahdi Army collapsed.

He was sitting in the passenger seat of a US Army truck in an escorted convoy when the truck in front of them exploded into a blinding fireball. McCord only had a moment to think *Incoming* before the next missile skimmed over them to hit the building beside them in a fury of sound and flame.

The driver, Corporal Morales, reacted quickly, going off road to avoid the smoking wreck in front of them. An armored vehicle would come back to search for any wounded, but they both knew there were no wounded to find. His heart pounding, McCord braced himself with one hand on the dash and a second on the door handle, peering out the windshield of the truck to try to spot the next incoming missile. He'd never actually see it coming in time to react, but he had to do something.

As they drove past the flaming truck, oily black smoke poured in the open driver's window, along with the smell of charred meat. McCord's stomach rolled; he'd never get used to the smell of burned victims.

Another explosion, this time behind them, and Morales swerved back onto the road and hammered the accelerator. They shot onto a cross street and the truck pulled up to a clay-brick building as machine-gun fire rang through the streets.

"Get out! Stay down!" Morales yelled, grabbing his rifle from where it lay beside him, propped against his seat. He went out the door firing.

McCord had a helmet and bulletproof vest, but no firearm. His only weapon was speed.

Move before they hit the truck.

He laid his hand on the door handle and calculated the distance to the door of the building. About thirty feet. He slammed open the door and flew.

The rapid *pop-pop-pop* of automatic-rifle fire filled his ears, but whether it was from the Mahdi Army or the cavalry, he wasn't sure . . . until the wall to his right shattered into a blizzard of razor-sharp shards and a cloud of dust.

Definitely not our guys.

One of the outward-spinning shards sliced along his cheek and he felt the warm trickle of blood, but then he was crashing into and through the door. Soldiers poured in behind him, spreading through the structure, setting up at every window and firing back.

McCord leaned back against the wall, breathing hard, adrenaline rushing through his veins, his hands shaking and his knees feeling like they were made of water. Now he was safe—or as safe as he'd be in the middle of a war zone—ugly terror rose. In the heat of the moment, there was never time to panic, only to react. But afterward, that was the time to second-guess his decision to spend years reporting from a war zone.

After an attack was when he had to find the courage to stay, to not call his editor to arrange for transportation back home.

Every time he'd been in a life-or-death scenario, he'd sworn he was done.

Every time he'd found the courage to stay.

Friday, August 23, 7:45 AM
Russo Logistics Group
Yardley, Pennsylvania

He jolted from his reverie, freezing as he heard the sound of footfalls coming down the hallway toward him. The bottom dropped out of his stomach, but he forced himself to go slack, letting his head loll forward, to feign unconsciousness as he dug deep to find the courage that served him so well more than a decade before.

There was a laugh as someone stepped into the room. "I think you worked him over too well last night. He's still out."

"That's okay, I can fix that. Rise and shine, reporter boy."

Blinding pain exploded in McCord's left side, wringing a cry from him as his body jerked and the chair started to tip. Only the hard grip of a hand on his shoulder kept him upright at the last second.

He looked up to find Falconi planted in front of him. The man was tall, but seemed even taller from McCord's seated position, and McCord had no illusions that Falconi towered over him as an act of intimidation. Falconi wasn't dressed in Russo Logistics navy, but instead was in all black from his Italian loafers to his summer-weight linen slacks to his perfectly pressed shirt. *Doesn't usually get his hands dirty. That's for his enforcers.* He stared into Falconi's hard, dark eyes, and his courage wavered at the cold calculation. But he didn't allow the gut punch of fear to show as he stared Falconi down without blinking.

"I see you're with us again." Falconi strolled around the room, running a hand idly over items on the shelves. "You're in some trouble, Mr. McCord. For starters, you're trespassing. How did you get in?"

McCord simply looked at him and didn't even attempt an answer through the gag.

"Of course . . . the gag." Falconi pulled a switchblade from his pocket and let the blade spring free with a *snap* an inch from McCord's face.

Clenching his fists and holding firm, McCord didn't allow himself to flinch.

Falconi slipped the blade under the band of the gag, just in front of McCord's ear, and the material parted easily under the pressure of the keenly honed blade. Falconi dragged the cold metal down McCord's cheek before dropping it away, then moved to stand in front of McCord, legs splayed and the knife still held in one hand. "Let's start again. How did you get in?"

McCord's mind was whirling. How best to handle this? Answer, and risk coming off as a smart-ass, because that tended to be his natural tone? Or remain silent so everything about him remained shrouded in mystery?

He'd go with silence, for as long as he could. Which would bring on the violence, but if they really wanted information, they'd have to temper that violence or risk losing their prize completely. He just hoped he'd be able to hang on.

Hurry, Meg.

He clenched his jaw shut and stared up at Falconi.

Falconi's eyes narrowed. "I asked you a question."

Even though McCord thought he was prepared, the backhand was shocking in its speed and brutality. His aching head jerked sideways, making it spin with vertigo and waves of pain, but he bore down, trying to breathe through the pain, air sawing audibly through his clenched teeth.

"Answer the question." When McCord remained quiet, Falconi looked around the room, one eyebrow cocking as something caught his eye. "Okay, let's try this, then. Why did you come here?"

McCord struggled to get his breathing under control, but let all the hatred he felt show in his eyes. And stayed silent.

"So that's how you're going to play this? I'll have to up my game then." Falconi wandered over to the huge spools of tubing and then looked over McCord's head. "Push these over to the chair. Two on the right side. Two on the left." He folded his knife and slipped it into his pocket, then pulled a heavy mallet off a shelf and turned, slapping it into his open left palm.

Another man came into view—the same dark Italian coloring, but this one was wearing heavy boots, jeans, and a black T-shirt. *Classic enforcer. Of course Falconi was once an enforcer, so he's got the chops to do whatever he'd ask of his own men.* The man picked up the spools, two at a time, lifting them like they were made from cardboard. But when he dropped them with a *thump* on the concrete beside McCord's chair, their weight was obvious.

Slap slap slap. The mallet continued to rise and fall against Falconi's palm as if it had no heft.

That was nothing more than an illusion.

"Untie his hands," Falconi ordered.

The *shoosh* of a knife pulled from a sheath sounded behind McCord's head, and then the pressure holding his hands evaporated for a fraction of a second before the pressure returned, but even more forcefully, painfully crushing the bones of his wrist.

Falconi set down the mallet, carefully leaning the handle against one of the two stacks of spools. "Retie the left hand." He grabbed McCord's right hand, dragging it around to hold it on top of the spool. McCord fought them both then, even as his abused shoulders screamed at the change of position, rocking back and forth in the chair. But it was two against one and they were too strong, and in moments his left hand was bound to the back of the chair.

The goon came around to take his right forearm, pressing it into the top of the spool.

Falconi grabbed a roll of duct tape from a shelf and ripped off a couple of pieces. Then he hammered his fist down on McCord's wrist, holding him in place while his goon immobilized his hand with tape. Then they untied his left hand and, together, taped it on top of the second stack of spools.

Oh God oh God oh God. McCord knew exactly how they were going to convince him to talk. And he honestly wasn't sure he wouldn't babble like a baby.

You can do this. It was Cara's voice he heard in his head. Cara, who knew a thing or two about survival. Cara, who'd nearly died at the hands of a man who was killing her sister, over and over again. He internalized the sentiment, holding it tight. And raised his chin an inch higher.

Bring it on.

Freed from having to hold on to McCord, Falconi stood in front of him again, the mallet held in both hands. "I'm going to ask you again why you're here. And you're going to tell me. And if you don't, I'm going to break your fingers." He smiled, but there was no joy in the expression, just feral aggression. "I understand you reporters live by the keyboard. And maybe die by it. So I'm sure you'd like to be able to do your job. And you can, as long as you answer my questions." One more slap of the mallet for emphasis, then, "Why are you here?"

McCord closed his eyes for a moment, gathering himself as he pulled in a deep breath. Then he opened his eyes and met Falconi's.

And said nothing.

Falconi shook his head, his lips twisting. "Arrogant bastard. You could have made this easier on yourself." And raising the mallet to shoulder height, he brought it down on the pinky and ring fingers of McCord's left hand.

McCord thought he was braced, but the shocking pain was nauseating and he couldn't stop the cry that burst from between his clenched teeth. Lips pressed together, breathing hard through his nose, he battled back the pain, and raised his head to glare at Falconi again.

Falconi looked down at him, amused. "So you don't like that question. Let's try another one. Who knows you're here?"

McCord hoped his flat stare conveyed his message. *No way in hell am I giving you anything.*

With a sneer, Falconi brought the mallet down on his middle and index fingers.

This time McCord was ready and kept his jaw clenched, only a grunt trapped in the back of his throat marking the strike. The worst of the pain over, McCord hung his head, panting, as his fingers throbbed to the rapid pounding of his heart.

"Who else knows why you're here?" Falconi pushed, not interested in giving him time to recover.

McCord didn't even bother to look up, so when the mallet fell again on his right hand, he wasn't totally prepared, the burst of agony somehow startling him and making him jump, his teeth clamping down on the inside of his cheek, warm blood spurting into his mouth.

The room was starting to spin, but he raised his head and fixed bleary eyes on the man in front of him, on the weapon he held.

"I don't know what you think you're fighting for." Falconi's gaze ran over him, reviewing each injury, large and small, as if to revel in it. "You'd have better luck trying to talk yourself out of this than being silent. Be smart, give yourself a chance to survive."

You'll never let me go voluntarily after this.

No way out.

"Answer the question this time. You must be doing an investigation for a story. What are you specifically investigating?"

McCord shook his head, almost detached from the process, his eyes on the mallet as it rose and then fell.

So much pain, but at this point, pain was beginning to be relative, his brain not able to fully process it anymore. He stared down at the destruction of his hands, and realized that Meg wasn't going to come in time.

He was on his own.

But he still refused to go down cowering.

Falconi turned the mallet around in his hands, choking up on it like it was a baseball bat. "You're a stupid son of a bitch, and you've thrown away your writing career. One more question, and I'd recommend you answer it. Have you left details of your investigation for anyone else to find?"

McCord looked at the solid wooden handle and knew this could be it. He was already concussed. Another hit might be enough to scramble his brains permanently. Hell, the strike itself might be enough to crush his skull.

Time to let loose the reins on his inner smart-ass and go out in a blaze of glory with his head held high.

He gathered the fluid pooling in his mouth and spat it at Falconi's Italian loafers, splattering them with a combination of blood and saliva. "Haven't you ever heard of 'voice-to-text'?" he rasped.

Falconi muttered something vicious in Italian.

McCord had one brief moment to think *Cara* as the handle swung.

The room burst with brilliant streaks of light and then darkness claimed him again.

CHAPTER 29

Feather: A small fracture inside a diamond that may be completely enclosed or extend up to the surface.

Friday, August 23, 8:06 AM
Stony Hill Road
Yardley, Pennsylvania

Brian was pulling his SUV to the side of the road, just past McCord's abandoned car, when Craig called Meg's phone. She put the call on speaker so Brian could hear as well.

"Are you there yet?" Craig asked.

"Sort of." Meg scanned the cornfields that hugged the road on both sides. "As close as we're going to get before we start walking."

"I wanted to catch you before you went in. Addison and I just got off the phone with Kate."

Meg glanced at Brian in the driver's seat to find his puzzled eyes locked on her face. He mouthed, *What's going on?* and she returned a shrug.

"Is something wrong?"

"Not sure about 'wrong.' Possibly right. We think McCord identified the FBI leak."

"That man was on a roll."

"More importantly, he thinks the leak is how Giraldi found you."

"Now *I* want to know," said Brian. "Who is he and when can we arrest him?"

"First of all, it's a woman. Special Agent Abby Taylor. And she's already being brought in for questioning."

"How did McCord figure it out?" Meg asked.

"There are likely more details McCord could fill in, but he was suspicious of how they found you. He theorized some possibilities about how you might have been found—through him and your sister, through Webb or maybe a friend, but he kept circling back to the idea that the most efficient way to get your address quickly was through the FBI. He looked into Giraldi's background, and Falconi's, and even Cianfrani's, but he couldn't nail anything down. Then one of his contacts told him of a connection—an FBI agent normally in Philadelphia, but who had been transferred temporarily to the Baltimore office. That's what led him to Taylor. And then he figured out the connection backward."

"Someone was having an affair with Taylor?"

"No, he thinks someone was blackmailing her. Taylor has a sealed juvie record."

"She was accepted into the FBI even with that record?"

"It doesn't happen often, but it does happen. Individuals who've had their records sealed or expunged, but who have then become model students and citizens, can be accepted to Quantico. We looked up her record in the FBI. She's been an exemplary agent out of the Philadelphia field office."

"Convenient to the local family," Brian muttered.

"But if she'd still been there, she'd have known about Pierce. She must not have or else he'd have been taken out. She must have been transferred to Baltimore before he went undercover."

"She's been there over a year, and is due to come back in

the next month or two. But her transfer to Baltimore and lack of connection to the Philadelphia field office kept Pierce safe."

"But not Meg."

"She still had access to Bureau records, and that's how she tracked down Meg's information and sent the address to Giraldi. Or at least that's the theory. Someone in the family had dirt on her and threatened exposure if she didn't help them out."

"How is that a threat?" Brian asked. "She'd already been accepted into the FBI."

"Sure, the sealed record got her into Quantico. But her supervisor and colleagues don't know about it, because it's a *sealed record*. Or maybe they know there's a record, but don't know what's in it. And keep in mind, there are some fossils who still think women don't belong in law enforcement. Tie that kind of information to a subordinate someone doesn't like and they could find a reason to get rid of her. At the very least, people might look at her differently and not trust her in the same way. She probably felt that information getting out would have ended her career as she knows it."

"Or it might not have. One thing is certain, she's ended it herself now."

"Definitely. She's on her way here, and Kate wants her locked down until she gets back, because she wants to handle it personally."

The doors of the SUV in front of them opened and Kate got out on the driver's side.

"Craig, we need to move. Anything else for us?"

"Just that Pierce confirmed something went down last night at Russo. He doesn't have specifics, but extra men were called in, first thing this morning. So be prepared for numbers."

"Kate has numbers too. And a warrant. We'll have the

place surrounded and then get in there before they know what hit them."

"Copy that. Kate's got this, so depend on her. And be safe."

"Always." Meg ended the call and pocketed her phone. She looked over at Brian. "Ready?"

"Always," he echoed. "Let's go get McCord." He opened the door, froze momentarily, and slammed it again. "Oh my God. Is that the stench you were talking about? The chickens?"

"Sure is. You can't mistake that smell."

"I don't know how the dogs are going to manage it. How are they going to find a single McCord scent particle through that overpowering stench?"

Meg turned to look at Hawk and Lacey, both sitting up and alert and watching them in the passenger compartment. "They'll do it. They're pros. They'll focus on the bagged scent and work it. It may take longer, but once one of them finds it, they'll lead us right to him."

Hopefully, alive. Meg couldn't help the thought whispering through her mind, and pushed it firmly away. *Focus.*

Brian took a deep breath, as if it was his last gasp of breathable oxygen, and opened the door again. "This is inhumane . . ."

They got out of the SUV, popped the back to retrieve their go bags, put on their earpieces and throat mics, shrugged into Kevlar vests, checked their sidearms, leashed the dogs, and then met Kate as she gathered with a similarly attired group of FBI agents. Lauren and Scott walked over from their vehicle parked ahead to join them. They stood at the side of the road, partially hidden by their vehicles, trying to take shallow breaths despite the humid August heat that only intensified the stench.

"The fully executed search warrant is good for the entire

property," Kate said. "Once we get the front gate open, we're going to fan out and hit all the warehouses at the same time. We're looking for two things—*Washington Post* investigative reporter Clay McCord, and any indication of illegal activities by the Philadelphia crime family. McCord's notes indicate a grow op, at the very least. We have the legal right to access, so don't let any door stand in your way. If you run into trouble with entry, Wallace and Marchand have the rams. Dalal, you're with me serving the warrant. Stanley, you and your guys will take the outer perimeter when we go in with the warrant. Everyone else, wait at the main gate. Once we're in, split up and spread out to cover every building. Where are the dog teams?"

"Back here," Meg called.

Kate spun around to face them. "When the gates open, do your thing. We all have comms, so if you pick up McCord's trail, report in. Or if you need help, or backup because you hit on something big, report in."

"Will do."

"We have one team from the Yardley-Makefield EMS here on-site, and more on standby. And the last thing to know is we're a go at 08:30, so we need to get into position. Also, at 08:30, Russo's service provider will cut their outside access—telephone and Internet—to reduce their ability to bring in outside support." One of the agents started to protest and Kate cut him off. "I know, cell phones. I'm sure some, if not all of them, will have them, but we can't block cell signals to only take out that facility. All we can do is reduce communications as much as possible." She checked her watch. "Let's move."

As a group they jogged down the road. They didn't even attempt stealth, simply speed. There were no sirens to announce them, but as soon as they surrounded the complex, it would become clear to those inside the fence that something big was happening.

As they approached the driveway, a team of agents split from the main group in two arms, each circling the facility through the adjacent cornfields from opposite directions. Kate and a second agent broke away, jogging up to the main door and disappearing inside, as the rest of the group held back from the front gate in an attempt to avoid raising suspicion.

"Everyone ready?" Meg asked, pulling out a plastic bag from the side pocket of her go bag as the other handlers did the same.

"We're ready," said Scott.

Meg bent and offered Hawk the bag. "It's McCord, Hawk. We need to find McCord." When he looked up at her, she could have sworn she saw the same grit and determination she felt. *We can do this.*

The tall chain-link gate rattled and then started to roll back.

"Hawk, find McCord!"

They all flowed forward and through the ever-increasing gap, fanning out to cover the complex. But Meg wasn't watching the agents; her eyes were locked on her dog at the end of the leash. Hawk had his head up, his eyes bright, and his tail waving as he trotted forward. *In the game, but doesn't have him yet.*

As the teams scattered, all moving in different directions, Meg scanned the complex, trying to put herself in McCord's shoes. *What would he do?* Her gaze ran over trucks at loading docks and into warehouses bustling with early-morning shifts packing trucks for the day's deliveries. *McCord would have been looking for the grow op, and you're not going to find something like that in a busy warehouse.* More than that, Meg knew McCord would have studied the facility before going in. He was thorough, sometimes to an enormous degree, so if he was trying to sneak onto the property, he'd study to find the quietest spot.

Her gaze drifted to the two smaller warehouses at the rear of the property, which were quiet and sat apart from what appeared to be the normal hustle and bustle of the average business day.

There.

"Hawk, come." She tightened the leash to keep him beside her and sprinted for the back of the property. However, within fifteen seconds, she had to slow because Hawk was head down and weaving through a scent cone. *So much for the stench of the farm next door handicapping the dogs.* "Good boy, Hawk. Find McCord." She touched the button for her throat mic to activate it. "This is Jennings. Hawk has the scent. We're headed for the two smaller warehouses at the rear of the property, aiming for the north structure."

Hawk was no longer weaving back and forth, but running straight out. Straight for the door on one side of the building. When he reached it, he sat.

Alerting.

McCord went through that door.

Meg tried the door, but it didn't budge. "Jennings again. I need agents and the ram at the northernmost of the smaller rear warehouses."

"This is Marchand. I'm nearby."

About twenty seconds later, two agents ran into view, one of them holding a compact battering ram. Meg moved Hawk out of the way and let the agent work, using brute force to demolish the lock and then they jerked open the door. The skunky smell of marijuana rolled out.

Bingo.

She drew her Glock. "Hawk, find McCord."

Hawk didn't hesitate, but ran inside, passing doors on

the right-hand side without a second glance, as he arrowed down the hallway.

The boom of a gunshot echoed in the open space and Meg whipped around.

Marchand stood with his back against the wall near a door on the far side. "FBI! Drop your weapons." He nodded at the agent on the other side of the door and the agent grabbed the handle and yanked the door open. Another blast echoed and Marchand swung in. More gunfire. More agents running in.

Stay on point.

She turned around to find Hawk, sitting at a closed door. Meg glanced down the hallway—those agents were busy fighting for their lives—dropped the leash, and grasped the door handle with her left hand, keeping her Glock trained on whoever might be on the other side of the door. She eased the door open a few inches to peer inside.

She froze at the sight that met her eyes. McCord, badly beaten, his head lolling, slumped limply in a chair, held upright only because he was tied there. Blood and bruising washed his face with color, and at first glance his nose was clearly broken. But was he unconscious? Dead? She couldn't take any time to assess him because her attention was locked on the man standing behind McCord, using him as a shield while he held the barrel of a handgun to McCord's temple.

The man was large and muscular, and had eyes that reminded her of Giraldi's—flat and cold. Willing to snuff out a life in seconds without another thought.

For a moment they simply stood staring at each other as Meg pointed her gun at the man, and he pointed his at McCord.

"Open the door." The man's voice was as flat as his

eyes, not conveying any alarm or undue pressure, like it was just a moment in another ordinary day. "I want you where I can see you."

Behind the door Meg gave Hawk the hand signal to move back, then opened the door all the way, once he was out of sight.

"I suggest you put that down on the ground, or I'll be forced to shoot," he said. "You'll survive, but he won't."

An idle threat because McCord was already dead, or the truth because he still hung on?

She put all her chips on life and bent to set her gun down on the floor. As she did, Kate came in the far door, but Meg immediately turned away, straightening and putting both hands in the air, knowing Kate would immediately read the situation.

"Now kick it over toward me."

She did as he asked, but purposely put little effort into the motion so the weapon only moved halfway between them. If he wanted to get it, he'd have to pull the muzzle of the gun away from McCord's head. "This place is surrounded," she said. "It would go easier on you if you just surrendered."

"It would go easier on him if no one came near me."

"You're losing the whole operation. There's no way out for you."

"He's my ticket out. You don't want me to kill him, you need to do as I say."

Through her peripheral vision Meg had been tracking Kate creeping closer, but now she dropped to the floor just past Hawk and inched forward on her stomach, leading with her sidearm.

Keep him talking. Keep his attention focused on you.

Meg shrugged, trying to make it loose and careless, a feat considering tension was coiling her as tight as a spring. "Who's he and why would I care?"

"You're part of the FBI team; you're telling me you don't know who this is?"

"No idea. Is he important? Is he so worth keeping that we'd let you live?"

Her disinterest actually seemed to throw the man off balance and he took his eyes off her long enough to look down at McCord, as if to confirm who they were talking about.

The *crack* of the gunshot from the floor right beside her, echoing through the high-ceilinged corridor, made Meg jump, even though she'd expected it. The force of the bullet caught the man in his right shoulder, jerking his hand and the gun up and away from McCord to reflexively fire a round toward the ceiling. But Meg was already in motion, leaping into the room, reaching down to grab her Glock and turning it on him even as he staggered. Then Kate was shoulder to shoulder beside her, after rolling to her feet.

"Drop the weapon," Kate ordered. "Or I'll go for a second shot."

The gun dropped from his hand to skitter across the floor; then Meg covered him while Kate slapped on the handcuffs.

Only when he was secure did Meg drop to her knees in front of McCord's slack form. "McCord? McCord!" Ignoring the blood, she clasped his face in her hands, gently eased his head upward—his skin was warm, not cool with death—and leaned in to try to detect breath sounds. She held motionless for a long moment before she finally heard the quiet rasp of his indrawn breath. "He's still with us!"

Kate passed the man off to another agent, then activated her throat mic. "This is Agent Moore. Send that ambulance in now!" She looked over to Meg. "You'll stay with him? I need to find out what happened, now the shooting has stopped. And I'll direct EMS to you."

"I'll stay with him." Meg felt the warm press of fur and the cold slide of a wet nose as Hawk squeezed in between her body and McCord's, trying to comfort a hurt friend.

"Good boy, Hawk." She scanned McCord's face, looking for any sign of awareness. "McCord? McCord, stay with me. Help is coming. You need to hang on."

But there was no answer.

CHAPTER 30

Skydiamonds: Synthetic, eco-friendly diamonds created from atmospheric CO_2, using wind, solar energy, and rainwater.

Friday, August 23, 12:06 PM
Thomas Jefferson University Hospital
Philadelphia, Pennsylvania

Meg kept vigil at McCord's bedside.

She had sent Hawk home with Brian and had accompanied McCord in the ambulance to the hospital. He hadn't regained consciousness, even hours later.

She was comforted by the regular rhythm of his heart monitor, but remained concerned by his continued stillness. He lay motionless, propped up by the angled head of the bed. The leads to the heart monitor spilled out of the left sleeve of his hospital gown, and an IV dripped fluids into the tube that ran into the vein on the inside of his left forearm. All of the fingers on both hands, except his right index finger, were wrapped in silver-and-blue foam splints secured with bands of white medical tape. A black splint enclosed his left hand. A thicker band of foam-padded tape was secured over the bridge of his nose, the stark white contrasting sharply against the deepening bruising under his eyes. Other than several splotches of mottled black-and-purple bruising spreading across his jaw and forehead, his skin was sheet white.

As she sat beside McCord's bed, it came home to her that this was Webb's greatest fear—the result of one of her searches being a grievous injury or death. He was used to her cuts and bruises, but this case highlighted that the risks of her job weren't merely out on search. She'd brought violence into their home—not on purpose, but, still, it came—and she deserved the anger he wouldn't show her. He internalized so much of his fear and worry, not letting it out because he knew she had to carry the same concerns about him in his career. But that didn't negate his feelings, and it was high time they sat down and talked about it. Not here, not today, but both of their careers affected the other, and, someday, might affect a child. They might not be able to change that level of risk, but she needed him to see she recognized what he went through.

She glanced at the time. Webb and Cara had been on the road for about two hours at this point, and Meg expected them within a half hour or so. Cara had reacted to the news of McCord's condition with a calm that only barely vanished over panic at hearing he could be so badly hurt his life might be in danger. Webb, always rock solid in a crisis, had called Chuck Smaill to come take care of the dogs, and then had packed Cara into his truck and lit out for Philadelphia as fast as he could without getting pulled over for speeding, once he cleared the beltway.

Meg had checked in with them a few times en route, and had a handle on their approximate location. But each time Cara had asked about McCord, Meg had hoped she'd be able to tell her there was a change.

Not yet.

They'd transferred McCord out of the ER and into a private room about a half hour before, and the ER charge nurse had cleared Meg's way up onto the trauma ward so she could stay with him. She'd been sitting by his bedside ever since.

Restless, she got up and wandered over to the window, looking out over the parking lot stories below, and past it to S 10th Street. The sun was just sinking over the tops of the buildings, washing the world in a soft gold glow.

A soft rustle behind her had Meg whirling around to find McCord's head moving restlessly on his pillow as his eyelids fluttered. "McCord?" She hurried to the side of the bed, laying a hand gently over his shoulder. "McCord, it's Meg. Come back to us now. You're safe."

He slowly blinked a few times, trying to focus on her face.

She smiled down at him as his gaze finally fixed on her. "Hey."

"Hey." His voice was raspy and the single word sounded like his tongue was coated in sand.

"Let me get you something to drink. They left you some ice water." Reaching over, Meg picked up a capped Styrofoam cup with a bent straw. She bent it a little farther and then held it out for him. "Here, have a little water." She held the straw to his lips and he took a small sip, then a longer one. When he nodded that he was finished, she set the cup on the table.

"What happened?" He sounded a little more like his old self now.

"Your little system with Cara worked exactly like you wanted it to. She gave you two more hours, but she finally couldn't stand it any longer and showed up in our bedroom at three thirty in the morning."

McCord winced. "Only days after the attack. Did she set off alarm bells?"

"No, because Hawk knew exactly who was in the house. He wasn't on alert, so neither were we. But once we

suspected you were in trouble, especially following the attack on Monday morning, we moved fast. We had everyone, including Martin Sykes, at the Hoover Building before
five this morning to make plans."

The corner of McCord's lips tilted slightly. "Sykes must
have loved that. He's *not* a morning person."

"Interesting. You'd never have known it. He was pretty
worried about you."

McCord let out a short laugh and then winced. "I didn't
know he had it in him."

"Apparently, he does. When I called him this morning
to tell him we'd recovered you, he was absolutely over-
joyed."

"Time to hit up the old codger for a raise." At her
pointed stare and raised eyebrow, he chuckled softly, not
able to hold the straight-man routine. "Kidding, obviously. Actually, I'm touched he got so involved."

"*Involved?* He was the linchpin. He got into all your
notes on the *Post* server and they told us where to
find you."

"You found Russo Logistics. And the grow op. I . . . I
wasn't sure you would."

She rubbed his shoulder comfortingly, knowing all too
well the terrified isolation of thinking you were going to
die on your own. "We went in with all four dog teams and
a full complement of agents. Hawk found you."

McCord blinked in surprise. "All four? You mobilized
the whole team?"

"That's not my call. But Craig didn't hesitate. Congratulations, McCord, you're officially a part of this team.
You mess with one of us, you mess with all of us."

A little color warmed his pale cheeks. "I . . . I don't
know what to say to that."

"You don't have to say anything. Just remember you're
a part of the team next time I have a massive research re-

quest and then tie your hands on a story for weeks or months. Speaking of stories, I think this could be that Pulitzer story you're always going on about."

"It might be. Granted, I missed the end of it."

"Yeah, you gave us a hell of a scare. I thought we'd taken too long and you were already dead." She raised a hand to her still-bruised, swollen cheek. "You look worse than I do. I look like amateur hour by comparison."

"Giraldi's no amateur. He just didn't have enough time to perfect his technique."

"And your guy did?"

"Guys. And yeah. Although I'm pretty sure they intended to come back for round three and you must have beat them to it." He looked down at his injured hands. "How about we hash it out when it doesn't feel quite so close."

Meg squeezed his arm. "You got it. But this should make you feel better. We got them and their whole operation. The grow op. The luxury goods. The diamonds."

"All of it?"

"All of it. And we got a lot of the players. Starting with Tony Peluso, the underboss who came on-site when he got the news you were there and they had a problem to deal with. And then there's Vittore Falconi." Meg paused when McCord's eyes went to slits. "Wait. Was that who did this to you?"

"Yeah." The single word was a short bite.

"When we came in, he tried to use you as a shield so I wouldn't shoot him. But Kate pulled this amazing move. While I kept his attention up with me, she army crawled down the hall and shot him in the shoulder from the floor, around the corner of the doorjamb. The shot knocked the gun up so he fired at the ceiling instead of at us." She didn't bother to tell McCord that Falconi's gun had actually been trained on his temple. He'd had enough trauma. "That first shot gave me time to get my gun on him, and then Kate took him into custody. I didn't even know who he was until later, just as I was about to leave in the ambulance with you."

"Yeah, he's a real sweetheart."

"Oh, totally. We got Peluso, Falconi, and eight other soldiers. Kate thinks she can get a number of them to dish because they'd rather give up the bosses than go to jail for them, and there's less risk to them, now Peluso is caught. Kate is hopeful we'll get enough out of this to bring Cianfrani down as well. Look what you did, bringing all those nasty guys down." A sound out in the hallway attracted her attention. "I think they're here."

"Who?"

"Cara and Todd. I think I hear Cara's voice."

"You made them drive up?"

Meg rolled her eyes to the ceiling, as if asking for strength. "You're an idiot, McCord. Have I told you that lately?"

"Not for a while."

"I'm telling you now. I didn't *make them* drive up; I didn't have to. Did you really think Cara would sit around and wait for you to come home in your own good time when she'd been that terrified for you? And Todd wasn't about to sit tight either. As soon as they heard we'd recovered you and what sorry shape you were in, they headed for Philadelphia." Movement in the doorway caught her eye. "And here they are."

Cara stood in the doorway, Webb standing behind her, easily seeing into the room over her shoulder. Cara flew across the room to bend over McCord.

Meg stepped back several paces, giving them some privacy, and turned when she felt Webb's hand on her arm, letting him tug her to the far side of the room. She turned to face him, going up on tiptoes to wind her arms around his neck, and then kissed him, lingering for a second or two longer than she normally would in a public place.

His eyes stayed fixed on hers as she dropped down to the floor. "What was that for?"

"For being you. For putting up with all the stress I add to your life."

"You don't add stress."

"Says the man who just drove over two and a half hours because of yet another emergency. You're a terrible liar and I love you for it. But thank you for bringing Cara. She was too upset to drive herself."

"I would have come anyway. For better or for worse"— he gave her a cockeyed smile, belying his words—"he's family."

"Definitely." She glanced over to where Cara sat on the edge of the bed, carefully cradling McCord's right hand in both of hers, her eyes locked on his face, nodding at something he was saying. "If you'd told me a year and a half ago that this is where we'd all be, I'd have never believed you."

"You'd have never believed me because you didn't know me a year and a half ago. I guess we can thank that maniac Mannew for bringing us all together."

"Not that I'm ever going to tell him that. He won't ever be eligible for parole with all his stacked life sentences. But yes, he's responsible."

Webb pulled her arms from around his neck and stepped back a pace to give her a quick once-over. "I don't see any new injuries, so I assume the raid went okay?"

"Yes, thank God." She gave him a quick rundown. "We came in Brian's SUV, and he offered to take Hawk home with him in exchange for regular updates, and so I could ride in the ambulance with McCord. We'll get him later."

"He'll be happy as a clam hanging out with Lacey." He assessed McCord over her shoulder, his eyes flat and his jaw locked. "They beat the hell out of him."

"It's not good. A head injury, a broken nose, and they broke almost every finger on both hands."

"They wanted to make him suffer. He's a man who writes for a living. They wanted to take that away from him. Or make him think they could."

"At least. I'm not sure how bad his injuries are, though."

"That's easy." Webb walked to the doorway and did a quick, cursory look up and down the hallway.

"What are you doing?"

"Grabbing this." He returned with McCord's chart from where it had been left in a metal folder mounted outside the door. "If we know exactly what's wrong with him, we'll know how to help him."

"You may be a paramedic, but this isn't your jurisdiction, or even your state. You're not supposed to read that."

"As far as I'm concerned, the only permission I need to read this is McCord's." He looked over at the man in the bed. "McCord, you mind if I take a look at your chart?"

"Hell no. That might be my best way to find out how I'm really doing, since I haven't seen a doc yet."

"You've been unconscious," Meg said. "Even if the doc had come in, you wouldn't have heard the report. And they weren't going to tell me. I'm lucky they let me stay with you."

"You flashed your FBI ID, didn't you?"

"I may have."

"It gets results, so why not?" McCord looked back at Webb. "Go for it. Tell me what they did to me. I know the damage they intended to inflict. Not that they thought that through."

"What do you mean?"

"He was threatening to take away my ability to write for the *Post*. But you could see why he'd been an enforcer as he worked his way up the Mob ladder. He's got brawn, but not so many brains. The last thing I taunted him with before he knocked me out cold was that he'd never heard of 'voice-to-text.' " He looked down at his hands, his lips folding into a flat line. "Still, this isn't good."

Cara ran a comforting hand over McCord's forearm. "Whatever it is, we'll deal with it."

"Let's see what you need to deal with." Webb flipped open the metal folder and scanned the pages inside. "Grade three concussion. X-rays show no skull fracture and they don't suspect a subdermal hematoma." He looked up to meet McCord's gaze. "That's a brain bleed that builds up and puts pressure on the skull. Can happen immediately following a head injury, or days or even weeks later. Rarely, months later."

McCord groaned.

"Good thing you share a wall with a paramedic who knows all the classic symptoms and can check on you daily if need be," Webb said lightly, and went back to the chart. "A number of phalangeal fractures." Raising one hand into the air, he wiggled his fingers. "You've also got a couple of metacarpal fractures behind your left palm, up near the fingers. Yet, somehow, they managed to miss your right index. You'll be back on the Internet and mouse clicking like a pro right away. And they didn't go after your thumbs, so texting remains a possibility. They did kind of a half-assed job."

"The half they did was still pretty efficient. After my fingers heal . . ." McCord seemed to be struggling to put his worst fears into words. "Are they so bad—"

"That you won't have use of your hands? Don't jump to conclusions. I don't have the X-rays here, but if they've set them well, they should heal nicely. But I know an orthopedic surgeon in DC who feels like he owes me a favor. I pulled his dog out of a fire before it could die of smoke inhalation, and he was so grateful at the time he would have given me anything I asked. We can get a second opinion to make sure it's all set properly. If not, he can work his magic. And I can help you get the hand back into shape afterward. The next six weeks will be a pain in the ass because you're going to have to let it heal, but then we can start to work it and get the strength back. Three months from now and it will be like the fractures never existed."

McCord had been holding himself so tightly, relief collapsed him back onto the bed. "Good. Less important, but what about my nose?"

"Broken and manually realigned. Should heal fine, but you're going to look worse than Meg by tomorrow. The double black eyes are already starting. You have a couple of cracked ribs, but nothing some rest and care won't heal. Which is good because that's exactly what that concussion needs, as Meg will tell you from her experience."

"Or Todd, from his," Meg shot back.

"Add to all that, generally lots of bruising." Webb slapped the chart closed. "They worked you over good."

"They sure did. I have to admit, I wasn't sure I was going to get out of there alive." McCord looked over at Cara. "But I had faith you'd raise the alarm." His gaze slid up to Meg. "And faith you'd figure out how to find me and get me out. And that kept me going almost all the way to the end."

"It wasn't just me, but yeah, we figured it out. You owe Sykes big-time. Without him, we wouldn't have been on time even if we'd somehow figured it out. Because of him, we were on time, and we got the family members and their contraband."

"How many diamonds were recovered?"

"The entire remaining cache. The warrant allowed us to search every building. The warehouse next to the one where we found you? That was where they kept everything. Handguns, automatic rifles, heroin, cocaine, cigarettes. A fortune in oxycodone. Even a couple of art pieces. This was the hub from where they distributed their illegal goods, though I admit we weren't expecting the grow op. Pierce just wasn't high enough up the chain yet to know this was where they kept it all."

"What about their books?" asked McCord. "Were those there too?"

"Oh yeah. When we told Doug Addison, he was thrilled. This is going to be the first domino to fall, and it will take the rest of them down." Meg grinned down at McCord. "You done good, McCord. You ferreted out not only their stash, but their distribution system, and led us right to it."

"Fortunately, I didn't die for my trouble."

"But it sounds like you thought you might," said Cara softly. "You said faith kept you going almost all the way to the end. What happened then?"

"I was pretty resigned to not making it. I knew the dogs could find me if they knew where to start. I just wasn't sure I'd given the teams enough information to find the starting point. So I thought that might be it. I know they wanted information from me, but I'm pretty sure it wouldn't have been much of a loss for them if they'd beaten me to death."

Cara pressed a kiss to his cheek. "You're too ornery to kill. It's a burden we'll all just have to bear."

McCord gave her a crooked smile. "It's a tough job, but somebody's got to do it. Speaking of jobs . . ." His gaze darted up to Meg. "Do you remember after the Mannew case that I asked you to let me write a story about you and Hawk?"

"I remember. I said no."

He looked up at her, all bandages, bruised skin, and serious eyes. "Look at me, lying here in this bed, practically at death's door. Now will you finally take pity on me and let me write it?"

"Not a chance. And you're laying it on a little thick with the 'death's door' routine, don't you think?"

He chuckled. "Probably, but it was worth a shot."

Meg patted his leg through the blanket. "Good try. Maybe next time."

"*Next time?* I don't want there to be a 'next time' like this."

"Not like *this*." Meg spread her hands wide, as if to indicate the entire experience. "The next case. Because you know there'll be one."

"Because I'm an honorary team member now?"

"Craig would probably never come out and say it, but yeah, you are."

McCord settled back on his pillow, looking self-satisfied as Cara leaned down and whispered something to him that made him smile, while Webb stood beside Meg, ready to help McCord slowly make his way back into the light.

Colleagues. Teammates. Family.

A messy and convoluted combination of all three.

She wouldn't have it any other way.

Acknowledgments

One of the joys of writing is the collaborative process that brings a final novel to fruition. Sincere thanks go to those who helped shape *Under Pressure* and to bring it to publication:

Shane Vandevalk, for his continuing role as my weapons expert for both firearms and knives, as well as advising on gun safety measures. He also assisted with fight choreography and advised how to best batter Meg without giving her yet another concussion. Assistance with the grow op setup was also greatly appreciated.

Jordan Newton, for her good-natured willingness to stand in for Meg during the Meg/Giraldi fight staging. We only pretended to beat you up!

Rick Newton, for early research assistance on gems and grading, as well for the initial germ of the idea of McCord's disappearance that kicked off a large part of this story.

Jessica Newton, for her ongoing artistic support, always producing any social media or promo images I need, and for patiently putting up with my constant can-we-move-that-just-a-little-more-to-the-left requests on every image.

Paul Vanderlaan, for driving almost 700 miles each way to deliver the new computer he helped me plan and build, so I could work on this manuscript.

My critique team, Jenny Lidstrom, Jessica Newton, Rick Newton, and Sharon Taylor, for sharing your time and talents, and for your sometimes brutally honest opinions as we journeyed together to make this novel a coherent, consistent, and thrilling final product.

Nicole Resciniti, my agent, for all the magic she does in the background to keep my career running smoothly. Your counsel is always appreciated. And to the rest of the Seymour Agency team, including Marisa Cleveland, Lesley Sabga, and Leslie Nunez, for all the support you give your authors.

Kensington Publishing and its many teams, including Louis Malcangi and the art department for once again taking my vision of the book and producing another wonderful and evocative cover, editorial support from Norma Perez-Hernandez, and publicity and communications support from Larissa Ackerman, Vida Engstrand, Lauren Jernigan, Kait Johnson, Alexandra Kenney, and Alexandra Nicolajsen. It is a pleasure to work with you all.

Esi Sogah, my wonderful editor, for her continued insight and assistance throughout this series, and in this book specifically for her flexibility through an accelerated publication schedule. You are always ready and able to take on any bump in the road, and it's continually comforting to know I'm in such good hands.